CW01551801

# Twenty

# Five

By C.E. Graham

Also by C.E. Graham

# Fear's Burden

Copyright © 2015 C.E. Graham

Sometimes you only have a fleeting moment
in time to grasp an opportunity,
as fate may never again line up a set of
circumstances in the same way…..

# Chapter One

# Generate

As an early morning mist slowly descends and curls around the city buildings, Kym's head moves restlessly from side to side on a tear stained pillow.

'Mum, Mum please,' she shouts. 'I can't hear you. Twenty what?' The pale face and bright eyes of the well-dressed lady with long blonde hair, glides further away into a white haze. Kym rushes towards her mother with outstretched arms, but she's almost disappeared.

'I can't hear you, stay still. What are you saying? Mum… please, twenty… what about twenty?' Her mum's gentle voice continues to fade in and out, the words repeated in slow motion. Then she's gone and a cold chill fills the air. Kym looks at the empty space and sinks to her knees, trying to remember. Twenty four? Five? Five, yes it was five. Twenty five.

Sitting bolt upright in bed, shaking, sweat dripping from her forehead, Kym cries out his name and a sob catches in her throat as she reaches across the bed. Her fingers stroke the place where he once lay and she wraps her arms around herself, hugging her thin frame.

'Tom, oh Tom,' she says over and over, trying to remember the warmth of his body next to hers. He'd disappeared a month ago and now on her thirtieth birthday Kym cries openly for everyone she has loved and lost from her life. Swallowing hard and breathing deeply she whispers,

'Stop it, come on. Try to be strong.' But it's not over yet and the tears keep flowing.

Most people would think Kym had everything. A successful career as a research scientist, expensive apartment in London and plenty of money. However, work dominates her life leaving little time for anything else. Even today on her birthday, Kym is forced to attend a meeting at Downing Street in London not knowing why she has to go there. An email arrived two weeks earlier, giving no information about the meeting, or attendees, which seemed very mysterious.

Concerned by its lack of content, she spoke to her Head of Department at the time.

'Why have I been invited and not you? Did you recommend me for this?' she asked raising an eyebrow.

He was an intelligent man, quiet and thoughtful, often approaching her saying,

'I have a new opportunity for you,' with an optimistic look on his face. Generally his "opportunities" turned out to be a way of dressing up a mundane task. However, it worked as his approach and light heartedness always persuaded her to take on whatever he had in mind. He read the email, clearly not knowing anything about it.

'In the national interest,' he said slowly. 'How intriguing. Doesn't sound like you have any choice, you'll have to go. Good luck.'

'Great, that's my birthday and I just wanted a relaxing day off,' she replied, hoping he'd offer to go instead.

'A relaxing day, what's one of those?' he chuckled, before leaving hastily.

Still sitting up in bed Kym feels the slow chill of a shiver run down the length of her spine even though the apartment heating is on. She tries to put Tom and her mum out of her mind and tosses back the warm quilt before walking unsteadily towards her wardrobe.

Checking through several business suits, she picks out a soft grey jacket and skirt with a pale green top. Brushing her long blonde hair, whilst scrutinising the sorrowful face reflecting back from the mirror, Kym sighs as golden strands fall past her shoulders.

Whenever Kym feels sadness sweeping over her she tries to keep busy and not think about Tom, but it doesn't work. Every day is the same, followed by cold, silent, lonely nights. She stays at work as long as possible so she's not on her own. The technicians who clean the Lab's during evening hours always stop for a chat, but as they move away only the distant sound of whirring hoovers remains.

Tom is everywhere. Crossing the road, in crowds, whatever she does or hears, triggers more distressing memories and inevitable tears. The girl who believed she was special, has now discovered has flaws. His persistent absence hurts more than his actual leaving, with the agony of self-doubt constantly shadowing her every move.

Pulling back her silver, silk bedroom curtains, Kym watches as muddy puddles of heavy rain swirl towards overflowing drains on the street below. People are rushing around, clutching umbrellas, with coat collars pulled up to gain some protection from the gusting wind. Kym sighs, remembering the mornings when you couldn't move on the crowded city streets, as a sea of people jostled and pushed their way towards the station. Now it's quieter, calmer and cold. Raising her voice slightly she speaks to her apartment computer for the first time, shattering the silence.

'When is the next train to Westminster?' she asks, whilst carefully applying makeup. Her dad had installed a rapid response system which could pick up voices in any room. A cheerful sounding male replies,

'Good Morning Kym, it's Monday the 4th February Happy Birthday. The next train leaves in ten minutes for Westminster and then every fifteen minutes after.'

Kym remembered the day she first named the system, when Tom moved in seven and a half years earlier. He'd wanted the sultry female voice of an actress he'd fancied and sulked when she refused to instantly do what he asked. Ignoring him she continued to alter settings on the large screen which adorned her lounge wall. Sitting back on the floor next to Tom, who as usual was monopolising the settee, she asked the computer a question.

'What's your name?'

'Tom's an idiot,' it replied right on cue, Tom stared at her,

'Ha, ha very funny, I can't believe you've called

5

it that,' he remarked shaking his head in disgust. Kym had shrugged, not caring, he hadn't paid for it. She looked towards the man sprawled over the settee, feeling her face twitch with tension, realising that she couldn't remember the last time he'd paid for anything. Yet he was always there, by her side, her man. Kym changed the computer's name to "Mr. Right" from then on, naming it after him, though it obviously hadn't worked.

Picking up her bag and umbrella she asked for the front door to be opened, instantly hearing the sound of bolts releasing as it swung slowly inwards.

'Thank you Mr. Right lock up please,' she says, watching the door closing behind her and hearing the squeal of metal bolts sliding securely back into place. Kym fastens her jacket and carefully walks down the stairs to the street below. With her umbrella up she crosses at the traffic signals ahead and makes her way to the underground station.

Upon entering the delicatessen, next to the station, the seductive smell of freshly baked muffins and rolls cause her stomach to rumble. Kym looks longingly at the soft, golden croissants just placed in front of her, still warm from the oven. Resisting their appeal she quickly picks up a polystyrene cup of coffee and hurries away from the comforting aromas of the shop.

Though short of time she stops for a moment and

her face softens as she glances at the flower seller's display in front of the station. On a cold February morning the vibrant, bright petals along with the heavy sweet scent filling the air stir a memory as she passes quickly by to catch her train.

Easily finding a seat Kym sips warm, soothing coffee, whilst thinking about what might lie at the end of her short journey. Remembering that during the flu pandemic five years earlier, crisis meetings had been held at Downing Street every day, but recently the news reports had been less frequent.

The rain has stopped by the time she steps out of the depths of the underground and rays of sunshine, provide some welcoming brightness for her short walk to Downing Street. Approaching the gates that screen the area off, she pauses momentarily, her heart skipping a beat, before moving towards a waiting Police Officer stood on the other side.

'Can I take your name and see some identification please?' he requests in a cheerful voice. Kym searches her purse for her driving licence, whilst the officer smiles broadly.

'Thank you Dr. Clarke.' He opens one of the tall, wrought iron, black painted gates, gesturing her through before promptly securing it again. Kym looks at the buildings ahead, feeling a surge of unexpected excitement as she walks towards them.

'Looks like the weather's improving,' another officer says, before knocking lightly on the door.

'Yes, let's hope it continues.' Kym replies, before entering, wondering how many times a day he uttered the same words. Once inside the building she takes a deep breath and tries to focus on steadying her nerves.

'Good Morning Dr. Clarke please follow me,' a smartly dressed young man asks. Kym follows, picking up her pace, trying to keep up with his long strides. After being led down a hallway displaying portraits of previous Prime Ministers, she's ushered towards a room filled with lockers of various sizes. Two other people have already filled lockers and left the room, neither acknowledge her as they leave. Unfriendly and stuffy, she thinks, just how she'd imagined the day would be. A thick, luxurious cream carpet covers the ground floor of the building and her heels sink into its deep pile, making a pleasant change from hard laboratory tiles.

A tall smiling man is guarding the entrance to the locker room. As she turns to go past him, he looks directly at her, as if preparing to say something. Kym walks briskly by, in an effort to keep up with her escort who is already holding a locker door open, his sense of urgency is unsettling and she tries to remain calm. Kym remembers from the email that no recording or photographic equipment is allowed at the meeting and reluctantly places all her devices inside the locker. He bangs the door shut and hands her the key.

'Just the final scanner,' he says, gesturing towards two black wall panels. His face relaxes, when she doesn't set the damn thing off, then he leaves her at the door of the briefing room with a curt nod. Good start. Scanners, unfriendly staff and speed walking all in one morning. Whatever next, she wonders, smiling slightly.

Kym doesn't recognise any of the delegates sitting at the long, polished wooden table inside the room and her heart sinks as she pulls out a chair at the nearest vacant space. Glancing around she notices that the other attendees are of varying ages. None of them smile or make eye contact with her, whilst they sip coffee silently. Occasionally a cough, or the sound of china cups sliding onto saucers break the quiet, tense atmosphere in the room.

The meeting begins with the arrival of three Government officials. They all look to be in their thirties and dressed in grey suits. After introductions, one of them reads out a statement detailing the required level of secrecy that the group must adhere to. He seems articulate and familiar with the process then he asks his less confident colleague to give a copy of the Official Secrets Act to each person for them to sign, before continuing.

9

'Welcome … you are the Generate group.  The form you are about to sign, prevents disclosure of the content of the group's meetings with any other parties,' he explains, hesitating to allow attendees to read through the Act.  When the forms have been completed, the third official touches a wall mounted screen, which bursts into life showing several blocks of information at the same time. The presenter has an impressive tone, commanding attention, although the information about the highly contagious flu pandemic isn't new to Kym, who swallows hard, fighting back tears.  Millions died, including her parents and a pain rises in her chest as she looks down at the solid dark table.  She attempts to pick up her coffee cup which slides from her fingers and rattles on the saucer, drawing the attention of everyone around the table.

'Sorry,' she says quietly as the presenter hesitates momentarily before continuing.  Kym shifts her weight in the leather chair and tries to focus and block out the memories which are never far from her mind.

She re-reads in disbelief the figures displayed on the screen from the previous year.  Only ninety thousand new births had been registered surely that wasn't correct.  The birth rate had settled at three quarters of a million each year, during the last decade, but the figures before her show a steady fall over the past five years, with many couples choosing to remain childless.  However, only ninety thousand births last year, Kym's face twitches slightly as she considers the implications of this staggering fact. The figure was left up on the screen to reinforce the point. The "official secrets act" speaker, made his way to the front, clearing his throat.

'The Government feel that now is the right time to radically increase the birth rate. That's why we have brought you all here today. As members of the Generate group you need to find a solution which will enable the birth rate to start increasing from next year.' He pauses before continuing. 'The birth rate needs to increase at a sustainable rate to ensure our country can recover and grow as a strong nation into the future.'

Compelled by the authority of the speaker, Kym is unable to move. She wants to stand up and say – *hold on when exactly did I agree to become a member of the Generate group?* None of the other delegates seem concerned that they were all now compulsory members, so she remains silent looking around her in disbelief. Not one of them speak, but you can feel the tension hanging in the air. The speaker is in full flow, not pausing to allow questions.

'The next meeting will be held here in fourteen days and you are all expected to attend.' A few members complain about the short timescale causing the first spokesman to stand up again, anticipating their concerns.

'Presentations and documents won't be required for the next meeting,' he answers, raising his voice.

'Any ideas need to be treated with complete secrecy. Don't discuss them with anyone. Don't send any emails or save notes on computers. Just bring your ideas. Remember not to record any evidence anywhere, as it could be intercepted and misunderstood.' His tone had been calm and convincing, as he once again takes his seat at the top of the table. With no further comments or questions he closes the meeting.

Everyone looks deep in thought as they leave. Apart from the noise of chairs moving and departing footsteps, nothing else can be heard. Still nobody speaks. Kym is just relieved to be leaving the room and the haunting emotions which had been rekindled by the presentation. She walks briskly towards the locker room, arriving there first, anxious to get away.

Once safely seated on the train home, her thoughts are filled with the strange task the group have been given. Previously when epidemics have been contained, populations increased at their own natural rate. It all sounded a little ominous to her. How could they possibly increase the birth rate dramatically from next year and why all the secrecy?

Walking from the underground back to her apartment, Kym realised the importance of becoming involved with the Generate group's challenge. She couldn't miss out on the opportunity to convince the Government to embrace the benefits of stem cell storage.  Stem cells had cured many cancers and hundreds of diseases.  Kym dreamt of a time when every baby born would have their stem cells stored and was determined to get the message across to the people who could make this happen.

When she arrived at her apartment two cards were waiting on the doormat.  Tears cloud her vision as she studies them.  The bright pink envelope was from her friend Jacqui and its loud shade perfectly reflected her personality.  Kym could always rely on Jacqui to send her a birthday card, she never forgot.  They'd met at university when they both joined the same queue for the research science group and began chatting.  Physically they were total opposites.  Jacqui was much shorter than Kym.  Her big smile, dark curly hair and curvaceous figure could brighten up any dull moment as did her entertaining stories that would send listeners into a ripple of laughter.  Kym admired Jacqui's social skills and wished that she could be more like her.  They had graduated together and both lived in London.  Jacqui chose cancer research for her career, whilst Kym had pursued stem cell research which she found fascinating.  Both worked long hours and after Kym settled into a relationship with Tom, they had sadly drifted apart.

'So long ago,' Kym whispers, pressing Jacqui's card to her cheek, before putting it on the shelf above the fire.  Sitting back down heavily on the settee, she knows that Jacqui needs to be back in her life and decides to ring her tomorrow and explain what's happened with Tom. Maybe if she apologised for neglecting their friendship, they could arrange to meet up.

The other envelope was from him and she rips it up, unopened and throws it in the bin, which vibrates loudly as she slams down the lid. Kym can feel her face and neck tightening. Why couldn't he just leave her alone? A card wasn't enough. If he still loved her he would be there now, not sending a reminder in the post.

Sitting back down on the settee, deep in thought, Kym reflects on the last time they were together at the beginning of January when she was getting ready for an important dinner. They had attended several lately, due to the success of one of her published papers on stem cell development. She was really looking forward to the event, just wanting to dress up and have some fun. Tom only had a part time job working mornings at a small local gallery. After he'd spent the afternoon lying on the settee watching television, she tried to encourage him to start getting ready.

'Come on Tom, we need to get going, it's nearly six,' she urged, noticing he looked half asleep. She kissed him lightly on the lips, hoping to persuade him into some sort of movement.

'I'm very tired, would you mind if I didn't go with you tonight?' he said, closing his eyes.

'I can't go by myself,' she protested, frowning as her good mood evaporated.

'I'm sorry, but I'm just not up to it tonight, you'll be fine on your own.' He didn't move, but opened his eyes to look at Kym and could tell she wasn't happy that he wasn't escorting her. 'I feel like an idiot at these sort of evenings anyway, I never know what to say,' he continued, studying Kym's face for a reaction.

Her face fell and her eyes flashed angrily at him.

'Well thanks Tom, I've gone to all this effort and now I can't go. If it wasn't for the hours I put in to support both of us, we would be struggling to survive on the pennies you bring home. Is it too much to expect you to put on a suit occasionally and make a bit of polite conversation with my colleagues in exchange?' She took a deep breath struggling to control her anger at his apathy.

'Yes,' he snapped back at her. 'It's not occasionally, it's all the time and I'm sick of it!'

Kym was shocked by Tom raising his voice, he was always the calm and collected one. Knowing her words had provoked a reaction from him, she tried to curb her annoyance, but the words just kept coming. Reaching the height of her anger Kym wanted to hurt him and couldn't stop herself.

'It's times like this when I miss my dad most,'

she shouts, her voice breaking as she chokes back tears. 'He was always proud of me and my achievements. He would have loved to attend these events, sitting by my side, supporting me. He never let me down.' Kym felt better now that she'd got out what was really bothering her. Tom just didn't match up to the type of man he was.

'Well thanks a lot. You've just confirmed what I always suspected, that I'm not good enough for you and never will be.' Getting up he glared at her, his face full of rage, before going into the spare room and slamming the door.

Kym was too upset to attend the dinner and didn't speak to Tom again that night. He slept in the spare room and she retired to bed early, keeping out of his way.

When Kym came home from work, deliberately late the next day, the apartment was quiet and dark. Tom wasn't in. An hour later he sent her a text to say he was going away for a few days. Kym read the text over, what did he mean, where had he gone? She immediately rang his number only to get his voice mail stating,

*'Sorry I can't take your call, leave your details and I will ring you back.'*

When she went into the bedroom most of his clothes were gone. Her heart sank, finding his passport and other personal documents were also missing. With the now half-filled drawer hanging open, Kym sat on the bed in tears not fully understanding what had happened. They'd had a heated argument but so did all couples. There had been no warning that he was going to leave, no clues, or opportunity to discuss what was bothering him. He didn't ring after she left a message asking him to come back, not even to check how she was coping, displaying a callous disregard for her.

Kym had felt uplifted after realising she could introduce the possibility of stem cell storage to the Generate group. Now though, he'd crept into her head again and she started to cry. Kym cried for the loneliness and the disappointment from years of effort put into their relationship which had come to nothing. As her tears turned into long, deep mournful sobs, it was as if a wave of sadness had engulfed her and she couldn't stop. She cried for the loss of her parents and for the emptiness she felt inside at spending her birthday alone for the first time in her life.

Eventually Kym fell into a troubled sleep, exhausted from the stress of going through the many different scenarios in her head that had led to this moment. Waking much later to a room filled with darkness, her hands clutched the birthday card she'd binned earlier, searching for the words that weren't there.

'I miss you so much Tom, I can't do any of this without you,' she sobs, sinking further into the miserable depths of loneliness.

## Chapter Two

# Matt

Matt always tried to be a glass half full kind of person. Following a set routine every day, waking at the same time, ruffling his hair with his fingers before checking himself in the bathroom mirror. Turning sideways whilst sucking his stomach in, he'd frown, dissatisfied with slight changes to his lean, muscular torso. Promising himself to go to the gym after work and getting acquainted with the treadmill or cross trainer once again.

Matt liked to be organised, preferring simplicity and to have everything planned out in advance. He had five different coloured suits for work, wearing a crisp white shirt and smart black or brown shoes, depending on if it was a grey, black or dark blue suit day. He was a handsome man, tall at six foot three, with broad shoulders and bright blue eyes. His short dark hair was always immaculately maintained and he liked to greet you with a warm smile that perfectly reflected his fun, caring personality. At twenty nine years old he would be a catch for any girl but had decided it would be less painful for him to remain unattached.

He met the love of his life during his first week at university. With a list of well organised events, Matt went to the student bar to contemplate the week ahead. This would turn out to be the best decision, he'd ever made.

The place was crowded with students chattering excitedly with the prospect of a fun week ahead. Wondering where to stand and looking around for someone to start up a conversation with, he approached the bar and was stopped in his tracks by the laughter of an attractive girl whose face lit up when she spotted him. She was standing nearby and he could clearly see her smiling, pretty face which was framed by auburn hair. She was tiny, petite would be the correct way to describe her and stylishly dressed which Matt really admired. Checking over her neat size eight figure Matt thought she had a slightly European look. Not the type of girl that he usually went for, which was the tall athletic blonde, but he was drawn towards her. She immediately acknowledged him with a widening sensual smile.

Matt thought she was gorgeous and wanted to get her alone so that he could listen to her laugh and have her all to himself.

'Hello,' she said in a sultry voice, heightening his attraction.

'Hello I'm Matt where are you from?' he replied, whilst scrutinising her very pretty face.

'Manchester and I'm Lucy,' she answered, moving next to him with the most beautiful green eyes he had ever encountered.

'What about you, are you a southerner?' she asked mischievously.

'I'm from just outside London, would you like a drink?' Matt asked and was taken aback by her answer.

'No thanks, I already have one' she replied, turning slightly away from him to talk to the guy she was with before he came over.

Matt felt disappointed maybe he had misread the look she gave him with her welcoming "hello." He went to get a drink from the bar and talked with another group of students standing nearby. He just couldn't keep away from Lucy though, eventually finding himself magnetically drawn back to her side. Lucy noticed Matt returning and immediately turned to face him.

'I think I will have that drink after all,' she said, with another one of those absolutely gorgeous smiles.

It didn't take Matt long to find out that she already had a boyfriend back home in Manchester, sadly. However at only nineteen, free and single Matt decided that he would make it his mission to capture all of this incredible girl's attention.

Matt was not the kind of man who wanted lots of encounters with different women before he got into a steady relationship. He wanted total exclusivity with the woman of his dreams. After witnessing the failure of many relationships around him, he knew that you needed to take your time and really get to know a person first. Though there were no guarantees. However, chatting away to Lucy and listening to her bubbly, lively voice he was hooked. She was full of life, had lots of interesting and exciting ideas and was driving him wild with her lovely, sexy figure.

To be totally infatuated by a female was not a new concept for Matt and he constantly reminded himself to be patient, but he just couldn't do it. Instead he spent the next month trailing Lucy, inundating her with flirty texts, whilst finding out everything she liked. His prime motive being to eventually seduce her away from her boyfriend back home. Matt was a kind and caring person, he wouldn't hurt anyone intentionally, but he was also a hopeless romantic and had fallen for Lucy.

It turned out to be easier than he thought it would be as her long distance relationship was struggling. Lucy didn't make it home during the first term and a break up seemed inevitable. Lucy was extremely independent and would not give in to her boyfriend's emotional blackmail. She loved university and her new found friends and decided it was time to expand her horizons. Matt celebrated Lucy's break up quietly to himself. Secretly he made plans to make his intentions more than friendly as soon as he was allowed. However, a private moment with Lucy clarified that she didn't seem to be interested in heading into another relationship, at least not yet.

Matt adored Lucy, but felt a bit rejected by her lack of interest in romance with him. Later walking into the student bar, Matt noticed the tall blonde girl he'd also talked to on the night he'd met Lucy. She was very attractive and easy to get along with and it seemed natural to ask her out for a meal at a bistro he'd wanted to go to. What was there to lose? She was lovely. When she accepted, Matt felt elated, he was walking tall again and it had crossed his mind that the date could make Lucy jealous. It was worth a go, he thought, what did he know about women anyway?

Matt really enjoyed the date he had with his new lovely blonde friend, she was great company. Fascinating to talk to about science and medicine, which she was studying. From talking to her he realised she had a very serious work ethic, spending many hours in the university library. They drank far too much and laughed helplessly together. Matt felt she would make a great friend, there were sparks but he had already committed his heart to Lucy. This girl could be the best thing that would never happen to him but it was Lucy who enthralled him. They never got around to making another date which he felt guilty about. Luckily they didn't bump in to each other in the student bar, he wouldn't have known what to say to her. Whereas he was never stuck for words with Lucy.

Matt spoke to Lucy about his date in an effort to find out what she thought about it. Tossing back her head she laughed.

'Blondes don't have all the fun,' she answered, in a flirty, suggestive voice and continued to tease him over his choice of date. When they had finished joking, Lucy became serious, looking directly into Matt's eyes. They stood apart staring longingly at each other for several seconds.

'Anyway I would like to spend more time with you, perhaps if you fancy another night out, you could always ask me?' she revealed. Matt was elated, progress at last, he thought or was he getting confused and did she just mean spending more time with him as a good friend? Matt was finding it hard to figure Lucy out, but was feeling impatient and wanted to know.

'Any chance we could get together on Saturday night then?' he continued, half expecting a knock back.

'Yeah that would be great Matt,' Lucy answered before kissing him quickly on the cheek as she left for her next seminar.

Matt arranged for Lucy to come round at 6pm on Saturday and was planning a romantic evening. After they both had a few glasses of wine he intended to confess that he was falling for her. With growing excitement Matt went shopping for special touches that hopefully would surprise and delight Lucy. Buying candles, flowers, chocolates and a 'dinner for two' meal deal at his local quality superstore. Carefully scrutinising the cooking instructions and timings, Matt wiped sweat from his brow, wishing he'd booked somewhere instead.

After showering and dressing in smart but casual clothes and with the food all ready to serve, Matt poured himself a well-deserved drink, feeling smug that he'd done a great job. The self-catering accommodation he occupied at the university was more spacious than the small, basic rooms most first year students went for. Setting the table neatly and lighting candles, he arranged the large cream and pink striped lilies, bought earlier, across the table, before standing back to admire his work. All that was left to do was to carefully select slow sultry love songs and store them into his playlist ready to hit the play button when he heard her arriving. Everything was ready, it was just a case of waiting for Lucy.

Matt was totally infatuated with Lucy, he would have done anything for her and had planned this evening for weeks. She was due any minute, the thought of which made him feel slightly edgy. Once again he checked himself in the mirror, impatiently running his fingers through his hair. Just as he was putting the finishing touches to their meal, his phone vibrated to indicate a text message had arrived. It was Lucy, she was running late and would let him know if she could still make it in the next hour.

Matt was crushed, after all the effort he'd gone to, even rehearsing lines all afternoon and now felt a bit foolish. Sinking into one of the chairs he'd cleaned earlier, pouring himself another glass of wine, he drank it in one go. As he continued to empty the bottle Matt wondered if he would ever understand women. Perhaps I should stay single and concentrate on my university course, he thought. Matt blamed himself, it was always the same.

'Why can't I be a bit more patient?' he muttered angrily to himself. Throwing everything in to the evening without thinking it through first. How would it have looked to Lucy, it may have put her off, probably a good thing she hadn't arrived, he thought, turning the oven down.

Lucy did eventually knock on Matt's door. When he opened it and saw her standing there, he didn't care about anything else other than getting her inside. She looked stunning. Her petite figure looked perfect in a short red dress, with a close fitting black jacket. He loved the smell of perfume. Lucy's scent immediately turned him on and he fought back the urge to kiss her.

'Don't think you are going anywhere for a while,' he said in a deep, slow voice. 'I've got a surprise for you!'

Lucy hesitated to answer, wondering what Matt was up to. As she looked around at the candlelit table and the place settings she smiled widely.

'What a wonderful thing to do for someone,' she said, looking visibly touched by his efforts.

'It's not for just anyone,' Matt corrected her playfully, 'It's all for you.' Lucy was amazed by the effort Matt had gone to. She had no idea he was going to cook and had already eaten but decided not to let him know. As she went into the kitchen to help, Matt was leaning against a worktop and for the first time she realised how sexy he looked.

'Come here,' he said in a softer voice, looking intently at her.

'Why?' she asked teasing him. Putting his arms around her, he gazed lovingly into her green eyes.

'Because I think I love you,' he answered huskily.

They kissed, a long seductive kiss which completely emptied Matt's mind to everything but his lovely, sexy Lucy. All Matt's rehearsed plans disappeared in that moment. The talk he'd had to himself earlier about taking it slowly until you're sure she feels the same, was forgotten along with the food. He carried her to the bedroom and laid her down gently on the bed, removing his clothing, not taking his eyes from hers. He softly kissed her neck and shoulders, feeling her body shudder at his touch and slipped off her dress.

'You are so incredibly beautiful,' he whispered, whilst lightly tracing his finger over her body slowly and deliberately, keeping her waiting, until he could resist no more

Later when she'd gone, Matt reheated the dinner and ate both portions, he was starving. Things had gone much better than he'd planned but good food was not for wasting, he thought, finishing off the lemon torte. Blowing out the candles Matt noticed she'd forgotten the flowers he'd chosen for her.

'Damn,' he frowned gathering them up carefully. Then he had an idea, tomorrow morning he would place them outside her door, so they would be the first thing she'd see when leaving. Matt didn't know then that Lucy was an asthmatic.

After graduation, they married and lived in an apartment in London. Saving up for a house, they were both happy and content with their lives. Lucy's asthma rarely affected her and seemed to be under control with daily inhalers. It never caused a problem until the flu pandemic struck. Matt watched terrified as Lucy got worse and struggled to breathe although she insisted her inhalers took time to start working. Matt didn't know what to do to help so he stayed awake, watching her. At one point he thought she had stopped breathing, the whole of her body jolted, followed by uncontrollable shaking and she felt cold to his touch. Matt wrapped her in a blanket and carried her to his car, driving to hospital during the early hours of the morning. Lucy's lips started to turn blue and he gasped in horror, instinctively putting his foot down on the accelerator.

When Matt got within half a mile of the hospital he couldn't drive any further. Cars had been abandoned all over the road. Although exhausted, Matt carried Lucy, breaking into a run as he got nearer to the entrance. He couldn't believe the scene that met him there, it was complete mayhem. The waiting area was filled with hundreds of people desperately ill and in need of urgent medical attention.

Frantic to get their loved ones immediate treatment, people were shouting and holding onto members of staff, forcing them to help. Police and security men were overwhelmed by the numbers and could not bring order to an unruly crowd who had been waiting for hours. It became clear that no-one would be able to help Lucy. Patients were dying in the waiting area, without receiving any treatment. The noise was unbearable, the scene manic and the lack of air stifling. Lucy's condition was deteriorating rapidly. It seemed hopeless. Matt was fully trained in not only first aid but lifesaving procedures, he didn't want to leave Lucy but had to find the oxygen mask and supply she so desperately needed. He couldn't just wait around and do nothing, leaving her to die, without trying to save her.

When he found the equipment and rushed back to where he'd left Lucy, she had collapsed and was lying on the cold hard floor. Matt was horrified by the inhumanity of people, stepping over her as they hurried by, whilst she lay there dying. He picked Lucy up, she felt cold and didn't respond when he called her name. It was clear that she wasn't breathing. The next ten minutes were spent desperately trying to resuscitate her, though it seemed much longer to him. A nurse finally arrived with a defibrillator.

'Stand back please,' she ordered Matt. The device was quickly charged and administered, but after several unsuccessful attempts, it became clear that it was time to give up as Lucy had gone. 'I'm sorry,' the nurse said, touching his shoulder. 'I have to go,' she added, quickly moving to help another man lying on the floor near him.

Staggering backwards, Matt put his hand out, touching the wall to steady himself, not believing what had just happened. It was as though the whole world had gone into slow motion and he was on the outside, looking in, not part of the harsh reality around him. Feeling helpless, he didn't know what to do, but knew he couldn't leave her lying there on the floor in such a brutal, cold place. He felt himself sinking to the floor and remained crouched there, alone, cradling her in his arms. Sobbing into the strands of her soft auburn hair, he smoothed it away from her angelic, lifeless face.

'I'm taking you home with me,' he whispered, looking around, realising that there didn't seem to be anywhere safe to leave her. Eventually a porter came with a trolley, asked her name and took Lucy away from him. Matt was left standing there, unable to move, taking the force of people's bodies as they collided with him, desperate in their plight to find help. He wanted to scream, "What is going on? This is a hospital? Why are you allowing people to die like this?" No words came out of his mouth. Nobody spoke to him or comforted him, people continued to bump into him, as if he wasn't there.

Eventually he found himself standing next to his car, looking at the passenger seat which his beautiful wife had occupied less than an hour earlier. Staring at the now empty seat he visualised Lucy sitting there, laughing and singing, full of life. He quickly opened the car door to embrace her, but she was gone. Matt sat in the driver's seat banging his head hard against the steering wheel, only stopping when he saw it was covered in blood as were his face and hands. He then succumbed to the full brunt of his sorrow, crying uncontrollably into already soaked hands. After what must have been an hour, he drove slowly away from the hospital on the wrong side of the road, feeling totally numb.

Matt never really recovered from the shock of Lucy's sudden death. Knowing that he couldn't cope with experiencing such unbearable pain again, he decided not to allow anyone else to get that close to him. His torment never ceased, blaming himself for not taking her to hospital sooner, he continued to live with the consequences of an unchangeable moment that had wrecked his life so cruelly. Vowing to live his remaining years as a single guy, Matt knew he could take care of himself. However, he didn't think he was capable of taking care of anyone else.

After Lucy's death Matt went home and spent time with his family. After several months he got a job with a high profile security company who specialised in the protection of executive clients. When he'd completed training in Martial arts he obtained a firearms license. With his tall, strong frame, smart profile and easy going nature he quickly became a popular employee. After two years Matt was recommended for his current security position, which he felt had been his best job to date.

He'd been working in his new post for a month and everything seemed normal for a Monday morning. Delegates were due to arrive for a crisis meeting at 10am and he was on locker room duty.

Matt recognised Kym immediately. She was walking quickly down the corridor towards him and he was taken aback by seeing her again after so long. Today he'd been assigned to the locker room, how he wished he'd been picked as an escort, she looked beautiful.

She didn't even acknowledge him, glancing at him momentarily as he smiled at her, then quickly followed her escort into the locker room. Matt tried to get her attention but she just walked past him again on the way out without noticing him. Maybe he should have said something, but unless important guests acknowledged you first, it was part of the professional code of conduct they all followed to say nothing. Kym hadn't really changed, still tall and very slim, her long blonde hair was the same as he'd remembered. However, her face looked thinner and she looked a little sad. Matt had a quick look over towards her while she had been filling her locker. He thought about how well she'd done for herself, attending a Government crisis meeting. All those hours spent buried in science books had paid off, she was immaculately dressed in what looked to be an expensive suit.

# Twenty Five

More importantly though, for the first time since the loss of Lucy, Matt felt it could be time for some female company and the second date they never had. Matt knew he needed to find a way to speak to her and find out what was happening in her life, but how would he be able to do that? He decided to try and speak to her when she returned to collect her things from the locker room. The meeting attendees would be out eventually, he just had to wait for the opportunity to bump into her again by staying put.

A couple of hours had gone by which gave Matt the chance to do a reality check. It had been more than ten years since they were at university and their one and only date. She was probably already in a relationship and may have a family. Deep in thought as to what he was going to say to her, he missed his name being shouted by a colleague. Coming to his senses, he heard him approaching.

'Matt we need you upstairs, close the locker room, they will be a while yet.'

When Matt returned an hour later his heart sank finding that the locker room door was open and the lockers had been emptied. His opportunity to talk to Kym had gone as she and the other meeting attendees had already left.

# Chapter Three

# Kym

The only thing Kym liked about school was when the last lesson had been completed on Friday afternoon. Always one of the first to leave the building, she would race home unable to breathe easily until the front door was shut behind her.  Dropping her bag freed her arms to hug the three lively Labradors that almost knocked her over with excitement.  For the first time that day, Kym felt happiness fill her heart, knowing that the ordeal of Monday morning was days away.

Although an academic genius, with a kind and gentle nature, she found herself unable to keep friends. It wasn't through lack of effort, she often invited girls back to her house and attended their parties, but it never seemed to get her anywhere. Sat alone on coach trips or left out of arrangements to meet up at weekends, filled her with sadness which only served to decrease her popularity. Kym was left standing on the outside of a group of bubbly, lively girls making plans to meet up after school, not knowing how to get involved. Her voice remained quiet and unheard as they gossiped about boyfriends and clothes whilst she struggled to find any common ground with them. Instead it was easier to turn to books and spend time listening to music in her room, hiding away her unhappiness.

What's wrong with me? Why doesn't anyone like me? Kym couldn't work it out and accepted that she would never be one of the "in crowd", choosing to concentrate on her schoolwork instead. Teachers gave her the recognition she craved. One in particular Mr. Stuart-Jones took her under his wing, spending time during breaks giving her extra tuition in science subjects. He'd singled her out and in doing so led her to believe she was special. His prodigy, no longer a misfit. Kym had heard some of the malicious remarks made by girls in her class. Unable to defend herself, she continued to work hard and take all the credit that came her way. Much to the annoyance of her classmates.

After achieving the highest marks possible in the Sciences, it seemed a natural progression for her to study science in order to obtain a top degree. Her dad was a Doctor and had a great deal of influence over Kym, taking her to look at top Universities, even though she thought they were too far away from home.

Kym had dreams of her own, wanting to travel the world. Walk through the paddy fields of Asia, trek up to Machu Picchu in Peru and watch the cascading waters of Niagara Falls. In the future she wanted to move to Australia, fascinated by the country after seeing travel programmes exploring the many cities and beaches there. Although Australia would be her dream place to live, it was just a fantasy and she didn't actually believe that she'd ever move there. As her dreams seemed so out of reach, Kym would have settled for a job in a fast food restaurant locally, before going to university. Wanting to experience real life and desperately hoping to get to know other workers in her age group and make some much needed friends. Working alongside them, laughing and talking would have given her the chance to feel the warmth of friendship at last, but it wasn't to be. Daddy would never allow it. He'd never taken her to a fast food restaurant, even when she'd begged him as a child. Disappointed, Kym had given up asking over the years, which only increased her desire to eat there.

On the rare occasions that Kym went inside one of the brightly coloured diners, she'd loved it. Standing in the queue, waiting patiently to be served, gave her the chance to marvel at the atmosphere there. Voices chatting loudly, full of expression. Groups of friends huddled together socialising and laughing at their dilemmas. Families crammed around small tables, sharing pots of sauces and stacks of fries. It sounded great and it smelt even better. Sometimes Kym had gone in just to get a quick drink to take out. However, once inside her stomach would rumble at the spicy aroma of burgers with onions or freshly roasted chicken dripping in sweet honey. Looking around, all the tables were occupied and Kym would spot some of the girls she knew from school. Tears stinging her eyes, she'd wait silently for her drink and quickly leave. Never discussing with anyone how miserable and lonely she felt.

Kym remembered very clearly her first day at university. It was the last week in September and pouring with rain, as her parents helped move her belongings into the halls of residence. They both knew it was going to be a painful parting. Kym hugged her mum.

'I will miss you every day,' she said, choked with tears.

Kym's mum wasn't coping with the thought of her family breaking up, but was determined to remain strong for her daughter.

'You'll have a great time, meet lots of people and befar too busy to think of us. Get yourself down to the main hall this evening and talk to some other students. They will probably be feeling just the way you are, away from home for the first time,' she said gently, hoping to leave quickly before Kym became too emotional.

It wasn't to be though, as when Kym hugged her dad she burst into tears, traumatised by their parting.

'I think it's best if we go,' Kym's mum said quickly.

'Right,' answered her dad. He hated the thought of leaving Kym there alone, but knew it was inevitable and to delay would just cause them all more distress.

'If you need anything, no matter how insignificant, just call us, day or night,' he urged, his voice full of concern.

After they had left, she looked around the small, sparsely furnished room that was to be her home for the next year. Hearing giggling in the corridor outside, caused her to sigh deeply, as she unpacked her books and computer. Looking around and wiping a tear from her face, she sat on the single bed, wondering if she'd ever get used to being away from her family. It took all of her strength to drag herself towards the boxes containing some of her belongings. Luckily she'd bought a new quilt, cover and pillow case to brighten up the room. Its bare, whitewashed walls met a cold wood effect floor. The room was warm enough but it wasn't home.

On the small desk beside the window, was an invitation to a meet and greet event in the main hall, giving students the chance to sign up for the many social and sports groups available. Kym decided to head straight over to the hall and get involved. Determined to make a success of this opportunity, she knew that a busy social schedule would keep her from feeling lonely and homesick.

The main hall was noisy and full of students talking excitedly. Kym looked around desperately hoping she would spot someone who could be a potential companion. Everyone seemed to be engaged in conversation and she swallowed hard. Thinking it would be wise to choose someone with common interests she joined the end of the Science events queue. Managing to smile nervously at the person in front of her, she stood silently for several minutes until someone touched her arm gently.

'Hello, I'm Jacqui, what are you studying?' Jacqui's voice was warm and welcoming.

'Biomedical Sciences,' she replied, pleased that someone had spoken to her at last.

'Oh, I'm Kym, what are you studying?'

'I'm studying Medical Sciences, hoping to concentrate on Cancer Research,' Jacqui continued happily, 'I can't wait to start. Where are you going next?'

Kym hadn't really thought about anything else other than getting to the front of the queue and then returning to her room.

'Not sure,' she answered, 'What about you?'

'I think we should sign up here then go and have a drink, meet some other students,' Jacqui replied with a glint of fun in her eyes.

'Great. Where are you from?' Kym asked, relieved that Jacqui had invited her for a drink. They continued to chat as they waited for their turn to sign up for science events.

Kym and Jacqui continued to hang out together for the entire first week. Jacqui was lively and fun and Kym didn't mind doing what she wanted and tagging along. Friday night was a live band night and they flung open the doors of Kym's tiny wardrobe as Jacqui surveyed its contents.

'I'm thinking about wearing this.' Kym's face shone with excitement as she lifted her favourite turquoise dress from the wardrobe to show Jacqui. Jacqui crunched up her face in disapproval.

'It's a bit dressy, for a band night, let's have a look,' she offered, scanning the new clothes hung there that looked like they'd never been worn.

'What about these skinny jeans and this silver

halter top, they would look great together.'

'Ok,' replied Kym giving in to her new friends choices.

'You're going to look good,' added Jacqui smiling triumphantly. 'I'll see you later,' she shouted, banging Kym's door behind her.

Kym surveyed the jeans and halter top, whilst cutting the price tags off. The outfit Jacqui had picked seemed a bit understated but she'd been reassured that it wouldn't be a very 'dressy' night. When Jacqui knocked on her door a couple of hours later, her curvy figure was squeezed into a little black dress.

'I thought we weren't getting dressed up?' Kym said smiling, not wanting to upset her new friend in any way.

'I know but I tried to squeeze into my jeans and they didn't look right so I pulled on this dress instead,' Jacqui replied whilst moving towards the door.

'Come on then the night awaits, get your dancing shoes on,' she continued.

Kym put on her silver stilettos, not wanting to compromise, noticing Jacqui's disapproving look.

'Do you have any lower heels?'

'Oh,' Kym remarked, wondering why Jacqui was

being so manipulative.

'They do make you look a bit tall,' she added, a comment which Kym ignored, knowing she couldn't afford to lose her new friend with a sarcastic remark.

When they got to the dance hall, Kym was relieved that most students were dressed like her. Jacqui quickly launched herself into conversation with a nearby group of students and laughter soon followed. Kym watched her operate as she quickly isolated and chatted up a very young looking, dark haired art student called Tom. They were introduced and Tom gave Kym a lovely smile but as they start talking, Jacqui interrupted them and led him back to her side.

Not put off by events, Kym surveyed the room and noticed a tall, good looking guy who saw her and smiled. She looked at him again, he was in deep conversation with a pretty, petite girl. After a short time of exchanging glances with Kym. He came over to where they were standing, near to the bar and introduced himself as Matt. They talked for some time. Kym really liked Matt they chatted about his family life, which seemed similar to her own. After what must have been half an hour, Matt excused himself and returned to the petite girl's side. Kym felt a little disappointed by this, wondering if she had bored him into moving on. She hadn't planned on having a boyfriend, but he was definitely hot and she felt her gaze moving to where he stood, wishing he would come back and talk to her again.

Was he just be friends with the petite girl she wondered as Jacqui linked her arm, leading her off, talking excitedly about Tom. They shut the door to the ladies room blocking out the sound of the band, giving her the opportunity to ask Jacqui's advice.

'I'll find out,' Jacqui offered and before Kym could say anything to deter her she'd disappeared into the crowd and was introducing herself to the petite girl Matt was talking to. Jacqui knew Kym was inexperienced with men and because of this, didn't want her to be used foolishly and dumped. It was something that she'd experienced and although jealous of Kym's looks, wanted to protect her new vulnerable friend.

With Jacqui now absent Kym chatted away to Tom. He was a little shorter than her with a compelling charm and large deep brown eyes. Tom placed his arm around her waist, drawing her towards him, listening intently to her words. Kym felt comfortable with Tom and didn't want to leave his side. When Jacqui returned she gave Kym a stern look and put her hand on Kym's arm, steering her away from Tom.

'Don't worry Kym, Lucy has a boyfriend back home. Matt is therefore very much available and seems to be a genuinely nice guy.' Jacqui reassured her smugly. 'So, get yourself back over there and work your magic on him,' she said, moving her eyes in Matts direction.

Kym didn't have the confidence to go over and chat to Matt again, she wanted to stay with Tom, enjoying the comfort of his easy going nature. Jacqui had other ideas though, she wanted Tom to herself and expertly manoeuvered him away from Kym who was beginning to feel like she was in the way. Suddenly overwhelmed with tiredness, Kym touched Jacqui's arm lightly.

'I'm heading back,' she said. Jacqui groaned despairingly.

'Already, what about Matt, I thought you were interested in him?'

'I'm not so sure he likes me though,' Kym answered.

'Well Carpe Noctem, seize the night, or the man for that matter,' Jacqui added nodding insistently. Kym looked at Matt who seemed blissfully unaware of her presence.

'It looks like he's already been seized,' she sighed, noticing him laughing and standing close to Lucy.

'Fate will find a way...,' Jacqui added, turning her attention back to Tom.

Once back in her tiny room, Kym wished she had stayed with Jacqui and Tom. It was quiet in the room and she missed being in her cosy bedroom at home. Opening a book, she read for several minutes before falling into a deep and dreamless sleep.

Kym saw Matt again on several occasions. She knew what time he appeared in the student bar and would arrange to meet Jacqui there so she could bump into him. They'd been talking for weeks, but it didn't seem to be leading anywhere. Kym had done everything she could, spending time making sure she looked her best and had on outfits which would be sure to get Matt's attention, but it was still getting her nowhere. One night she had her casual jeans and checked shirt on, her hair was windswept from the short outdoor walk to the bar, when Matt arrived. She didn't feel or look her best and immediately wanted to hide away, but Matt quickly spotted her and came over with his big wide smile and his twinkling blue eyes. Kym couldn't believe it when he kissed her on the cheek.

'Are you doing anything tomorrow evening? Do you fancy a meal out somewhere?' he asked, smiling widely. She was speechless. Not quite sure what to say in reply.

'No, where did you have in mind?' she answered, noticing her heart had started to beat faster. Matt looked delighted.

'I know a quiet bistro we could try? How about we meet here first at around 7pm?' Matt continued, watching Kym's face, whilst waiting for a reply.

'Yes that's a great idea,' she answered blushing slightly.

'See you tomorrow then.' Matt turned and made his way quickly out of the student bar, not stopping to have a drink with them. Kym was very impressed, it seemed that he had only gone to the bar to find her and ask her out.

'At last,' said a thrilled Jacqui. 'Now we know he prefers the casual windswept look. Any idea what you're going to wear?'

'A dress,' Kym answered firmly, leaving no room for negotiation.

The next afternoon Kym went through her wardrobe planning what to wear for her date with Matt and picked out her short, clingy turquoise dress no matter what Jacqui's opinion of it would be. It was Kym's first date and she spent a long time getting ready. Although she'd talked to Matt many times, she was starting to feel very nervous about the evening. Kym wasn't used to drinking much alcohol and Jacqui had warned her against doing so. Maybe just a couple of glasses of wine with their meal and definitely none of the shots that the other students couldn't seem to get enough of.

Matt and Kym had a great first date, they really hit it off, but for some reason Matt hadn't arranged another date.  Kym waited for Matt to ask her out afterwards, but he didn't.  She felt really disappointed by this, but didn't have the confidence to contact him herself.  Kym consoled herself by thinking she couldn't have committed to a relationship anyway with all her course work piling up.  Sometimes Matt passed her in the university grounds, he would smile and wave, but never stopped to speak, which didn't help her low self-esteem.  Once again she felt like the girl that nobody wanted to spend time with.

Kym really missed her dad and wondered where she was going to find a protective man just like him.  However, the rugged, casual, outdoor type that was Matt would not have gone down well at home.  Kym's parents would expect her to bring a talented doctor home, although she was in no rush to bring any man home to be assessed by her dad.  Besides she had Jacqui, who seemed to like spending time with her and Tom who was turning out to be a reliable friend and a tower of strength when it came to needing a confidence boost.

The three of them spent time together most days, catching up, eating meals and planning evenings in the library or outings at weekends.  They enjoyed the closeness of their friendship triangle, joking and encouraging each other in a relaxed, cosy way.  Kym was a neat and tidy person, incredibly organised and liked to be in control of situations. If she didn't know what was going on, she became anxious, resulting in her constantly seeking reassurance from friends.

Kym didn't realise that Tom was falling for her. Jacqui made the odd remark but she instantly dismissed her comments.

'Jacqui there's absolutely nothing going on between us, we're all just good friends and that's how it will stay. I love spending time with both of you.' Kym was concerned by her friend's remarks,, she didn't want to risk losing either of them by starting a relationship with Tom. Besides with her studies and endless course work to complete, free time was becoming a luxury.

Things continued the same way until after they graduated and Jacqui went home. Kym and Tom found jobs in London. Kym at a research hospital and Tom in a small art gallery. It made sense to share an apartment. They became inseparable and spent all their spare time together.

It wasn't long before their relationship became physical, Kym could clearly remember the first time they had sex. She came in from a long tiresome day at work hoping to curl up on the settee. Tom had appeared secretive for several days, not wanting to discuss how he had been spending his time. He assured Kym that all was to be revealed that night.

He seemed very pleased with himself as he poured Kym a glass of her favourite wine. Then he produced a covered canvas from the back of the sofa. Although she was tired, Kym realised that she had to play along and unveil another of Tom's so called masterpieces.

Upon lifting the cover she gasped, finding a portrait of herself, smiling and looking happy. Tom could see that Kym was delighted with his painting of her.

'You have no idea how beautiful you are Kym. I painted you so that you can be reminded every day.' Tom moved closer and kissed her longingly. Kym touched his face lightly with her hand, tears filling her eyes.

'It's amazing. Thanks, nobody has ever done anything like this for me before.'

'Let's, see just how thankful you are,' he replied, taking the painting from her and unbuttoning her blouse.

'Hold on, I want to look at it for a moment longer,' Kym whispered, catching her breath, inbetween his passionate kisses.

'We can admire it later, come on,' he led her by the hand into the bedroom, his eyes full of desire.

That was the first night they spent together intimately. Cuddling up in bed afterwards, Kym could not help feel a little disappointed as it wasn't exactly the night of passion she'd imagined. But for the first time in her life she felt safe. Secure in the knowledge that she had someone who wanted to be with her and no-one else, ending her lifelong loneliness at last. For her the warmth and security she felt from their relationship more than made up for the lack of sparks in the bedroom. Over the next few weeks, Kym consoled herself with the knowledge that 'sparks' never lasted long anyway, a loving, caring relationship was what she really needed with a reliable, trustworthy man. Kym had read somewhere that most couples had sex once or twice a month and that was enough for her. She was often too tired after work and spent the weekends catching up on chores or working on a new presentation that needed completing for research purposes. Tom preferred to leave her to work and would watch television in bed most nights. He was usually asleep when she finally got to bed, which never seemed to bother either of them.

Jacqui visited them less often. She hadn't got a boyfriend and for the first time, in spite of their efforts, no longer seemed to be comfortable in their company. When Jacqui got a job in London, Kym offered Tom's old room, feeling that this would be a good opportunity for them to become close again. It seemed to be working, but after about a month, Kym came home to find Jacqui had moved on. It was probably for the best, Jacqui wasn't the tidiest of housemates and things were getting a little tense and crowded.

Tom was happy working during the morning in the art gallery. He continued to paint, mainly landscapes from photographs he took on afternoons out. Kym though, began to feel that things were unbalanced between them as she was working much harder than Tom. Putting in the hours, carving a career to create a large salary to pay for the majority of things they needed. Tom's part time job in the gallery didn't pay much and he never seemed to have any money left by the end of the week. Though she tried to hide her irritation, Kym was always having to bail him out, though he never repaid her and this started to cause some conflict between them.

When Kym got in from a long day at work, the place was always a mess. Dishes piled high in the sink, clothes strewn everywhere and paint brushes dripping bright colours all over the kitchen floor. Tom left all the housework to her and an exhausted Kym often spent an hour or more cleaning their apartment, whilst Tom remained sprawled out on the settee watching television. Eventually her frustration led to a heated confrontation.

'Tom, you need to help me a little more, I can't do everything on my own.'

'You only have to ask,' he replied, not taking his eyes off the television.

'Could you at least clean up a bit, before I come in from work, wash your brushes and any dishes, have a tidy around?' she looked at him with pleading eyes.

'I do tidy up, but you want everything done right away and I'm not like that, I've got a life and you're not exactly the easiest person to live with.' Kym felt the colour rise in her cheeks, he wasn't even looking at her.

'I'm fed up with this, would it be too much for you to put the dinner on occasionally and wash up afterwards?' Her voice was getting louder, she knew that if he didn't make any effort to agree with her then something would be said that would leave her full of regret.

'I never know what you want, how about you leave me some money for groceries and I can surprise you?' He looked at her and seemed to be half smiling as he said the words. Kym seethed with anger,

'How about you pay for something for a change, wouldn't that be nice?'

'Oh here we go, it's the…you don't earn enough or work as hard as me speech,' he mimicked her voice. 'Well done, I wondered how long it would take to surface.' He got up, annoyed that she was disturbing his peace, gathered all his paint brushes up, picked up canvases strewn across the floor and dumped them in the spare room. With a look of disgust on his face, he got his jacket and slammed the front door behind him. Kym's eyes stung with tears of frustration as she set about washing dishes, throwing the plates in the sink and smashing a glass in the process. As she carefully extracted a sliver of glass from her finger and watched a bead of blood swell up in its place, Kym wondered why she'd bothered. Now left feeling guilty for starting the argument, his words replayed in her mind. *"You're not exactly the easiest person to live with,"* she wondered if there wasn't some truth in the words.

When he finally returned he didn't apologise and he never made any effort to change. The next day all the dishes were waiting for her as usual when she got in. Kym continued to do everything for him, fearing that he would leave her if she didn't do exactly what he wanted. They settled into a routine with Kym trying to keep calm and avoid any further conflicts, until the flu pandemic shattered their lives.

Kym never got over the loss of her parents and in particular her beloved dad. Tom tried to help, but it was obvious that she chose to work through her grief to prevent herself from giving in to the pain which threatened to engulf her. Setting herself targets at work to regain some control in her life, enabled her to complete significant research for stem cell trials and write a report, which was published later that year.

She was reaching the peak of her career, attending prestigious venues and dinners every couple of weeks, loving the feeling of being important and successful. Tom however hated getting all dressed up and making small talk with people he didn't know and would do anything to avoid supporting her.

Now Tom had gone, the soul searching had continued all month. Kym was beginning to realise that he didn't love her and probably never had. Her fear of being lonely and craving attention had attracted her to him and she'd trusted him with her heart.

Kym simply couldn't bear to go back to the miserable loneliness that haunted her school days and wondered why Jacqui still hadn't responded to the messages left on her phone. Switching off the light and wrapping the quilt tightly around her, Kym prayed that she would see Jacqui again soon.

# Chapter Four

# Jacqui

Jacqui didn't believe in good or bad luck, she only believed in making choices and it had to be said that she'd made some bad choices in her life.

Living in a small market town in Lancashire, her childhood spent with her mum and grandmother seemed uneventful. On her sixteenth birthday she had a party at home with friends. All very tame for Jacqui who thought she was very 'street wise' and craved fun, risk and adventure. School had finished for the summer and Jacqui wanted to live a little.

A week after her birthday one of Jacqui's friends

asked her to an eighteenth birthday party in a neighbouring town. Jacqui didn't have much money for new clothes or taxis, so declined the invitation. Her friend Natalie pleaded with her as she fancied her older brother's friend Marc who would be going. Natalie was so insistent that Jacqui didn't want to let her down. There was no way she could tell her mum they were going to an eighteenth. Her mum would never allow it, so Jacqui decided it would be simpler to say she was staying at Natalie's house overnight. Natalie had co-erced her older brother into giving them a lift. Jacqui had nothing suitable to wear and used this as an excuse to try and get out of going to the party. She didn't like lying to her mum and felt that she would be on her own all night if Natalie spent time with Marc. Natalie solved the first issue by offering a black dress which she could try but Jacqui decided if it didn't look good she wouldn't be going, much to Natalie's dismay.

On Saturday night, Natalie's brother dropped them off at a pub in a nearby town, he could see they had too much make up on and that their dresses were very short.

'Where are you two going?' he asked, his voice full of concern.

'Just larking around, we won't be late, don't worry,' Natalie replied smiling. They seemed sensible girls so Natalie's brother assumed they would probably be trying to get into the local pub which was known for not verifying ages. He gave them money for a taxi back.

'Don't drink too much,' he shouted as he drove off.

'Look what I've got,' Natalie said cheerfully, producing a small bottle of vodka from her bag, waving it in front of Jacqui's face.

'How did you manage to get that?' Jacqui enquired.

'From Mum's drinks cabinet,' a very pleased Natalie said whilst quickly opening the bottle.

Walking tentatively on high heels half a mile to the house where the party was, they took turns drinking from the vodka bottle. It was very strong and Jacqui felt the strange tasting liquid burning her throat and causing a hot sensation in her stomach. Jacqui wasn't sure she wanted to continue drinking, but wanted to keep up with Natalie, even though she disliked the taste.

There was still vodka left when they entered the house, but the amount they had consumed was already taking effect. Plenty of people were crammed into the lounge where most of the furniture had been removed. Girls were dancing with their shoes off and boys were looking on whilst drinking beer and dipping into bowls of snacks. Jacqui was starting to feel a bit heady and dazed. She heard the strong rhythmic beat of the music, kicked off her shoes and started to dance on her own in the middle of the room. She felt very sexy, moving around in a slow, hypnotic way, everyone was looking at her and it felt great.

Natalie went into the kitchen and found her current love interest, Marc, who asked her who she had come with. A couple of boys next to Natalie heard her answer and surveyed Jacqui and one of them called Josh asked Natalie,

'How much has she had to drink?' Natalie laughed this off. Josh filled two glasses with fruit punch. He passed them both to Natalie before she went to check on her friend in the lounge.

'Jacqui come and have a drink in here, it's a bit quieter, I want to talk to you,' Natalie added pleadingly. She grabbed her friend's arm, leading a stumbling Jacqui towards the kitchen and what she thought would be a safer place. Med was there, he was a nice, quiet person who never drank alcohol and Natalie thought it would be good for Jacqui to talk to him for a while until she sobered up.

'Med, this is Jacqui,' Natalie said, hoping they would begin talking. Josh, was stood nearby and taking in Jacqui's inebriated state immediately moved to stand in front of her placing his hands possessively on her waist.

'Try this,' he said, passing her a glass of fruit punch. Med looked on disapprovingly, feeling slightly uncomfortable standing beside them.

Natalie was too busy flirting with Marc to notice anything else. He couldn't believe how different she looked tonight, much older than sixteen and very sexily dressed. He was having none of it though knowing her brother would kill him and thought about texting him, letting him know his sister was at the party. Her friend looked well out of it already and was moving closer than Marc would have liked to Josh. Whatever, he thought, the girls would probably be alright, they weren't his problem, he just wanted to relax tonight and enjoy himself.

The fruit punch seemed to be potent and Jacqui was starting to feel really drunk. Josh had commented on her ample boobs and she had offered to take her top off!

'Not here,' Josh said quickly, 'Upstairs in a minute,' he whispered in her ear. This was followed by lots of kissing and laughing. Natalie noticed out of the corner of her eye that Josh had taken Jacqui off for a dance, but she wanted to stay in the kitchen and continue to try and get Marc's attention.

Everything was becoming a bit blurred for Jacqui, who found herself suddenly lying on a bed, not knowing how she'd got there. Josh's weight pinned her down as he pulled her dress up past her waist, having already removed her underwear.

'Get off me,' slurred Jackie, quickly starting to come to her senses.

'We can't stop now,' Josh insisted breathing heavily 'you've been offering it to me for the last hour.' He'd already removed his trousers and was pushing her back down onto the bed. Jacqui was feeling very drunk and was in no position to negotiate. She screamed.

'No, stop it,' again and again, but the music downstairs was too loud and he was too strong for her, she couldn't get away and Josh looked like a man possessed.

He thrust hard into her for several minutes then it was over. Jacqui felt the room spinning round, she felt awful and was going to throw up. The urge got stronger and Jacqui couldn't stop it, she lost the contents of her stomach all over him.

'Aaagh, you bitch,' he shouted as he jumped up, his face twisted with anger. He resisted the urge to slap her instead wiping himself with the bed sheets, before pulling on his pants and leaving the room.

Jacqui couldn't believe what had just happened. Not having had sex before, he had really hurt her. She pulled down her dress and spotted her underwear thrown across the floor. Holding her head she attempted to pick it up feeling nausea rise in her throat once more, her hands stretched out as everything darkened causing her to collapse in a heap. After a few minutes she regained consciousness, quickly sitting up and grabbing her underwear as the room continued to spin faster and faster. Jacqui sat there crying tears of frustration and anger at Josh who had had sex with her even though she'd tried to stop it and due to her drunken state would probably get away with it.

After vomiting several times in the toilet a stumbling Jacqui found Natalie in the garden and told her to ring a taxi. Natalie could see Jacqui was ill, but didn't want to go home yet and suggested staying outside, hoping the fresh air would help sober Jacqui up. Marc offered to make some coffee, he seemed concerned, especially when he found Josh naked from the waist up standing at the sink.

'What have you been up to?' Marc asked in an agitated voice.

'Nothing,' said an annoyed Josh, sponging down his shirt 'she threw up on me that's all.' Marc seemed to accept Josh's explanation and returned to the garden with a glass of water. Jacqui took a mouthful and her stomach started to heave.

'Just get a taxi, I want to go home,' she pleaded with Natalie.

'I can't go back inside, you have to help me.' Seeing her friend looking so pale and physically shaken, Natalie wished they hadn't drunk so much vodka earlier.

'Ok I'm ringing one now, sit here with me until it arrives.' Natalie continued to comfort her friend, thinking she had never seen anyone that drunk before. After a further ten minutes the taxi appeared and Jacqui managed to walk towards it, assisted by Natalie. Neither spoke during the journey back to her home. It was only when Jacqui closed the front door and crawled into her own bed that she felt safe again. As morning broke she lay in bed feeling cold and numb, deciding to keep the terrible events of the night before hidden forever.

Jacqui somehow found the strength to put the summer behind her, not wanting to let what happened at the party ruin the rest of her life, although she had no interest in boys and didn't go to any more parties. Feeling lucky that no one had found out about what happened that night, she only left the house to go to school, never wanting to bump into Josh again. Jacqui didn't cry or reprimand herself, instead her focus was on getting good results, to gain a place at university so her mum would at least be proud of her.

Jacqui's efforts paid off and she achieved a place at Oxford University due to her high grades. Her plan was to move far away from Lancashire and the secret that haunted her, making a success of her life somewhere new.

She met Tom during her first week at university. He seemed quiet and nice, kind and caring, to her he was perfect. Jacqui who was deep down a lively, chatty, life and soul of the party girl, wanted to have some fun. Tom was drinking vodka and the smell of it made her stomach churn. Jacqui hadn't been able to drink it since that horrendous night at the eighteenth party, but was prepared to make concessions for Tom and his smiling eyes. Kym, her new friend, seemed to like Tom too but Jacqui was not going to lose Tom and was concerned this could turn out to be a problem between them. Kym was prettier but Jacqui was confident that she could get Tom's attention with her outgoing personality. As soon as Jacqui spotted Kym talking to Matt she aimed to get the two of them together, leaving Tom free to concentrate on her.

Over the coming weeks Jacqui noticed that Tom seemed to be getting closer to Kym. She couldn't believe it. Jacqui had slept with Tom several times already and now wished she'd waited until she knew him a bit better. They chose not to tell Kym about their relationship mainly as Tom didn't want it to complicate their friendship. Jacqui was beginning to worry that Tom had another reason for not telling Kym. What more could she do? She dressed how he wanted, did whatever he wanted in the bedroom, but he didn't want to tell people that they were a couple.

He'd commented once or twice that she talked too much and he needed more time alone. However, it was always her door he knocked on whenever he wanted sex.

After a few weeks Jacqui got fed up with Tom's attitude towards her. She decided not to sleep with him again until he officially made her his girlfriend. They rowed about it. Jacqui decided it was time to challenge him on the subject.

'Tom, what's wrong with us?' she asked, questioning his lack of public affection for her.

'What do you mean?' he replied, looking slightly annoyed that he was being put on the spot once more.

'You never kiss me in public, you act strangely with me when Kym is around, you're making me feel like some sort of dirty secret and I hate it.' She raised her voice as her irritation began to surface.

'I'm not the touchy feely sort, you know that, how would Kym feel if we were constantly all over each other in her presence? She would be embarrassed.' He added, resenting that Jacqui had such a lack of consideration for their friend.

'Enough about Kym, we are a couple and it's us that's important, isn't it?' she said raising her voice, her eyes flashing angrily at him.

'Do you fancy her?'

'Look I've got tons of work to do and I don't need this right now,' he shouted, moving away from her..

Jacqui turned towards him, searching his face for reassurance, but he looked down at the ground, avoiding her eyes. She fought against the urge to shake him, instead rushing out of the room, holding back tears until she'd slammed the door. Once back in her room she cried quietly, before deciding that he wasn't worth it and should be ignored, until he apologised. That never happened, leaving her feeling worthless once more. She had got over worse things in the past and never wanted to be used for sex again, which was exactly how he had left her feeling.

When they all graduated Jacqui felt ready to face returning home. It was wonderful to spend time with her mum and gran. She loved to be back amongst the familiar limestone buildings, along the river of her home town, although past memories often stopped her from walking alone amongst the streets she'd loved. It took two months before Jacqui knew it was time for her to move on, wanting to be somewhere livelier and different, each day her desire to leave grew.

Before returning to London, she took her mum and gran out for lunch to one of their favourite places on the coast. A couple of miles away from their home at the end of the bay, stood a white, curved fronted hotel next to the sea. The once derelict building had been completely restored some years ago, to its original art deco splendour. Jacqui was happy to be in her favourite surroundings once more, sitting at a table sipping a long conical glass of sultry creamy coffee. The waves looked spectacular as they crashed against the promenade in front of the hotel and she sighed deeply, content to watch the movement of the sea. Particles of sand blew towards the hotels tall glass windows which allowed unspoilt views across to the Lakeland Fells.

Jacqui felt at peace here and wondered if she was doing the right thing moving to London, but her thoughts were interrupted by the arrival of a sumptuous afternoon tea.

Before leaving Jacqui couldn't resist a final look at the hotel's round cocktail bar. Its curved walls were covered in red, pink and purple lit panels, merging into a cascade of bright colours. She took the curved staircase down to the powder room, walking through a large mirrored hallway with neatly arranged cream armchairs. A window was open and the room was filled with the scent of salty sea air. Sighing deeply, Jacqui knew she would miss this place but would always come back here, drawn to its remarkable location.

With her degree it was easy to secure a position at a hospital in London within the cancer research unit, but accommodation was expensive and she had little money. Kym had kept in touch, by text, during the summer and was delighted that Jacqui was returning to the area. The next day Jacqui's phone rang, it was Kym, they hadn't spoken for months and for some reason Jacqui hesitated to answer the phone, but eventually pressed accept.

'Jacqui I can't wait to see you again,' Kym announced. 'When are you coming back I've got loads to tell you.'

'Next week,' Jacqui replied, 'I've got to find somewhere to stay first.'

'Well you can stay with us, until you get settled. We have a spare room, now that Tom's moved into mine,' she sounded excited, happy.

'That's very good of you, thanks I'll let you know.' Jacqui's heart sank, Kym sounded elated that they were a couple, but she hated it. Sharing an apartment with them would be the worst thing she could think of, but starting her new job the following week meant it seemed her best option, until pay day. Facing Tom again would need to be handled carefully and Jacqui knew she would have to disguise her feelings for him, at least for a couple of weeks.

The first thing that Jacqui noticed was the long hours that Kym worked, she was never home during the early evening and they didn't appear to eat meals together, the whole arrangement seemed slightly odd.

Within days, Tom and Jacqui started going out for drinks after work and she quickly realised that Tom was frustrated by Kym's lack of interest in him, giving her the opportunity to reel him in once more. Jacqui knew it had been a mistake moving in with them, even for a short time. The closeness they had previously, soon returned and as they spent more time together, she wanted him back. One night after a few drinks, they arrived back at the apartment. Kym was still at work as usual and they couldn't keep their hands off each other. They waited for the apartment door to slowly close, not caring if anyone passing by saw them undressing.

They had sex and it was fantastic. Jacqui knew she wanted more and Tom disclosed that he'd never really enjoyed sex with Kym as she often left him unfulfilled. They couldn't get enough of each other and Jacqui felt that she was starting to win him back with the one thing that Kym was lacking, which increased her efforts to entice him. However, after a couple of weeks, she realised Tom still couldn't seem to make his mind up as to which one of them he wanted to be with.

'Together you're my ideal woman, but separately you both have your faults,' he confessed. They laughed at the time, he had to be joking, didn't he? Jacqui wondered, realising that he probably wasn't. During the next month he continued to sleep with her and love Kym. Eventually Jacqui accepted that he was never going to leave Kym and she would have to be the one to end it. One morning when they were at work, Jacqui packed up her things and left. Feeling guilty for what she had done to her friend, she felt unable to face her. Whenever Kym contacted her she would be busy, time went by and Kym gave up, Jacqui decided never to contact either of them again.

She continued to live in London, dating several men, but it never came to anything. Jacqui lost both her mum and gran to the flu pandemic and it was years before the devastating sadness that filled her days, began to diminish. Wondering where her life was leading and why she'd made so many bad decisions was a mystery to Jacqui who'd only ever wanted a fulfilling, stable relationship and a child of her own.

It would be seven years before she saw Tom again. It had been a mild and sunny September after a poor summer and Jacqui had missed most of the summer months, often not getting home until after 7pm. Looking out of the hospital window at the glorious blue sky increased her determination to take an hour off for lunch for a change. As she left the building, Jacqui was drawn to the local park, knowing it could be the last sunny day for a while as the weather would be changing soon, autumn was on the way.

She made her way to the park bench where she'd sat before, alongside the lake, admiring the cloudless blue sky. Quickly eating her canteen bought sandwich she relaxed in the sun, sipping orange juice, when he came strolling along. She spotted him straight away, even though he was at a distance from her. His jacket was off and he'd rolled up his shirt sleeves, just as he always did. Her heart stopped for a moment when she saw him. He hadn't changed it was still the same Tom. Her Tom. She would have let him pass by without saying a word, but he saw her and his amazing, bright sunny smile spread across his face as he approached the bench. It was as if he had planned that they would meet there at that time and Jacqui, for the first time in her life, was lost for words.

'Jacqui,' he said his voice full of emotion. She leapt to her feet and hugged him as if her life depended on it.

'Tom it really is you, how have you been?' Her eyes filled with tears with the realisation that she had never stopped loving him.

'Lonely. I've been missing you.' He held on to her as if he didn't want to let her go. His jacket lay on the ground where he'd dropped it, surprised by her sudden embrace.

'I never thought I would see you again,' she half whispered as her voice trembled, 'I can't believe you're here, you're really here.'

'Let's go somewhere private,' he replied, picking

up his coat and entwining his fingers in hers as he led her away.  Jacqui never did make it back to work that afternoon, taking some much needed time off.

Things seemed to be different this time around, it wasn't just sex, it had a depth of feeling that she hadn't experienced before.  They would lie together for hours afterwards, her head next to his heart, listening to its steady beat and to his dreams for the future including starting a family with her and not Kym.  After three months of meeting secretly and spending as many hours as they could with each other, they made plans to move in together.  Jacqui insisted that he tell Kym that they were a couple, but he never seemed to get round to it.  She knew he hated being pushed, so decided to leave things as they were though spending Christmas and New Year hardly seeing him, left her panicking that things would not work out for them once again.

It was a freezing cold January morning, just after celebrating the beginning of another year, when Tom reluctantly moved his things into her apartment.  He still hadn't told Kym and Jacqui began to wonder if he ever would.  A month quickly passed and he didn't contact Kym.  Jacqui threw all her efforts into making him happy.

She was beginning to relax and feel that he was hers and they would finally stay together.  They decided to send Kym separate birthday cards realising she would be alone on her birthday and it might help to get a couple of cards. The next day Jacqui had several missed calls from Kym and a text asking if they could meet up as Tom had left and she wasn't coping very well.

Jacqui couldn't risk losing Tom again so she put her phone in a surgical waste bin at work and bought a new one. She wanted to concentrate on her and Tom, nothing else mattered, Kym was part of their past.

Or so she thought until several weeks later, when they were on their way to have lunch at a small place they loved in Knightsbridge. Everyone has a moment in their life that they would change if they could. Jacqui had more than most but if she could, this would be the one that she would alter as the day's events unfolded.

Tom made breakfast for Jacqui that morning.

'What shall we do today?' he asked hoping that she would want to go out somewhere.

'Let's go to lunch at our favourite Italian, we haven't been there in ages,' she answered cheerfully.

Walking through Knightsbridge, with their arms around each other, they were talking intimately like any couple in love. Absorbed in each other's conversation they hadn't noticed Kym was walking towards them until it was too late. Kym stopped, standing dead still staring at them both no more than a few yards in front of them.

'Oh no,' Jacqui whispered to Tom as they dropped their arms from around each other. Kym just glared at them as if she was figuring it all out. Before they could say anything, she turned and disappeared into the crowd. Jacqui was shocked when Tom ran after her shouting her name. Leaving Jacqui standing there watching the scene as if she was totally unimportant to him, as he chased after his lost love.

## Chapter Five

# Fate

After a long night spent tossing and turning Matt woke up to rays of the morning's sunrise streaming in to his bedroom. It was Monday the 18th February and he smiled as a happy, contented feeling swept through his body. This was going to be the day he got another chance to meet Kym and he vowed not to let the opportunity pass by this time. The previous day he'd checked his work plan and discovered that he was down as an escort for the second Generate group meeting. Kym's name was on the list.

'Fantastic,' he'd said, at the time, his smile broadening.

'What is?' Sam, one of his colleagues inquired,

interested in what had cheered Matt up.

'Oh nothing,' he laughed, walking quickly away, leaving an inquisitive looking Sam guessing. Matt had wracked his brains trying to remember Kym's surname to try and establish if she was still single. Nothing came to mind, which was hardly surprising, as it had been over eleven years since their date at university. He breathed deeply, hoping his spirits hadn't been lifted only to be dashed again, remembering the previous week's disappointment. If fate was being cruel and he didn't get to greet her at the door he'd thought through a backup plan. As he escorted another person through the building, he intended to say a quick hello and stop to talk with her for a moment, if they passed in the corridor. Find out if she had time for lunch today, as unprofessional as it might be. Matt was going to take his chances and suggest the rooftop bistro in the Old Library building nearby. His lunch was at noon and he hoped that the meeting would be over by then, although he had advised Sam they might need to do a last minute swap, causing him to raise an eyebrow suspiciously.

It was 7am when Matt threw back the duvet eager to be out of bed and starting the day. The Generate meeting began at 10am and most attendees would be arriving up to an hour earlier, meaning he would need to be available in the reception area from 9am onwards. Matt had meticulously worked everything out in advance. He'd picked out his favourite light grey suit and spent longer than usual shaving and shaping his hair, although he always looked immaculate.

Kym meanwhile hadn't slept well either the night before the meeting, which had been running through her mind constantly over the last two weeks. Also, trying to contact Jacqui several times and leaving messages which hadn't been answered, was worrying her. Maybe Jacqui was away or had changed her phone number. That had to be it. Not to be put off, Kym decided to contact Jacqui soon, at the hospital she first worked at when they all left university. Luckily the Generate project was taking her mind off Tom.

Kym was going to raise the issue of abortion at today's meeting. It didn't seem right for new lives to be destroyed given the current situation in the country. Each and every life needed to be protected now. Which would lead perfectly into her next proposal for long term stem cell storage which was closest to her heart. If cells were taken from cord tissue at birth and stored they could be used in the future to cure cancers and hundreds of diseases. Sighing, her heart sank momentarily, realising that it would be difficult to convince the Government that they should commence a programme of storing stem cells, due to the costs involved. She also knew that restricting terminations would be a controversial issue, one which someone else would hopefully raise first. However, Kym thought that every idea discussed at the meeting would be filled with controversy. What else could they do? Ban the pill? This idea would only push up the sale of contraceptives over the Internet from other countries and condom sales locally. Charge for the pill? This might cause extra pregnancies but not in the numbers that would be needed to reverse the declining birth rate. It was going to be interesting to see what the other attendees put forward.

Looking out of her apartment window, the weather seemed to be calmer. The sky was powder blue with wispy clouds, promising a mild morning for her journey to Westminster. People were on the street below, walking hurriedly to their destinations. Kym couldn't remember the last time she'd seen a pregnant woman, or a new mum with a baby or a toddler in a pram. How things had changed during the past five years. Stopping for her usual coffee on the way to the station, she waited patiently for her train, hoping everything would go well today and that there wouldn't be any more uncomfortable surprises.

Walking towards Downing Street, gave her a fluttery feeling inside. It was quite a special place. She still felt strange going through the door, regardless of her many successes within her field of work. Kym was in a much better mood today, feeling positive about the meeting and in full control of her emotions. It wasn't like the first Generate meeting, knowing what to expect this time made her feel calmer and therefore happier.

Retrieving identification from her bag and walking towards the scanner, she looked up to see a tall, smiling man approaching her.

'Hello Kym. Do you remember me, Matt? We were at university together?' Kym was quite taken aback by this unexpected greeting and didn't know how to react. Looking at the sparkling blue eyes of the tall, good looking man standing there, her face immediately softened into a smile.

'Matt what a surprise, I had no idea you worked here.' With a bit of awkward conversation on the way to the lockers, Matt waited patiently for an opportunity to ask her to meet him for lunch. Other attendees had started arriving as Kym put several items into her allocated locker and he thought he might have missed his chance.

Matt knew more than anyone else that sometimes you only have a fleeting moment in time to grasp an opportunity, as fate may never again line up a set of circumstances in the same way. He had to go for it and as they left the locker room he took a deep breath.

'Do you fancy a catch up coffee when the meeting finishes?' he asked whilst searching Kym's face for a reaction. 'I could meet you in the Old Library rooftop bistro at about noon, if you can make it?' Time was short as they had already arrived at

Meeting room 'A' and Kym looked a bit serious.

'Yes, that would be great,' she replied hurrying into the meeting room and that was all Matt needed to hear.

Matt wondered if maybe Kym felt a bit cornered and had just said "yes" to get rid of him. She seemed very anxious to get into the meeting room. He decided he would wait ten minutes after the meeting had finished and then make his way over to the library. He'd picked the location remembering that Kym loved books and he'd taken his parents there when they visited recently. They thought it was a great place. It was a beautifully preserved building with a winding staircase leading up to a brightly lit rooftop conservatory which would be perfect for such a sunny, February afternoon.

Time dragged on, one hour became two as Matt felt at a loss for anything else to do other than wait it out. He stood with his back against the wall, just past the meeting room drumming his fingers at the side of his thigh. With another deep sigh he thought about how unwise it would be to get his hopes up as it was highly probable that she was in a relationship already. How could she not be, looking so good? Matt checked the time again, hardly five minutes had gone by. His mind wandered back to Kym and how he would love to spend time alone with her. Looking into her blue eyes, stroking that long blonde hair. Matt wondered what his chances were of ever doing that. Slim, he thought sadly. Reflecting on their date at university, he remembered the sparks between them, but he'd met Lucy first. After their one and only date they had continued to acknowledge each other. They hadn't fallen out and had always waved or smiled when they saw each other on campus. There was no reason why two old friends couldn't have a coffee together.

After what seemed like an eternity the door of Meeting Room 'A' opened and there was movement at last. Matt suddenly felt slightly awkward and asked Sam to escort the attendees back to lockers, instead busying himself in the control room. He felt this was a good move as it would not give Kym the opportunity to change her mind if he wasn't there.

When everything had quietened down he got his jacket, making his way out of the building into the sunshine, Matt felt a strange sensation of happiness flood through him. It continued as he walked briskly to the Old Library building, climbing the winding staircase two stairs at a time. When he got to the top he spotted Kym looking slightly uncomfortable sitting at a table in the far corner of the packed bistro, looking out at the London skyline.

Matt hesitated for a moment to look over at her beautiful blonde hair catching the light coming in through the long windows. Kym turned to see Matt approaching and got up to greet him. He kissed her on the cheek lightly, noting that her perfume was heavenly.

'It's good to see you again, you look wonderful and you haven't changed a bit,' Matt said, feeling slightly out of breath from climbing the stairs too quickly. His heart was racing.

'It's got to be at least ten years since I last saw you,' Kym replied.

'Eleven years and four months,' Matt added his eyes twinkling, hesitating before asking what he really wanted to know which was if she was unattached. Kym laughed.

'Well your memory is much better than mine. How did you get a job at Downing Street then?'

'They wanted a tall, good looking, single man, who was a trained security expert and spoke several languages!' Matt replied laughing. 'I was the only one who fulfilled all their criteria.' He hesitated, hoping that Kym would pick up on the "single" part which he had chosen to emphasise.

'What about you, how did you work your way up to a high level Government crisis meeting?'

'They wanted an intelligent, single scientist,' Kym responded, hoping to match Matt's wit. He smiled widely in disbelief, they were both single.

Elation flooded his heart and it skipped a beat. Matt decided to confess to Kym that he saw her during the original meeting, two weeks earlier and she'd ignored him at the locker room door.

'You walked straight past me and didn't even say good morning, I was mortally wounded,' he recalled, putting on a sad, hurt face.

'Why didn't you say something to get my attention then? I was trying to keep up with the man who was showing me around at the speed of light. I didn't have time to breathe, never mind time to check out staff loitering around in the corridor.'

They laughed and Matt caught both Kym's hands across the table.

'It really is good to see you Kym.' A move which sent pleasant shivers down her spine.

After time had dragged earlier, Matt couldn't believe that two hours had gone by when he checked his watch, thinking they'd only been chatting for less than an hour. He knew he had to leave her and make his way back to work but couldn't face tearing himself away from Kym. Everything had turned out perfectly. Before parting they arranged to meet on the following Saturday night at a nearby restaurant and swapped phone numbers.

Matt inhaled what seemed like fresher air as he

walked back to work, it filled his lungs, lightening his steps and broadening his smile. Kym and everything she said eradicated any other thoughts, leaving him wondering how he could possibly concentrate on the afternoon's security issues. It was only Monday and it would be a long wait until Saturday night. Be patient, take it slowly he told himself, she was trying to get over a recent breakup after all.

Kym had felt her spirits lift as soon as she saw Matt bouncing up the last couple of stairs to the rooftop conservatory. Thankfully she hadn't been left waiting for too long. Sitting there without a coffee, looking around nervously, Kym worried that other couples would be watching her and wondering if she'd been stood up.

When she looked up Matt was suddenly there with his rugged good looks and smiling eyes, greeting her with the softest of kisses. As his lips brushed gently against the skin on her cheek she quickly inhaled feeling her heart flutter. Somehow the awkward silences she'd envisaged didn't occur as conversation between them was natural and sincere. Trying not to linger too long on the sadness that had formed a large part of their lives they focused on their careers, likes and dislikes. This seemed to work, filling them both with laughter at times. There seemed to be a moment between them, unless Kym was imagining it. On a couple of occasions Matt had picked up her hands and held them in his across the table, stroking her fingers with his thumbs. Kym found this very stimulating, feeling a new wave of sensations sweep through her. At times he looked long into her eyes, providing another heart stopping moment as she discovered how alluring he was. Kym could have spent all afternoon with Matt, what a shame their time together had to come to an end.

On the train home her thoughts turned back to the meeting, the second unexpected thing that came out of the morning. It turned out to be a brief discussion with some attendees keen to talk about their ideas. Others didn't contribute anything but wanted to hand in papers at the end of the meeting. This meant that not everyone had disclosed their suggestions, the whole thing seemed extraordinary. At least she had managed to hand in her report recommending the storing of stem cells to protect future populations. As they packed up they were advised that no further meetings had been planned for the Generate group. However, members may be contacted personally to explore their proposals further.

Kym couldn't hide the look of disappointment that flooded her face as she walked slowly away. Her hopes to be heavily involved in any project work coming out of the Generate group's ideas seemed to have been quashed. It was strange how the meeting had turned out. Could it be that the Government had already decided what to do and just got them all together to waste their time? At least that was how it was appearing to her.  Putting this out of her mind, she thought of Matt, lifting her mood once more.  What a co-incidence that he worked there and now she was finally going to have a second date with him, the thought of which sent her spirits soaring.  Kym was stunned at feeling very turned on by Matt in the middle of the afternoon, it had startled her.  There were definite sparks when he touched her hands across the table.  She couldn't recall this sensation happening to her before, but wanted more of it.  Maybe it was time to throw caution to the wind, give in to her needs allowing the seductress inside to escape.  Could Matt hold the key?  It would be a long five days of sleepless nights before she would find out what fate had in store.

By Friday night Kym couldn't get her date with Matt out of her thoughts.  She poured hot water into her coffee cup and watched in a trance as it overflowed onto the worktop.  As she wiped down the brown stained puddle, a memory of cleaning up Tom's paints and brushes filled her mind.  Was it too soon to move on?  Scrubbing away at the mess, anger welled up inside her at how heartless he'd been.  His lack of contact had been cruel and Kym realised that she could no longer forgive him.

Matt had suggested meeting at a quiet restaurant near to her apartment and for the first time in as long as she could remember, Kym planned to spend Saturday spoiling herself.  Lying in bed, wishing the night would end so the next day could start, she gradually drifted into a long sleep. To ensure she looked her best Kym had made appointments to get her hair trimmed and her make up done in Knightsbridge early Saturday afternoon. Whilst there she was going to go shopping for a close fitting dress that had no associations with Tom, and new shoes, they were always a confidence boost.

At long last morning light entered her bedroom and her apartment computer reminded her it was time to get moving as its alert broke the quietness that surrounded her.

'Good Morning Kym, it's Saturday 23rd February the time is 9am,' Mr. Right announced promptly.

'Hmmm,' she muttered to herself, wondering if she'd actually found him at long last. Matt had sent her a text asking if he could pick her up.

'*I'll meet you there,*' she responded and then added '*I'm really looking forward to seeing you again*'.

Kym felt happier meeting him at the restaurant thinking it would be safer not to give out address details just yet. As the morning passed and it was time to go for her train, Kym's excitement surfaced and she collided with the settee when reaching for her coat. Dropping her bag and watching its contents spill out across the carpet caused her to pause for breath.

'Right, slow down,' she said out loud. Willing herself to conquer her nerves, Kym sat back down on the settee for five minutes before picking up her things. She closed her bag and tried to imagine Matt's strong arms around her and his calming voice. Still angry with Tom and the way her confidence had been affected, could easily prompt her to have sex with Matt later. It would feel good to be needed and desired by a new man and since their lunch she'd felt irrepressible tingles, whenever her thoughts turned to him.

Having missed the train she'd expected to take, Kym walked up and down the platform impatiently. Being a little behind schedule forced her to change her plans slightly and head straight to Knightsbridge to begin her shopping spree. Whilst listening to the groans and clatter of passing underground trains, Kym decided which shops to visit to select her seductive outfit. New dress, lingerie, she smiled to herself, feeling like a nervous teenager going on a first date. Kym hadn't shopped like this to impress a man before and found it very tantalising. Striding happily to the first department store, her good mood quickly evaporated as she looked in horror at a love struck Tom and Jacqui walking towards her.

The shock of seeing them together stopped her abruptly. They had their arms around each other, whereas Tom had never so much as held her hand in public! They looked so in love, giggling away as they moved nearer to her. A feeling of weakness flooded through her body, followed by lightheadedness which prevented her from moving away. They stopped as they caught sight of her, instantly dropping their arms from around each other. After remaining frozen to the spot momentarily Kym instinctively turned around and fled the scene, colliding with people in her haste to get away from them as fast as possible.

She could hear Tom shouting after her and hid within the crowd before darting into a store out of his sight. In an attempt to remain hidden from him she stayed there, picking up glassware like an ordinary shopper as tears filled her eyes. After some time had elapsed Kym left the shop with her head bowed and quickly made her way to the underground station.

'What a fool I am,' she whispered sadly, leaning against the cold tiles of the station wall, urging her train to arrive and get her away from the hell she'd just witnessed.

Devastated by seeing Tom and Jacqui together, Kym had lost the urge to shop for a new dress or shoes, thinking anyway that her date with Matt was going to have to be cancelled. Wiping away tears as she let herself into her apartment, Kym opened her bag which for the second time that day fell to the floor, along with her mobile phone. Hastily reassembling it she decided that a quick text to Matt would be the easiest thing to do, saying she was ill.

Kym knew it was wrong not to ring and explain,

but overcome with shock and emotion it was all she was going to be able to manage as speaking to him would give everything away. He would hear from her voice that something was wrong and would want to know what had happened. Kym didn't want to have to go through the misery of what had occurred that afternoon. She wanted Matt to see her as a happy, uncomplicated person, who would be fun to spend time with. Tom had done it again, he was still tormenting her and had managed to ruin everything.

She sent the text and it was some time before he replied.

'*Ok, no problem, I hope you're feeling better soon.*'

Kym read the words over and over which only increased her heartache as she struggled to find anything positive within them.

Lying in bed, the afternoon light faded as she tormented herself further, picturing Tom and Jacqui's smiling faces as they walked along arms around each other. Kym had always suspected that they had a thing going on with each other, but when challenged, Tom had just laughed it off. Then her thoughts turned to Matt, what would he be thinking? Though if she had gone ahead with their date and ended up in floods of tears he would know that she wasn't over Tom. That needed to be her secret as it could prevent Matt starting a relationship with her if he felt she still had feelings for someone else.

Wishing that she'd chosen her black halter dress to wear for their date and not gone shopping, Kym became distressed again. She was hoping that things could be different, the chance of a new start with a kind, caring man. Now everything had gone wrong again. Tom was with Jacqui and Matt probably wouldn't ask her out on a further date, just like last time. After feeling her life was starting to brighten up, she was now lost in a darkness that only years of deception can bring.

# Chapter Six

# Acceptance

Kym spent a restless night going over every conceivable scenario in her head as to how and when Tom had betrayed her. Had he always been having an affair? How long had they been sneaking around for, six months? A year maybe? She thought back to when Jacqui had suddenly moved out of her apartment seven and a half years ago, surely if hadn't been going on that long.

She couldn't believe that Tom had been unfaithful to her for so long without her realising. Hadn't they been happy and content? Tom loved painting and she'd always encouraged and supported him with his art. He'd never indicated that they had any problems in the bedroom. Then again why would he if he was getting plenty elsewhere and making a fool of her. As for Jacqui, they were supposed to be friends, although there hadn't been much contact from Jacqui over the years and Kym was beginning to realise why. Turning to Jacqui for support since Tom had left, had been a foolish thing to do. No wonder Jacqui had been ignoring her calls and messages, it all made sense now.

Since Tom had left Kym had been having a haunting, recurring dream which revisited her in the early hours of the morning. In the dream they'd gone to a shopping complex and Tom parked in the usual place.

'I have something to do,' he'd said with a mysterious smile, as if planning a surprise for her, arranging to meet back at the car an hour later. Kym gets back to the car park first, walking towards where they parked only to find the car is no longer there. Kym walks hurriedly around in circles searching for the car. Maybe I can't remember where we parked, she thinks, whilst searching different areas of the car park aimlessly. After what seems like hours looking for the car, Kym accepts that it's no longer there and must have been stolen. It then dawns on her that Tom hasn't returned either or contacted her, something has happened to him. Ringing his mobile, he answers with a strange unrecognisable voice sounding like he's miles away.

'*You'll never see me again,*' he says in a chilling voice, before ending the call. It felt strangely morose as if he was dead and Kym is terrified. Miles from home she doesn't understand what has happened to Tom and panic sets in. Upon waking she finds herself covered in sweat and feeling totally disorientated. It takes time for her to calm down, realising that she's safe in her apartment and not standing isolated on a car park searching for Tom.

Kym's vivid dream, still causes her to shiver as she pops two slices of bread into the toaster and listens to the kettle boiling ferociously. A cloud of steam flows towards her and she quickly moves away from its hot path. Gathering up toast and butter she sits at the table, still deep in thought about the previous days harrowing events. Tom isn't coming back, they no longer have a future together, it's just herself from now on. Yet she doesn't cry. Instead Kym tells herself she must face up to building a new life and forget him. Still feeling hungry, the trusty pack of chocolate biscuits comes under attack. Food shopping hadn't been high on Kym's agenda lately, however, there's always biscuits in the cupboard. After demolishing half a packet of milk chocolate digestives, her spirits lift a little and she turns her attention to Matt. He hasn't texted to ask her out again. It wouldn't surprise Kym if he didn't as letting him down without even a phone call, may have annoyed him.

However, Kym remembered the kind sensitive man she had chatted to at length earlier in the week at the Old Library. It was his understanding and caring nature that had appealed to her as well as his good looks and toned body. He seemed to enjoy their time together and was keen to see her again. Kym picked up her phone, wondering what to do, remembering the exciting expectation she'd felt at the thought of a date with Matt, before yesterday's shock had put an end to it all. She put the phone back on the table to avoid checking it constantly, deciding to give Matt until late afternoon to contact her. If he didn't, then she would text him and hope he would reply.

..................

Matt put his hands to his head, sighing deeply unable to hide his disappointment after reading Kym's text cancelling their date. It was the first time since Lucy's death that he'd felt such captivating attraction towards a woman only to be let down.

'Why, oh why do I bother,' he muttered out loud to himself. Then he remembered how she looked, the smell of her perfume and her enticing smile. Convinced he hadn't misread the signs, he whispered,

'She's worth it and I'm not giving up.'

Matt didn't have any other plans for Saturday

evening. During the week he spent an hour after work doing sit ups, press ups and some punch bag work at home. Now though he needed a change from the monotony of his weekday routine and decided to go to the gym. Grabbing his sports bag he found his membership card in the front pocket, which luckily was still valid as he hadn't been a regular at the gym for months. Finding his crumpled kit in a drawer, he pulled it on clumsily and for once didn't stop to check his appearance in the mirror before he left. When he arrived at the gym's car park he struggled to find a place to park, luckily he didn't have to wait long before two giggly ladies appeared. Matt beeped his horn impatiently as they applied lipstick in the car before eventually reversing out of his way.

Once inside Matt headed for one of the many treadmills which looked out onto the road below, wincing at the musty smell of sweat in the air. Saturday evenings appeared to be very busy at the gym. He hadn't been there on a Saturday before and was amazed to see the amount of people occupying the equipment. Probably all single like me he decided, selecting a fast speed on the treadmill, to try and overcome his bad mood.

'You're going for the burn,' said a young girl cheerfully on the treadmill next to him. Matt didn't answer as he ran on the treadmill for twenty minutes at the higher speed. It felt like torture, he was sweating profusely but refused to stop. Dropping the speed a little he continued to run at quite a pace until he was exhausted. His legs felt a bit weak as he stepped off the treadmill but it had done the trick, neither Lucy nor Kym filled his mind. All Matt could think about was getting a takeaway and getting home. His legs felt numb and he struggled to get out of the car. Relieved to be home again, he found a washed fork in the kitchen and dug into a high calorie Chinese meal. Not long after eating far too much food he collapsed on his bed and slept right through the night.

When he woke up on Sunday morning the first thing he felt was sharp pain as he tried to move his knees. Cursing himself for running too hard and long on the treadmill, he dragged himself out of bed and hobbled to the kitchen where he drank a large glass of chilled orange juice in one go. The coldness hit his stomach, waking his senses and thoughts as he stretched out on the settee with ice packs around his knees. What was he going to do about Kym? Should he stay single and maybe date a few different women first, although he'd never had the desire to play the field before meeting Lucy, so why now? Since Lucy's passing Matt could have had his pick of women if that had been his choice, but none of them gave him that sense of magnetic fascination, until now. Matt thought about how thrilled he'd felt when Kym had met him at lunchtime on Monday. How she looked, laughed, that gorgeous blonde hair and her sparkling bright blue eyes. He'd felt something stir as he hugged her goodbye, possibly a bit too close for friends and his heart lifted when she agreed to see him again.

With these thoughts running through his head Matt decided to send Kym a quick text asking how she was feeling.  If she replied then he would ask her out for drinks.  What the hell, he thought, tonight.  Badly needing a boost after the disappointment of yesterday, he needed to see her and didn't want the intensity between them to cool.  Matt sent a text considering that it would fit better than a telephone call, giving her the chance to decline, without any awkwardness, it was the gentlemanly thing to do.

................

To help the time pass on Sunday, Kym busied herself packing up any of Tom's things she found left in her cupboards and drawers.  Continuing to gather together the many paintings he had left behind in the spare room, she counted fifty.  Kym never really ventured in there it was a very messy place.  Coffee jars stood filled with various sized paint brushes in cloudy water, sketch pads and paper were strewn across the floor.  Canvases were piled up against the walls in several places.  Why couldn't he put all his papers and canvases in a pile together Kym wondered, gathering them up and throwing them into a heap with no regard for their fragility.  The pile collapsed, sending canvases across the floor.  Kym picked some of them up and stood them in the corner, pausing when she found her portrait.  Sitting down on the floor she held it in her hands and examined the face staring back at her. Tom had painted her as a happy, smiling person, capturing her beauty, he'd told her lovingly. Looking at the painting now, filled with hindsight, all she saw was a fool, who had been easily manipulated into what Tom wanted her to be. Their life together had turned out to be a deception, a bed of lies.

She looked again at the portrait, wondering if he'd ever loved her, then placed it clumsily in the middle of the other pictures, realising that she would never really know. Continuing to tidy his things away, Kym only paused to wipe her eyes and request her apartment computer to play classic rock songs loudly, thus reflecting her mood.

When Tom had completely disappeared from her view and was shut behind the spare room door, the kettle went on for more coffee and chocolate biscuits. The apartment smelt fresh and clean. Kym started to relax but then realised that having deleted his profile from her computer, Tom wouldn't be able to get in to pick up the rest of his things. She would have to face him one final time. Had she been stronger it wouldn't have posed a problem, a quick slap across his face would have done the trick. In her weak, vulnerable frame of mind, Tom would only see her tears, how could that be fair? Still deep in thought Kym was brought back to reality by hearing her phone vibrate. Picking it up her heart leapt as she saw that it was a text from Matt.

Quickly opening the text she read the words several times.

*'How are you feeling, fancy dinner later?'*

She put her hand over her mouth, stunned. Matt wanted to take her out in only a few hours' time. She gasped, not knowing whether to accept, it was very short notice. Then Kym considered that if she turned him down again he would probably give up, he was giving her a second chance and she simply had to go. Quickly accepting his invitation Kym vowed not to let anything mess things up this time.

# Chapter Seven

# Tom

Tom sat at a polished table with his head in his hands. After attempting to pencil some outlines onto a blank, cream A4 pad, his mind wandered. Looking down at a mass of patterns artistically filled with the names of the two women he loved, he reached for a piece of charcoal and obliterated one of the names with fast, dark strokes. Tearing the page and screwing it up into a tight ball he hurled it towards the waste bin, tutting as it missed, knowing that he'd have to move it before she returned. Reluctantly he picked it up and unravelled it, checking the name blackened out couldn't be deciphered, before adding it to the bin, already overflowing with similar discarded creations.

Passing the mirror, he looked at his neglected state, not surprised by the tired, sad image that stared back at him.

*How on earth are you going to be able to do this*? he asked himself, slowly shaking his head from side to side as his forehead creased with lines of worry. Tom ran his fingers through his thick dark hair, before returning to the table to waste another afternoon with his unresolved dilemma. There was no alternative, he was going to have to be the bad guy and just couldn't do it. All his life he'd avoided conflict, putting other people's needs before his own and avoiding making decisions until one was forced upon him, knowing it wouldn't be what he wanted.

Unable to choose between two very different women, Tom had been forced to make a start. Seeing the confusion and hurt in Kym's eyes, during his moments of antagonism reminded him of his mum and what she went through when his dad did exactly the same thing. Being closest to his mum, her anguish deeply affected Tom as he witnessed her struggle to cope with day to day life after his father left. A lovely woman, crushed and stamped on like a flower that once stood proud and reached out for the sun. Yet he reminded himself that his mum had learnt to cope eventually and by the time he went to university was looking slim and attractive and had found a new man. Lost in his thoughts, Tom remembered the one time in his life when he had made his own decisions and felt unburdened and free.

His room at university had been tiny and bare, compared to home, but it was unimportant as he walked with his head held high along the halls of Oxford University. He'd made it, studying art at what he considered to be the best place in England. With a spring in his step, he made his way to the main hall to meet other students, greeting anyone passing with a welcoming smile. Free from worries he'd arranged a large student loan to cover the cost of his course, although Tom never worried about money, if he had it he spent it and never planned on paying the loan back.

After an interesting few days he arranged to meet up with a couple of students from his course on Friday night, dressing casually in a striped shirt and jeans. There was a band playing in the main hall and as he walked there Tom breathed in deeply, thrilled with excitement and expectation. Standing around drinking vodka shots, listening to the band and noticing some of the girl students passing by caused his smile to broaden, loving every minute. Downing another shot he looked up to find a pretty dark haired girl had appeared from nowhere and was standing next to him.

'Hi I'm Jacqui, who are you then?' she asked smiling, with an enquiring look on her face. Taken aback he looked at her, startled by her enthusiastic approach, she oozed happiness and fun at the same time.

'I'm Tom, how are you, what are you studying?'

'Medical sciences,' she answered 'what about you?'

'You,' Tom said cheekily, watching her smile widen, he'd immediately got her attention. Jacqui was impressed by his response, not many people left her stuck for a quick, witty reply.

'Interesting, that's the first time I've heard that one, are you using it with all the girls you meet?'

'No,' Tom answered looking slightly embarrassed. 'It's the first time I've said it.'

'Sorry,' Jacqui responded. Tom actually looked hurt, which appealed to her. 'Can I buy you a drink as a peace offering?' she asked.

'I'll have a vodka shot please,' Tom replied. 'Maybe I could buy you one in return,' he offered not wanting to appear ungentlemanly.

When she returned with the drinks, they soon fell into a comfortable banter with each other. Tom thought she was funny and lively but maybe a little overpowering. She introduced Tom to her lovely friend Kym, who seemed shy and lost. Although taller than him, he would have liked to get to know her. Jacqui however, wanted to talk solely to him in a flirty manner which he was happy to go along with.

Hearing that the first few weeks at university could be wild his chain of thought was why not? This sexy girl seemed to be very interested in him and it was intriguing as to where she might lead him. Tom very much liked the idea of being lead anywhere by an attractive, fun female. It was much easier than him having to do all the hard work and getting things wrong, as had happened with his limited past experiences with girls.

As the night wore on Tom realised that Jacqui was flirting with him but there didn't seem to be anything else on the cards, until she turned to face him looking as if she had something on her mind.

'I could be a model for you,' she said, adding 'nude,' which stunned him into silence. Tom knew she was probably only joking but wondered what it would be like to draw her naked. Imagining her curvy body taking shape with charcoaled strokes onto his canvas, excited him. They exchanged mobile numbers before she left. Should I call her? Tom wondered, though it seemed more likely that he wouldn't have to wait long for her to call him. After a few more drinks with his new found friends, Tom decided to head back to his room. He couldn't be bothered to get undressed instead just pulled the quilt over himself, noticing the room was slowly spinning. The start of university life,

'Excellent,' he said out loud before falling into a deep sleep.

After her initial enthusiasm, Jacqui seemed to back off and kept him waiting for a while. Whenever they were together she was always full of flirty innuendos. It was like a game to her, reeling him in and dropping him again.

Whatever her method it was certainly working. She had awakened his senses and he was producing some of his best artwork to date. Her friend Kym was lovely too. Although quieter and always buried in books, she was becoming a good friend.

Tom enjoyed being with them both and wasn't missing home at all. After a couple of weeks playing her on and off games Jacqui offered to pose naked for Tom to sketch. He couldn't refuse and set aside Saturday afternoon to make a start.

Still thinking she was joking, Tom couldn't believe his luck when she started to remove her clothing.

'Where do you want me,' she said in a sexy, flirty voice.

'Erm over there, on the bed,' he answered feeling his temperature rise and wondering if this was another game. He was expecting her to pull her top back on at any moment, saying "got you" in her fun way. She didn't though and when he looked at her she smiled knowingly, obviously enjoying the whole experience.

'Keep still,' he whispered, unsettled by her movements as he began to mark his sketch pad with her curvaceous lines.

Trying to get Jacqui to remain quiet and serious for a couple of minutes was proving difficult. Trying to draw Jacqui when he just wanted to touch her was unbearable. It was becoming clear that the drawing would not be completed that day. Jacqui seemed to be in a naughty, suggestive mood. Tom was on the bed next to her, telling her how to pose for him. She was leading him into one of her games, enjoying the domination, as did Tom. He had never met anyone like Jacqui before, she seemed inexperienced and experienced at the same time. Unable to resist her teasing, led to them kissing passionately and giving in to their desires. Afterwards they lay wrapped around each other on the tiny single bed and Tom knew he didn't want this to be a one off thing.

'What about finishing your drawing?' he asked, raising an eyebrow.

'If this is the way you treat your nude models then it may never get finished,' she answered. They both laughed. He never did get to complete the drawing of her. It was always an intimate joke between them.

Sometimes Tom found Jacqui annoying, always talking over him, leading conversations and deciding what they were going to do. Tom loved to have peace and quiet to spend hours drawing or painting and Jacqui was getting to be too much for him. Looking for ways to avoid Jacqui he started to spend more time with Kym. She was gentle and kind, much quieter and always listened to Tom completely. Not butting in on his answers or trying to end his sentences with her own. Tom confided in Kym that he wanted to spend less time with Jacqui.

'We're all close friends but she's always hanging around me. I don't feel like I have any time to myself and she chats non-stop,' he complained to Kym.

'Tell her that you have work to complete and agree which nights you need to be alone, like I do.' Kym suggested.

'I've tried that but she wouldn't listen, can't you spend more time with her?' He pleaded with Kym, no longer able to cope with Jacqui.

'Not really, I've got a ton of work to do, to pass this course. You need to make her listen to you,' she answered sympathetically. Kym understood Tom's dilemma, Jacqui was a handful. It was an advantage for her that Jacqui was absorbed with Tom. She was getting loads of work done and didn't want that to change anytime soon.

Tom continued to try and detach himself from Jacqui's grip but she didn't seem to be taking him seriously. The sex didn't seem to be working anymore either as he was fantasising about Kym more and more when he was alone in bed at night. Still choosing not to do anything about it, he was relieved when it finally became blatantly obvious to Jacqui that he wanted Kym and not her. Jacqui stopped visiting his room and ceased her relentless texts. They spent less time together and Tom felt happier as he began to escape from her grip.

After they graduated, Tom knew he wanted to be wherever Kym was. It wasn't down to luck that he got a job at a small gallery in London near to where Kym would be working. He applied to every gallery in the area as they often recruited art students over the summer months on a part time basis. Tom was so intent on staying close to Kym that he visited each gallery in person, hoping to impress them with his enthusiasm. His efforts were rewarded with a temporary job offer at the seventh one.

Things could not have gone better when Kym suggested that they move in together. Her dad had bought the apartment she lived in as an investment opportunity, although he hadn't expected to be in the spare bedroom. Kym wanted to take her time and he tried to be patient but struggled to get her to respond to his advances. Then he had an idea to impress her with a personal portrait and entice her into bed. It worked and they were officially a couple, Kym's shyness meant she struggled to relax during sex, but he liked her lack of experience which seemed to boost his ego.

Everything was going fine. Kym was making good money with her new job, working late most evenings, leaving Tom lots of time to paint and draw. The arrangement suited him perfectly. Until the day that Jacqui showed up.

Kym had offered the spare room, without asking him what he thought. Even expecting him to be at home to let her in. His palms were sweaty as he opened the door and as soon as he saw her something inside him stirred. His heart leapt as he embraced her and judging by the way they were looking at each other, she felt the same.

'I'm sorry Tom,' she started to say.

'Shush, it's ok we can make this work,' he silenced her with a kiss on the cheek, followed by a close hug. His body started to respond to the feel of her curves.

'Can we?' she replied moving her eyes down towards his trousers. They both laughed.

'It really is so good to see you Jacqui,' he answered with a huge smirk on his face.

Tom spent many restless nights struggling with his conscience. Did he love Kym or Jacqui or neither of them? Who did he want to be with and how could he possibly decide without upsetting one of them? Not finding the answers and with Kym out of the way during the day, he couldn't resist Jacqui, the attraction was too strong. A few drinks at a local bar meant they were both ready and kissed passionately as they walked back to the apartment. Kym wouldn't be in for hours and he put her out of his mind whilst enjoying having wild sex with his uninhibited Jacqui. Tom's happiness filled him with life, everyday seemed new and invigorating, prompting him to keep the arrangement going as long as possible.

Then Jacqui confronted him, it was totally unexpected, after they'd spent the afternoon in bed together. After sex he'd noticed her looking a little sad and unusually quiet.

'Do you love me?' she whispered. What could he say, he didn't know the answer.

'I love being with you, you are gorgeous,' he replied whilst gently stroking her hair, not at first seeing the trouble that was brewing.

'When are we going to tell Kym then?' His face must have given his unease away, because she got out of bed abruptly, with the covers tucked underneath her arms, hiding her nudity for the first time that he could remember.

'Wait Jacqui, come back to bed. We can't tell her, it would break her heart.'

They had a very heated argument after he

admitted thinking they were just having a bit of fun. Tom had never said he would leave Kym and as fast as it had started it all came to an end. Tom, saddened by her leaving had no option but to settle for a return to the dull, boring, quiet days before Jacqui's warmth and vibrancy filled his heart. He had a good life with Kym and was desperately hoping that she wouldn't find out about his intimacy with Jacqui. If she did, then he would be out of her life forever and he certainly didn't want that to happen.

Tom's reluctance to meet Kym's parents perturbed her, so unable to put it off any longer he agreed to go out to dinner with them. Upon meeting them he got the impression that they weren't very impressed with him, so just sat there sweating, as they ordered lavish courses and expensive drinks. Thankfully her Dad offered to pay the bill, but not before making a point that only served to make him feel inadequate.

'I'll get this, until you get a proper job,' he told Tom. 'Only joking,' he added, patting his back as he went to pay. Tom would have loved to say, "no, let me," but he simply couldn't afford it. Her dad had insisted that they go to this particular expensive restaurant. If they had gone to the place he suggested, he could have easily afforded to pay and they would have had a better evening in a more relaxed atmosphere. Kym ignored his suggestion and sided with her dad's choice and although he'd laughed at

Kym's dad's remarks, felt that he wasn't good enough for their talented daughter.

Things didn't seem to improve between Tom and Kym's parents. It was getting to the point where Tom refused to visit them and Kym started going more often on her own. Kym would come back and it was obvious they had been talking about his faults. Kym insisted he got a full time job or changed his career path, complaining that they didn't have an equal partnership. Tom tried to stay positive in front of her.

'There could be a masterpiece in me yet,' he'd say defensively, continuing 'chances are I will only get some credit for my work when I'm dead like a lot of artists.' She'd just glare at him saying nothing.

Tom's misery continued when Kym's parents died, she wouldn't let him touch or comfort her. Feeling unwanted he thought about leaving but enjoying all the free time he had and the money, had no motivation to try and start over. Enduring four more years of their relationship, Tom finally had to face up to the reality that things were coming to an end between them. He couldn't seem to do anything right and didn't think he could make her happy, plus he was starting to miss the warm intimacy that he once had with Jacqui.

They had lost touch but Tom knew where Jacqui worked and knew there was a park nearby. They used to meet there for lunch when she moved in with them temporarily years earlier.  It was her favourite place and if she was still working at the hospital, there was a chance that she still went to the same park for lunch.

After a period when he had hardly seen Kym for nearly two weeks, Tom convinced himself that he needed to be with Jacqui again.  His painting had ceased and he felt fed up and in need of some new stimulation.  He remembered his wild, fun Jacqui who seemed able to motivate him in a way that Kym couldn't.  He decided to visit the park after working mornings, each day in an attempt to bump into her.

Tom wrestled with his conscience again.  Was he being cowardly?  Shouldn't he just leave Kym and set up on his own?  He didn't relish the thought of ending up in some dodgy bedsit if he did, which would be all he could afford.  Tom couldn't go back home to his mum either.  She had remarried and lived with her new partner in Spain.  He'd lost touch with his dad, they hadn't been in contact for years and Tom wasn't sure where he was.

There was only Jacqui, she would be his last hope to escape from his mundane life.  He remembered how angry Jacqui had been when he last saw her.  How would she react if she saw him again?  It had been seven years since then and much may have changed with her.  He remembered her words the last time they parted, she was crying.

'It's me who loves you, Kym doesn't and you are

making a big mistake staying with her.' She was right and Tom needed to find her and hope and pray she was still single and still had feelings for him.

The more Tom thought about this idea the more it seemed to be the right thing to do. What was once just a small idea was now engulfing him, it was mushrooming in his mind and he had to find her. The only problem would be if Jacqui was not free and if that was the case he would end up staying with Kym and have to make the best of it.

After taking the underground to the park every day after work for almost two weeks Tom was ready to give up. Things had been frosty at home with Kym. This was due to Tom not going to another important dinner one evening. She didn't realise how hard it was for him to share conversation with medical people who seemed to look disinterested when he told them what he did for a living. He ended up feeling inferior and useless and often sat in silence whilst they talked amongst themselves.

It was late September and a warm sunny day, though Tom hadn't found Jacqui yet, he didn't want to go home and sit there all afternoon alone. He took the usual path along the river and slowed to a near stop as he saw his lovely, sexy Jacqui sitting on a bench just ahead. His heart raced, there was no turning back. He looked at her dumbstruck and she locked eyes with him, unable to speak.

'Jacqui,' was all Tom could manage, completely overwhelmed by the emotion he felt at seeing her again.

They hugged closely and he could feel her warmth and the softness of her body against his.

'Any chance you could pose for me, I have a drawing to finish,' Tom said to her softly, he had rehearsed this moment for weeks.

'Still the same old Tom,' she said smiling through tears. 'Always thinking about getting me naked.'

'That wasn't what I meant,' Tom replied looking serious.

'The drawing of you that I never get to finish, is our story, which we abandoned abruptly, all those years ago. We need to complete it, our story needs finishing.' His face started to break with emotion as he said the words convincingly. He could see in Jacqui's face that she understood what he meant.

'Are you in a relationship?' he asked suddenly realising that he hadn't established if Jacqui was free, being so keen to create the perfect romantic moment between them.

'No,' she replied. 'I've been waiting for you to come to your senses.' She looked away momentarily, unable to prevent tears flowing.

'It doesn't matter how many years have gone by, you're still mine and we deserve to be together.' Tom managed to answer, fighting back tears.

Tom couldn't face telling Kym about Jacqui. They had been together for three wonderful happy months and inspired by her, Tom had started painting again as each day seemed new and bright. Kym had noticed the change in him and it was lifting her spirits as she looked forward to spending Christmas and the New Year together. Jacqui though was acting strangely, concerned that Tom wouldn't leave Kym in the New Year, although he had done everything he could to reassure her.

'Don't let me down again Tom,' Jacqui told him, after they had spent a passionate afternoon together. 'I can't bear this anymore, we need to start building a life together.' Tom tore himself away from Jacqui and went home to Kym, he knew what he had to do.

The night before he left Kym, Tom was full of doubt. Was he making a big mistake? Kym had spent more time at home in the evenings since Christmas and Tom started to see signs of the old Kym he knew and loved. He was torn between the two of them, knowing he would be breaking Kym's heart and clearly remembering the pain and torment his mum had gone through when his dad left. Tom still wasn't sure that she'd recovered from the death of her parents and worried that his leaving would be a huge shock, with her having no-one to turn to.

Tom decided to instigate an argument by refusing to go to another science gathering which he had been dreading for weeks. Kym wouldn't listen to him, nastily spelling it out that he was useless and not the man she needed. It worked well and gave him the opportunity to leave, although he did feel a slight pang of guilt for letting Kym think it was her fault he'd left.

However, Tom could never have anticipated that they would all be in Knightsbridge, on the same day, at the same time, in the same place. He couldn't bear to see the look of pain on Kym's face and his immediate reaction was to comfort her. It confused him when he realised that he still had feelings for Kym and wanted to try and explain what had happened, not wanting Kym to jump to conclusions and shut him out of her life forever. He searched frantically for her, but she had disappeared into the crowd and after spending some time looking, had to give up. Tom turned around, suddenly remembering Jacqui. She would be really mad with him and would sulk for days. This was going to cost him dear. Jacqui didn't seem to trust him lately and would not take well to the fact that he had left her and chased after Kym.

When he got back to the place where he'd left Jacqui, she'd gone. He looked around for a bit and tried her phone but there was no answer. Tom didn't know what to do and standing alone with his hands in his pockets, tried to decide which one of them would be more likely to forgive him?  His fingers found several notes there which he quickly pulled out and counted, before crossing the road and heading towards the nearest pub.

# Chapter Eight

# Decision

Jacqui soon arrived home, slamming the front door behind her before locking and bolting it. Tears of frustration stung her eyes as she banged her back against the cold hardwood door.

'Aaagh,' she cried out. A bolt of pain shot through her body and she slid down onto the floor, with tears running down her cheeks. Tom had done it again, chosen Kym, plunging her into the depths of humiliation for the third time.

Wiping her eyes she stood up.

'How could you have been so stupid,' she screamed, clenching her fists before wrapping her arms around herself and sobbing loudly.

After several minutes she dried her eyes and poured herself a glass of wine from a bottle that had been open for several days and had a strong acidic taste. Not caring she downed it in one go and sat on the settee thinking of Tom and his inability to maintain a lasting relationship with only one woman. Sitting there she realised that her love for Tom wasn't going to be enough, if he still loved Kym, then they couldn't have a future together as all her efforts to keep him would be futile.

Jacqui had heard stories about relationships that had formed whilst one of the parties had still been in love with someone else. They often turned out miserably, with the needs of both people in the relationship unfulfilled. She wasn't prepared to be involved in anything like that. Her mum had brought her up to be a strong, confident person who could stand on her own two feet and cope alone.

Jacqui had worked hard since leaving university eight years ago. Buying and furnishing her own apartment had been very satisfying. As her breathing returned to normal, looking around it seemed very different from the space she knew and loved. It was him, he was everywhere. The soft, bright sand coloured carpet she had lovingly chosen to match her chocolate suite, looked dirty, marked with splatters of paint. Art magazines had been discarded untidily on the floor and his jumpers and socks, dangled from chairs. Canvases and sketch pads covered her polished oak table, once a favourite place to eat by the window, now claimed by him as a dumping ground. Jacqui shuddered as she realised it wasn't her apartment anymore. It had been invaded by a messy, disorganised thief, who was stealing her sanity.

Why had she allowed him back in her life? It wasn't as if she'd needed him, with plenty of friends to go out with at weekends, she always had a full social diary. Jacqui loved having her large, comfy bed to herself, tucking up within its soft, warm quilted layers, whenever she felt in need of comfort. Glancing over towards the half open door of her bedroom, she couldn't even see her luxurious, silk hemmed quilt. It was covered with the mess of a man who was incapable of putting anything away.

Calming down, Jacqui's thoughts turned to six months ago, when she bumped into Tom in the park. Was it just a coincidence, she now began to wonder. Did he really love her or was it just the thrill of meeting in secret that attracted him. Returning to the fridge she managed to get another half glass from the leftover wine bottle. Taking a mouthful she winced at its bitter taste, but still swallowed the rest, realising it was helping her to relax. Jacqui tried to figure out if it was love or just a battle between her and Kym which she had to win. Hadn't she knowingly tried to split them up by making herself easily available for sex whenever Tom was bored with Kym? Whatever the reasons, it wouldn't be happening again, Jacqui knew her demons had to be faced and defeated.

He'd tried to call her several times, but she didn't want to speak to him yet. If he turned up now, they would just end up yelling at each other. All the past things that had bothered her about his lack of commitment would appear like a huge storm, smashing everything in its path, leaving destruction behind it. Jacqui had to be in control of her emotions before speaking to Tom. If not it could be over, something she might end up regretting.

She sent Tom a text telling him to find somewhere else to stay that night, thinking this would be the first time she had ever turned him away. Although she just wanted to shake him at times, Jacqui had made every effort to bite her tongue and let him have his way, acting like a kind and caring girlfriend. Now though, enough was enough and she had to show him that he wouldn't be allowed back into her life so easily this time. It was her apartment, not his and he needed to respect her. Still it was a huge risk, after all they had been very happy lately and Jacqui didn't know what had actually occurred when Tom caught up with Kym. Had Kym welcomed him back with open arms, after he groveled as only Tom could? The only thing Jacqui was sure of was that she was not prepared to be the loser again, that would really hurt.

After a few hours of soul searching Jacqui started to miss Tom.  Her anger had subsided, though her back was still hurting from the collision with the door.  After tidying up his things in the lounge, her apartment was starting to look like home again.  Should she have been less harsh with him and a bit more understanding?  He'd replied to her earlier text with,

*'I love you, can I please come home, I just needed to check Kym was ok, it's you I love not her, please believe me.'*

Reading his words over Jacqui started to mellow.  Shouldn't she listen to what he had to say before making a decision?  If he came back to her then he hadn't chosen Kym, or could it be that Kym had told him she didn't want him anymore and that's why he wanted to come back.  Jacqui decided what to do.  She texted him back.

*'I don't want to see you at the moment.'*  Turning her phone off, she walked towards the bedroom, intending to put her phone out of reach, aiming to leave him sweating a bit longer.

Jacqui sat down heavily on the bed and that's when she spotted Tom's wallet, partially hidden on his unmade side.  Picking it up, she softly touched the leather case, then flicked it open.  He'd put a picture of her inside and she smiled looking at the background of the park where they had recently reunited.  Then her face darkened and she threw it back on the bed in disgust, realising that he couldn't get any cash without his bank cards or pay for anywhere to stay.

'Typical Tom, he has all the luck,' she muttered disappointed. Taking a deep breath she selected his mobile phone number and waited for him to answer.

Tom's distress was obvious as he stood in the road, turning in the direction of the underground only to turn back and look towards the pub. Nervously running his fingers through his hair, he decided it wouldn't be wise to go straight home to face Jacqui, as all hell would break lose if he did. It was the right choice giving her some space and him time to think. Noticing the pub was quiet for a Saturday afternoon, he made his way to the bar. Standing there waiting at its glossy black, clean surface he became mesmerised by the totally miserable face reflecting back at him, before sitting down heavily on a tall bar stool. No sign of a barman anywhere, though he could hear crates being stacked in the back. Tom thought if he sat there long enough with the amount of pressure hammering away at his temples that he might just explode into midair and not exist anymore. How good would that be, he thought, a kind of self-combustion, tainting the shiny unspoilt bar's surface. Not feeling a thing and not to have to go through a long groveling exercise to try and fix everything again.

'What can I get you?' enquired a tall, slim young man, who had appeared somehow unnoticed to Tom, still deep in thought as to how to tackle the day's events.

'A double vodka and coke, no ice,' Tom answered impatiently, pulling a ten pound note from his pocket, noting there were only four more left there.

He took a long drink, slowly swallowing the chilled dark liquid. It felt good, first good thing that had happened that afternoon. The day had started badly enough with him forgetting his wallet, due to Jacqui rushing him out the door. She wanted to go to their favourite place for lunch and wanted to get there before it got too busy. When they got to the station, he noticed his wallet was missing. Jacqui made a big fuss about that, but wasn't prepared to let him go back for it. It wouldn't have taken long. Luckily he had enough cash on him to pay for lunch, but everything else would have to go on her credit card again and she wasn't very happy. What was the big deal? He would have paid her back on pay day. As they walked through Knightsbridge he put his arm around her and gave her a bit of a cuddle. She seemed to cheer up after that and was her normal bossy self again.

With his glass quickly emptied, Tom wondered where the barman had disappeared to, didn't he recognise a man in despair when one sat at his bar? When he returned Tom stared at him.

'Oh, you're back, how about another drink, or would it be better for me to order several if you are going to keep disappearing?'

'Sorry, short staffed today, same again?' the barman replied.

Tom ordered another double vodka and coke feeling the whole world was against him.

'Bad day?' offered the barman, wondering how many vodkas his customer was going to consume, before leaving.

'Oh yes,' replied Tom. 'I'm the bad guy again,' he answered looking totally disillusioned. 'I just wanted to relax and take my girlfriend out for a nice lunch, but not to be, everything has turned into a major drama. C'est La Vie!'

Draining another drink and placing the empty glass a bit too hard back on the bar. He decided that if Kym and Jacqui both thought he was a useless idiot, then he might as well act like one and roll in drunk to one of their apartments. Let's see which one shall I pick? The thought of which tickled Tom and he smiled broadly, amused by the idea.

'Maybe tomorrow will be a better day,' the barman suggested, hoping to inspire Tom with his positivity.

'Bloody women,' Tom answered looking fed up. 'Always giving me a hard time.'

Tom ordered another double vodka and coke, which was placed in front of him.

'You're getting through the vodka's a bit quick,' added a smiling, older looking barman, who had been watching Tom from the other end of the bar. Sensing his mood changing.

'Last one,' replied Tom raising his glass, but this time sipping the strong but soothing liquid a little slower, whilst waiting for solutions to magically come into his head.

Deep in thought he wondered why Kym had run off without letting him explain. He had come up with a story, during his search for her, about him and Jacqui bumping into each other recently and becoming friends again. He was sickened by the pained expression on her face as she stood there, staring at them. Tom liked that Kym was needy, it made him feel strong, heroic, coming to her rescue. Why hadn't he been allowed to come to her rescue? Scoop her up in his arms and kiss her. Tell her that she had got it all wrong, that he was here and would take her home and make everything alright.

Somehow though he didn't think that would have worked. It was too late, Kym knew! He could tell by the look on her face, by the way the colour had drained from her cheeks. It was as if in that split second her heart broke in two in front of him. He had turned into his dad and now it was over between them. Tom picked up his empty glass and beckoned towards the barman.

'This is definitely my last one,' he added, noticing the barman raising an eyebrow at him.

Tom couldn't understand why Jacqui was taking things so badly either. What did she expect him to do? It was obvious he would want to check Kym was alright. They had been together for over seven years, he couldn't just switch off caring for her. Why had Jacqui disappeared, why hadn't she just waited for him to return? They could have had lunch as planned and discussed what had happened over a bottle or two of wine.

Jacqui's *'don't come home tonight'* text was a bit over the top. Where did she expect him to go? He had no wallet or credit cards on him? What was he going to do?

For the first time in his life Tom felt very alone and didn't like it. Unable to free himself from the bonds that he'd forged with both women, filled him with anguish, shaking him to the core. Realising he may have lost them both caused his heart to tighten and he put his hand to his chest until it relaxed again. What if Jacqui wouldn't take him back this time? He had treated her badly in the past, maybe she wouldn't believe he loved her, but why wouldn't she after all the effort he'd put in to find her again? Visits to the park, walking up and down for two weeks hoping to bump into her. Sneaking around for three months, nearly losing his job due to taking sick and holiday leave to meet and spend days with her. What about Kym? Why had she let him behave as he did, never once asking where he'd been all day? All the lies and deceit could have been for nothing, what a mess it all was.

Tom shook his head slowly from side to side, as he considered what had gone wrong with his life. He couldn't afford to live in London and had no possessions to his name. At thirty years old, with no savings or assets his heart sank, realising that he was a complete failure.

Failing to make it as an artist, failing in his relationships and failing to make a good standard of life for himself. What had he actually achieved? Not very much, Tom thought, a place at Oxford but nothing more than that. Why had he allowed himself to be tied up in all these knots? Relying on someone else to haul him up and support him, meant he would never be able to stand on his own two feet and break free. He simply couldn't do it, going it alone was not a viable option. Tom needed to get Jacqui back, there was no other alternative available to him he had too much to lose.

'What's that old expression?' he shouted towards the barman. 'Love two women at once and you won't end up with either of them.' The barman looked at him with a blank expression, knowing that his customer didn't require an answer. 'Last one,' Tom said a little too loudly, waving the empty glass in the air.

One more drink then he'd go and confront Jacqui and make her believe that he loved only her. Suggest finishing her nude drawing, which always seemed to work. After his fifth vodka he rose unsteadily.

'Oops,' he muttered as his coat slid onto the floor. Picking it up he felt light headed and then realised it was because he'd missed lunch with all the afternoons distress. Then he smiled broadly as an idea came into his head.

'Eureka,' he announced, picking up his coat. He would ask Jacqui to marry him and put an end to all of her doubts forever. Kym wouldn't have him back now, it was Jacqui who would be his future.

Tom wanted to get a move on now that he had decided what to do. If he hurried he could pick up some flowers at the station and just make it to the art shop before it closed to get a sketch pad. Pretending he was going to finish drawing her, Tom intended to get her to pose and then turn the pad around with the words "Marry me" showing. Jacqui would be delighted, he could picture her face now. He had quite a bit to do before he got home. Feeling more confident now that he had a few drinks inside him, he felt sure the flowers would get him through Jacqui's door.

Tom managed to put his coat half on and walked quickly out into the street as his phone started ringing. Hurriedly pulling the rest of it around him whilst retrieving the phone from his pocket, his face lit up. It was Jacqui at last! Quickly trying to press the accept button he stepped into the road, right into the path of an oncoming lorry. He was killed instantly.

# Chapter Nine

# Unknown

Tom's body had suffered horrific injuries.  Police
searched what was left of his clothing for any sort of
identification, wallet or a mobile phone.  They couldn't
find anything to identify him.  This was very unusual
leading them to think that he may have been a victim
of theft.  He didn't wear a wedding ring so they listed
him as single.  Without an address, they couldn't
contact anyone to inform them of his death.  He was
only wearing a watch and had no identifying marks
that were visible, although bits of him were
unrecognisable.  The lorry driver insisted that the
victim had stepped out right in front of him and he
could not avoid hitting him.  Eyewitnesses backed up

the lorry driver's statement and the possibility of a suicide was noted. After investigations had been completed, his corpse was put in a body bag, zipped up and transferred to the city mortuary. The mess at the accident scene was cleared up and the road re-opened later that evening.

...................

Tom hadn't answered Jacqui's calls and as the evening wore on she was beside herself with worry. Where was he? She kept trying, leaving messages, but eventually had to give up. Maybe he had turned off his phone and decided not to speak to her after her last text. Jacqui couldn't do anything about it, it was now her turn to sit and wait until he chose to contact her, although it did seem a bit unusual that he was taking control. At the very least Jacqui expected him to come round for his wallet. Maybe she had been a bit too strong with her '*Don't come back here tonight*' text message and wondered if she'd driven him right back into Kym's waiting arms?

'What a fool I've been' Jacqui cried out. She disliked the weak, vulnerable image that Kym portrayed to Tom. Kym would always win and stupid Tom would always run back to her huge bank balance. Knowing him as Jacqui did, he was bound to just cancel all his cards and order new ones, not wanting to face her by coming round to pick up his wallet. After all he wouldn't be needing the photo of herself that she had put inside. Jacqui looked at her photo before tearing it in half, how could she have been so stupid to think it would last? Discarding the pieces into an overflowing waste bin she decided to shed no more tears for him, he wasn't worth it. How unexpected, that he'd adopted his usual cowardly approach by not telling her in person. Well, Jacqui thought, he'd have to pick up his favourite paintings and clothes eventually and she would be at home when he did. She had a few things to say to him.

. . . . . . . . . . . . . . . . .

Matt was waiting for his phone to buzz with Kym's reply to his text and as he read it, a wide smile spread over his face,

'Yes,' he cried out in his excitement, she had accepted his invitation and they would be meeting in less than four hours' time. Then he wondered if he'd done the right thing and decided to leave his phone switched off until nearer the time. Women were hard work. If Kym cancelled again that would be it, he would just give up. It had been almost five years since Lucy had died and the main thing was that he felt it was finally time to move on, with or without Kym.

Matt arrived first at the restaurant, standing in the doorway waiting impatiently he constantly folded and unfolded his arms, looking tense and uncomfortable. Kym had texted to say she was on her way and as he looked out at the pouring rain, wished he'd thought about bringing an umbrella. Matt wanted everything to go right tonight, taking a few deep breaths was helping him to relax a little, but his chest pounded with nerves. Dealing with many precarious situations and dodgy people during his career hadn't prepared him for this, as waiting for Kym made him feel very hot under the collar. He cursed himself for being so long out of the dating game and tried to figure out what they could talk about. Relax, he told himself, listen carefully to her answers and remember to compliment her. He tried to think of some topics they could cover but his mind had gone blank, just as a black cab arrived and Kym stepped out of it.

She looked gorgeous. Should he tell her? Matt was lost for words as they approached the bar. She had a mid-length black halter dress on. Her hair hung down her back, hiding some of its curve. Matt imagined stroking the length of her back with his fingers. She looked elegant and very sexy at the same time.

'You look absolutely gorgeous,' he whispered to her as they were shown to a table.

'Thanks,' she whispered back, smiling at him and holding his stare. They sat down at a small candlelit table. Kym's heart skipped a beat as she admired his firm body when he removed his jacket.

The waiter left them to study the extensive wine list.

'Should I choose for us?' Matt suggested politely, he wanted to impress Kym with his vast knowledge of fine wines.

'I'm not much of a drinker, but a glass or two would be great,' she answered, remembering she was working in the morning.

The waiter looked impressed with Matt's selection and quickly returned, pouring dark red velvet liquid slowly into their glasses.

'Thank you,' they both said in unison not taking their eyes off each other.

They took their time over deciding what to eat, exchanging flirty innuendos.

'What do you fancy?' Matt asked mischievously.

'Whatever you feel like,' Kym teased him, finishing her glass much too quickly for not much of a drinker, Matt thought.

Whilst demolishing pate, followed by fillet steaks, they discussed most things that had happened in their lives during the eleven years since they first met at university. Kym was feeling confident enough to ask why Matt hadn't asked her out on a second date, after finishing another glass of wine. Matt delayed answering.

'Do you think we should risk another bottle?' he

said hoping to distract Kym from her question.

'Maybe just one more glass for me,' Kym replied smiling.

Matt ordered two large glasses of sparkling wine for them. When they arrived he picked up his glass.

'Here's to the most stupid man in the world, who took eleven years to ask the most beautiful woman in the world for a second date.' They laughed loudly at this, the wine was taking effect, causing witty remarks to follow as to why they had failed to see each other again. Conversation between them flowed easily and all too soon it was time to get the bill and move on.

'Halves,' said Kym, used to paying restaurant bills.

'No, I'll get this,' Matt offered looking slightly offended by Kym thinking she should contribute. 'Then we can get a cocktail.' He was also feeling a little drunk and put his arm around Kym when they moved to the cocktail bar as she seemed a bit unsteady. When attempting to sit on the bar stool, she almost missed it completely. Matt caught her and they both looked at each other's lips, imagining, yet containing their passion.

'Would you rather go somewhere else?' he asked huskily. Kym wanted to say, yes, please, your place or mine, aiming to ask Matt back to her apartment for coffee and much more.  Thinking it would be heaven to feel him wanting her and to show him how much she wanted to be with him.  Hesitating to answer his question, she thought that being too forward might put Matt off.  He'd been the perfect gentleman all evening and she didn't want to ruin things.  Yes, having sex with him would be fantastic, who wouldn't want to?  He was a very handsome man.

Imagining feeling wanted, with his strong male arms around her was making Kym blush, thinking, why not.  If Jacqui was a seductress then she too could learn to be one and seduce Matt in a way that would steal his heart and cure the ache inside her.  However, she decided that the waiting and anticipation would only enhance their attraction, so the best thing to do was to go home alone and leave them both wanting more.

Matt waited for Kym's answer wondering if he'd said something wrong.  He had meant going to another bar and not to bed, although he most certainly would not have refused the latter.  His desire was to undress Kym, feel her silky skin against his, twist her hair in his fingers, kiss every inch of her body and show her his passion.  However, rushing into sex could ruin the great evening they'd had, patience would be his ally after all he'd endured a long two weeks to even get to this point.

'It is getting late,' Kym answered, 'and we both

have work tomorrow.'

Her taxi arrived promptly and with a hug and a quick kiss on the lips, Kym was gone. Matt had felt good, energised, but now standing there waiting for his taxi, he felt a bit deflated, not relishing the thought of going back to his place alone, but that's the way it had worked out.

'Damn,' he muttered, exhaling deeply, as he realised that concentrating on making the evening perfect meant he'd forgotten to ask Kym for another date. Reaching for his phone and pressing keys clumsily, Matt remembered to check the text before sending.

'*Kym, I had an amazing time, can't wait to see you again. Are you free for a walk next weekend, Sunday?*'

Within seconds he received a reply.

'*Matt that would be great. XX*'

# Chapter Ten

# Missing

A chilling wind sent a swirl of debris into the art gallery as Anton opened the door on Monday morning. Kicking the pieces of litter outside again with his designer shoes, he shivered. Early mornings were not something he normally tolerated even though he'd arrived late at almost ten o'clock. Mornings were Tom's domain, but not today. Anton and his partner were going away for a romantic weekend break on Thursday and Tom was needed to run the gallery. Tom normally only worked mornings, but this week had swapped his Monday to Wednesday mornings having agreed to work all day Thursday, Friday and Saturday instead to cover Anton's absence.

Anton yawned as he turned the open sign around

on the door.  He was in his mid-thirties, looking taller than his six foot height, with a thin frame causing him to appear slightly underweight, although he ate very well.  Every day he carefully shaved his head to hide his thinning blonde hair.  Anton always wore expensive aftershave and liked wearing stylish hats, which he had a varied collection of.  He enjoyed cooking with quality ingredients, matching his culinary creations with his favourite wines.  His lavish waterfront apartment, overlooking the Thames had been lovingly filled with many antiques and paintings. He was a quiet, caring man with a gentle nature and was a successful artist.  Anton loved nothing more than going away for long weekends to mainly city destinations, where he could explore different cultures and look for artworks for his gallery.

'Only three days to go, then I'm off to sunny Barcelona,' he muttered happily whilst making himself a coffee.  He couldn't wait to be on the plane, not having had a break since before Christmas, needing to relax and eat and drink to his heart's content.

Monday and Tuesday's were often very quiet at the gallery, so he busied himself with framing to pass the time, which was turning out to be a very lucrative business.  Wednesday produced a few more browsers and a sale of one of his more expensive paintings.

'All money for the weekend,' he uttered, turning the closed sign around on the door.  On Wednesday evening he texted Tom to make sure everything was in place for him taking over the following morning. After trying several times throughout the evening, without a reply, he left several messages for Tom to return his calls. Getting into bed at midnight, he sighed after checking his phone and finding Tom still hadn't replied. This concerned him slightly but as his employee was so reliable he felt sure there would be a response in the morning and didn't worry.

By 9.30am the next morning, Anton's concern grew as he constantly rang both Tom's mobile and the gallery phones, whilst packing. His flight was at 1 o'clock and he needed to leave for the airport by 10.30am. As Anton wheeled his case to the waiting taxi, he felt a bit annoyed that Tom hadn't bothered to get in touch, not even to wish him a good holiday. On the way to the airport he tried to figure out what the problem could be. Tom had explained about leaving Kym and moving in with Jacqui but he didn't have a contact number for Jacqui and didn't know where they were now living. Anton continued to try both phones during the taxi ride, watching raindrops dripping down the cab's soaked windows. Eventually deciding he didn't need the hassle, put his phone away in an attempt to steer his thoughts to the weekend ahead. When he met his partner, they had a couple of cocktails in the bar, both were in good spirits and Anton started to relax as they chatted about their plans for the weekend.

Before boarding the plane, his anxiety got the better of him and he turned his phone back on. Still nothing from Tom. Tutting loudly, he walked up the steps and entered the plane, resigned to the fact that he couldn't do anything now and would have to leave the problem until they landed.

When Anton returned on Sunday morning, he still hadn't heard from Tom. It had certainly put a bit of a dampener on the weekend. Anton headed straight to his gallery, the closed sign remained in the same place on the door where he'd left it.

'Damn,' he muttered, heading for the tea rooms next door. He knew one of the ladies there, who was busy setting out homemade cakes on stands, before placing them into glass display cabinets. The place was always very busy, one of the reasons Anton had opened his gallery next door to attract browsing customers.

'Take away coffee Anton?' asked the owner. Her name was Irene, she was in her fifties an attractive blonde lady with her hair tied back and a smart apron wrapped around her middle that looked immaculately clean. She reminded Anton of his mum and the shop smelt like the home he once loved and missed. The cakes were decorated with iced flowers, chocolate strands or a dusting of icing sugar. They were beautifully presented and smelled of freshly baked vanilla.

'Have you been away anywhere nice?' Irene enquired in her cheerful voice. Anton gave Irene a quick summary of his fun weekend in Barcelona. Explaining that the hotel had been well located for Las Ramblas.

'Las what?' laughed Irene, placing freshly baked sausage rolls onto a tray underneath the counter. Anton would have relished the opportunity to describe the seedy and contrasting conventional sides of the boulevard which cut through the city to the gothic quarter, where they'd spent all their time. However, reminding himself that it was Irene he was conversing with, just laughed along with her. Describing instead the many art galleries and museums he'd visited there.

'I got several new artworks for the gallery, as well as a suntan!' He answered happily, remembering the weekend, before his voice changed and became more serious when asking if she had seen Tom.

'He's not been around. We noticed the closed sign on the door and thought it was a bit unusual.'

'So the gallery has been closed for all three days?' Anton asked, keen to find out if Tom had opened it up at any time while he was away.

'Yes all three days,' she added before disappearing into the kitchen area.

Anton's face twisted with frustration. If Tom

had bothered to tell him that he wouldn't be at the shop, Anton could have put up a notice saying he was on holiday until Monday and moved some of his more expensive pieces to a safer location. Sales had been poor at the gallery and he didn't want to lose any business or leave customers thinking they had closed down. Stomping out of the shop he exhaled sharply, Tom better have a good excuse for disappearing without a word.

Annoyance soon turned to concern. This was not like Tom, he was never late and had never let him down like this before. At the end of last year he had taken a few last minute holidays and had been sick more often than Anton would have liked, but things had been fine since then. It couldn't be a problem with his phone as he'd failed to open up the gallery for days. Strange, Anton thought, walking towards the underground, perhaps he should call round and see Kym later, she may know what's happened.

Anton wanted this to be a last resort, knowing it could be very awkward speaking to her, now Tom had moved out. Frowning, he decided to wait and see if he turned up for work tomorrow. Yes, that was what he would do. Tired from travelling and with other things to organise, he decided to sort it out tomorrow with Tom when he saw him.

It was pouring with rain on Monday morning when Anton reluctantly got up. Dressing hurriedly, he cursed Tom for spoiling the lazy morning he'd planned, watching television and reading magazines in his warm dressing gown. Striding towards the gallery, cold raindrops dripped from his umbrella down the back of his collar and he shuddered, wishing he'd stayed in the warm Spanish sunshine. Within minutes he was in range of his gallery, expecting it to be open and the coffees on. It was still locked up with no sign of life. Anton picked up junk mail and flyers off the floor as he opened the door and sighed deeply. He couldn't understand why Tom had left him in limbo when they were such good friends. Anton hung up his dripping overcoat and tried unsuccessfully to fold his soaking umbrella before dumping it in the sink. Deep in thought he sat down on a leather upholstered chair, filled with an ominous feeling that something bad had happened to Tom. He flicked to the contacts menu on his phone. Kym's number stared back at him. Anton didn't relish the thought of speaking to her, but had no other options. Leaving a message on Kym's mobile asking her to ring him, he tried to keep his tone friendly. They'd met on several occasions and she knew him, however, Anton was concerned when she hadn't responded by the time he shut up the gallery at four o'clock. Frowning he knew there was nothing else for it and would have to go to her apartment that evening, probably at about eight o'clock, giving her the chance to get in from work.

Later that evening, Anton reluctantly climbed the stairs to Kym's apartment and knocked hard on her sturdy, wooden door.  No answer.

'Damn,' he muttered to himself, what was going on everyone seemed to be missing!  He continued to knock persistently and loudly for some time and eventually Kym answered.

'I'm sorry to bother you,' he said and began to explain that he was concerned about Tom.

'He hasn't turned up for work in the past week, I have been away and he was supposed to run the gallery for three days, but he didn't open it up,' he hesitated, giving her the opportunity to respond.  Kym looked down at the ground, disinterested.

'Tom moved out six weeks ago and I haven't heard from him since,' she replied, speaking firmly as if to hide her emotions.  Anton felt uneasy, Kym hadn't invited him in, seeming a bit preoccupied.  He contemplated just leaving and returning home.  Knowing that wouldn't help him locate Tom and solve the mystery of his disappearance, he had no other choice than to stand his ground.

'I'm sorry to have to ask you this, but I'm really worried about him, have you any idea where he is?' Anton's voice was filled with concern and he was trying to be discreet in case Kym didn't know about Jacqui.  Kym's face darkened, she looked embarrassed.

'Yes,' she answered in an irritated tone.  'He's

living with someone else.' This is turning out to be painful, Anton thought, but had to continue.

'Do you know where he's living?' he asked risking the wrath of Kym's anger in her reply. 'I'm just worried that something may have happened to Tom and I'm at a loss as to what to do about it. I need your help to find him.'

Kym looked at Anton who was beginning to feel like a nuisance.

'He's living with Jacqui Lewis. She used to work at St. Katherine's cancer hospital, that's all I know.' Anton could see by the look on her face that Kym felt totally humiliated by having to tell him this.

'Thanks,' Anton said, relieved that he finally had a lead to Tom. It had been very awkward, but thankfully she knew about Jacqui. He would have hated to be the one to break the news to her on that matter.

Tuesday came, still nothing from Tom. Anton rang St. Katherine's hospital, luckily Jacqui still worked there so he left a message for her to contact him. Jacqui rang the phone at the gallery at 3pm. She sounded fed up too. Apparently she had been trying to contact Tom since she last saw him over a week ago. They'd argued whilst out shopping and Tom hadn't returned home afterwards. The last time Jacqui saw Tom he was running after Kym and Jacqui suspected from his lack of contact that he had moved back in with her.

Anton explained that he spoke to Kym the previous evening and Tom wasn't there. Kym hadn't heard from him since he left her either. Jacqui was beginning to wonder if something had happened to Tom and asked Anton what he thought they should do next.

'Do you think he may have had an accident, should we check local hospitals?' she asked with all sorts of possibilities running through her mind.

'No,' said Anton calmly. 'We need to go to the Police and report him as a missing person.' Jacqui felt faint,

'Do you think that's necessary, he may have just gone off somewhere on his own,' she replied anxiously.

'Yes, I'm going to report him missing today,' Anton insisted. 'I know Tom and he would never let me down, he knows how important the gallery is and he hasn't been in touch. I've left it long enough and am going around to the Police Station now.' He swallowed hard affected by the enormity of the situation.

'I'll get my things and meet you in half an hour,' Jacqui said her voice breaking with emotion. Anton's reaction was causing her to panic and she started to feel ill, but had no idea why, knowing Tom would probably turn up soon.

After introductions, they walked silently into the Police Station, neither of them knowing what to do or say. Jacqui had never been into one before and the formality of it all wasn't helping the feeling of nausea that swept over her. Together they filled in a missing persons report with a sympathetic female officer. Describing the clothes Tom had on when she last saw him was distressing. The officer asked for details of his parents but all Jacqui could remember was that Tom's mum had moved to Spain several years ago. He'd lost contact with his dad, although he could still be in the UK, Jacqui didn't know his christian name for tracing. Thinking she was managing to answer all the officer's questions calmly, Jacqui started to explain that she had his wallet and her heart quickened, noticing the officer's face change. The WPC listened more intently, as Jacqui described the watch he was wearing, scribbling away as if she knew more than she was saying. This caused Jacqui to think that something was very badly wrong and she started to cry. Now that she had started she didn't seem able to stop. Anton put his arm around her in a reassuring way.

'Do you know which dentist he goes to,' the WPC asked Jacqui gently.

'No,' was all she could reply, feeling the lump in her throat turn into a huge choking rock as she fought back tears.

The officer left them alone temporarily and Jacqui muttered quietly, between sobs,

'Where are you Tom? Why don't you let us know where you are?' Anton wiped a tear from his eye, fearing the worst scenario possible had happened to his friend. The officer returned and looked at them sympathetically.

'We have your contact details and will be in touch as soon as we have any news. In the meantime if you think of anything this is my number, don't hesitate to contact me.' They both thanked her and got up, feeling they had just been dismissed. It looked like they would have to spend another night worrying about Tom and what had happened to him as they hadn't received any reassurance from their visit.

Anton gave Jacqui a lift home, noticing how quiet she was.

'I'm going to ring round the local hospitals, when I get in,' he advised. 'Tom could be lying in a coma somewhere and we don't even know about it.' Anton, rubbed his eyes, exhausted from the stress of the day's events, but knew he had to continue until Tom was found.

When Jacqui arrived back at her apartment, she flung down her coat and dashed into the bedroom, searching through Tom's personal documents to try and find his parent's details. She found nothing, not even his doctor or dentist's numbers. Remembering that he kept his dentist and all other important numbers on his mobile phone jogged her memory that she hadn't checked her own mobile since Anton rang. Opening her bag she saw the pregnancy test she'd bought earlier that day. Jacqui was never late and two weeks had gone by. Feeling nauseous and light headed, meant she didn't need to be a scientist to know that there was a good chance she was pregnant. During the turmoil of the afternoon it had gone right out of her head until now. Not wanting to take the test, Jacqui decided to leave it until she knew Tom was safe and they could share the news together. They'd talked about having a baby and when he returned it would be the first thing they would celebrate. Jacqui would need to put aside their troubled past, they needed to plan for the future and prepare for the arrival of their first child. Although she was filled with a sinking feeling that something was badly wrong, she tried to console herself thinking Tom had just gone away for a while, probably to stay with family.

Jacqui couldn't face going to work on Wednesday and stayed in bed until almost noon, hoping the nightmare of not knowing what had happened to Tom would go away. She had read before about loved ones who simply disappeared and were never heard of again. They were never found and remained filed under "missing". Sometimes they changed their names and started new lives miles away from where they had left. They lived happily ever after and their relatives lived in the misery of not knowing what had happened to them for the rest of their lives. She picked up her mobile phone, texting Tom.

*'Please, please let me know that you are ok. I went to the Police yesterday to report you missing, just send a quick text to me.... please Tom.'* She wiped away tears as she sent the text, praying that he would answer.

Jacqui eventually gave up waiting for a reply and got dressed, feeling sick again she settled for a piece of dry toast for lunch. Just about to eat it, she nearly jumped out of her skin, startled by a loud knock at her door. Hesitating to get up and toying with the idea of ignoring it, she put her head in her hands, scared of what may be waiting for her on the other side of the door. It was a persistent knock, the sort of knock which meant trouble and wouldn't go away. She reluctantly walked towards the door. The same police officer she met yesterday was stood there with a colleague.

'Jacqui can we come in, we have some news.'

Chapter Eleven

# Fire

'Good Morning Kym, it's 9am on Sunday 3rd March,' a familiar voice interrupted her deep sleep. Moaning and touching her head, Kym wished she'd remembered to cancel the alarm.

'I've got a headache,' she cried out, kneading her left temple gently. Mr. Right launched into action, with his cheery voice listing remedies for a sore head.

'Shut up!' Kym shouted, burying her head under a pillow. Her apartment fell silent once more. Reaching for the bedside cabinet she grabbed at a pack of painkillers, which fell to the floor.

'Damn,' she cried out, fumbling for them whilst trying not to fall out of bed. In the process she located a half filled bottle of water, rolling around towards her. Picking up both she swallowed two tablets and gulped them down before falling back asleep. The next time she woke up it was 10.30am.

'Oh no,' she cried jumping out of bed in a panic.

She had arranged to go for a walk with Matt today and he was due to arrive at 12.30 which meant only a mere two hours to change herself from the frumpy wreck she had spotted in the mirror into a seductive goddess.

After a quick shower Kym chose the same body lotion she had worn for their previous rendezvous, which Matt said had smelt heavenly. Generously massaging it into her body, felt very sensual and made her skin soft and silky. Next the arduous process of drying and straightening her long blonde hair began. As a teenager she wanted to get it cut into a shoulder length bob, which would have been far less work. Her mum wouldn't allow it though and as she sprayed a fine mist of anti-frizz treatment onto her hair, was grateful for her mum's foresight.

Looking out of the window, it was raining quite heavily and it felt cold in her apartment.

'What's the outside temperature?' she asked her computer.

'Six degrees,' was its cheery response. That was the good thing about having a computer to talk to, Kym thought, it never got temperamental if you insulted it with the occasional "shut up."

'Six degrees,' Kym repeated startled by the low temperature but then remembering it was only the beginning of March. It was looking more like a jumper and jeans day than the flimsy underwear and laced clingy top she'd chosen. In her mind Kym blamed the failure of her relationship with Tom on their lack of having sex. If it had been her and Tom going for a walk on a cool March afternoon, she would have pulled on her favourite old sweatshirt and baggy jeans. Topping this off with a long, plain, wind and waterproof jacket. Not very flattering but highly practical. However, this time she was going out with Matt, not Tom and she was picking her outfit for a different reason today.

Kym had no idea how couples managed to keep the sex thing going through years of togetherness. Did all couples just end up as companions, no longer having sex in later life, Kym wondered. Was that the reason why Tom had left? They didn't have sex very often and it had never seemed adventurous, always following the same routine. More of a pleasing Tom session, as she was often too tired and never really felt like it. Kym would put it off as long as possible, until Tom insisted. Then she'd resign herself to just getting it over with, hoping he wouldn't bother to ask her again for a while. Was there something wrong with her, was she frigid? Kym shook her head, dismissing the idea, they were both at fault.

She smiled, recalling a typical Sunday afternoon at her parent's house in the Lakes. It was a cold day and they had just got in from walking the dogs on the fells. Her dad set about lighting and stoking the huge log burning fire they had in their lounge. It was warm, bright and very comforting. Kym loved the smoky, woody aroma from its embers, she could sit staring at the fire for hours, taking in its warm glow. Once they had warmed up, her dad launched into one of his witty quotes.

'Marriage is not that much different from a log burning fire.' Kym laughed at this remark.

'What do you mean?' she enquired, her voice full of anticipation.

'Well' her dad continued, 'you constantly have to feed and nurture it to feel its warmth and keep it burning. If you neglect it, well, it will fade and eventually die.' Kym looked thoughtful then her face lit up as she replied with a witty remark of her own.

'But, it goes out most nights,' she said, with a self-satisfied grin. Her dad always had an answer for everything and he didn't disappoint.

'Yes, so you have to make the effort to re-light it

again and that's usually me in this relationship.' He looked at Kym, making an imaginary ducking movement with his upper body as if to dodge something his wife might throw at him. Kym laughed at her dad's attempts to try and defuse the impact of his comments. When she stopped, her mum put her hands on her hips.

'You could always get a new one, if you're not happy with things,' pausing, waiting for her husband's reply.

'That's a good idea,' he answered, winking at Kym mischievously. 'Let's see, one that's less work would be an improvement,' he continued smugly, knowing he'd got the last word in. Seeing the look of mock terror on her dad's face, before he hid behind his newspaper, sent them all into fits of laughter. Kym remembered thinking that constantly stoking and relighting a fire seemed like a lot of work, but hadn't thought about its significance until Tom left. However, she knew more than anyone that anything was better than being alone.

It was simple, relationships had to be worked at, something which she hadn't spent much time doing previously. Now though Kym was changing, wanting to be the seductress, as Matt awakened her interest in sex. Searching through her underwear draw, she tossed knickers and bras onto the floor in her haste to find the desired outfit. Surveying the few items she'd placed on the bed caused her to groan in despair, none of them were good enough for Matt. Her stomach started to churn with nerves, as past insecurities surfaced, causing her to pick flimsy underwear and a thin clingy top. Shivering in her bedroom, Kym picked out her tightest jeans and high heeled boots. Now I am ready for Matt she thought, I've learnt my lesson.

It was still raining when the doorbell rang and her heart felt like it was going to explode. In her eagerness to be ready on time she had forgotten to breathe and gasped for air just before opening the door. It was Matt as expected, he was grinning.

'Hello,' was all he seemed to be able to manage. He looked a bit dumbstruck as his eyes surveyed her from top to bottom.

Matt was feeling a bit disappointed because of the weather. He had planned the whole day out including a picnic, wanting to impress Kym. His spirits lifted earlier when he found an old picnic blanket in the spare room giving him the idea. As he dashed round to the local express food shop, he started to plan what he would buy. It was surprisingly well stocked with a variety of small crusty rolls baked with cheese, garlic and sun dried tomatoes. He found a good selection of Spanish hams and smoked cheeses on the deli counter and a decent bottle of champagne. All went into his shopping basket along with pasta salad, plates and plastic cutlery. Matt's smile was wide as he packed up his shopping, satisfied with his selections.

Rushing round to Kym's, his initial elation faded into annoyance at the persistent rain falling onto his windscreen. Watching his car wipers moving back and forward in a steady motion, made him swear. Feeling like it was his responsibility to have a backup plan, he tried desperately to think of one. As he approached Kym's apartment, time was running out, he needed to think of something fast.

After closing the door, they had a long kiss. Matt inhaled the sweet scent of her body, which tensed as he touched her. I'm not the only one who's nervous, he thought taking her hands in his.

'You look fantastic,' he exclaimed whilst admiring her long legs, in tight jeans which clung to her perfectly formed body. Matt's mind was suddenly working overtime, he'd thought of a plan and a smug grin spread over his face.

'What are you up to?' Kym asked, noticing Matt was looking very pleased with himself.

'I've got an idea,' he replied reluctant to give out any more details other than to hold up two filled shopping bags. Kym's face shone with delight as Matt unpacked the shopping bags in the kitchen, proudly showing off his purchases.

'Mmm,' she said whilst surveying, fresh bread rolls, slices of Serrano ham, chorizo and a selection of cheeses, which all looked mouth wateringly appetising. Matt's perfect, gentlemanly approach from the previous evening had somehow departed, as he picked Kym up placing her gently on the worktop and kissed her passionately.

'Are you hungry?' he asked in a rugged, sexy voice.

'I missed breakfast,' replied Kym, missing his innuendo, but then he hadn't had anything to eat either in the rush to get to her apartment.

'It's pouring with rain unfortunately,' Matt announced looking towards the window, 'have you ever had an indoor picnic before?'

'Never,' she answered breathlessly, wondering what was going to happen next. They set about piling plates with rolls, meats, pickles and cheeses, slicing cakes and pouring champagne into glasses. Matt thought that things were shaping up very nicely as Kym looked thrilled with his efforts. He gazed into her eyes as he poured her another glass of champagne. They clinked glasses.

'To us and our afternoon in,' he added his voice full of anticipation. Matt spread the picnic blanket onto the carpeted floor in front of the fire Kym had turned on in the lounge. It was hardly a fur rug but it was feeling hot, sexy and romantic enough for their needs.

Kym noticed that she was drinking more champagne than Matt and started to feel a bit tipsy. He was talking softly, whilst his fingers gently stroked her arm with a feather like touch.

'Would you like some coffee,' Kym asked thinking, I need one!

'Let's leave it,' Matt replied looking longingly at Kym. He stood up holding out his hand gesturing her to join him.

'Where's the bedroom?' he whispered huskily. Kym didn't resist.

'Over there,' she mouthed, brushing her lips against his neck. He picked her up and placed her gently on the bed, not taking his eyes off her. Kym felt an aching sensation rising within her, longing for his touch, as she unbuttoned his shirt. He kissed her passionately, removing her top and kissing her body gently. He couldn't wait to undress her completely and Kym relaxed for the first time, letting passion consume her as the intensity of their desires left them lying sated in each other's arms.

Kym recovered first and whispered to a breathless Matt,

'That was the best time I've ever had.' He smiled then kissed her intently. 'I was just wondering,' she continued raising an eyebrow. 'Did you really want to go out for a walk today or did you have this all planned?'

'I had no idea what was going to happen,' Matt replied honestly, 'but when I saw you in those tight jeans and high heels there was no way I was going out!' They both laughed and he kissed her, more gently this time, as they stayed locked in each other's arms. Kym began to feel a little nervous, aware of her nakedness as the alcohol started to wear off. She was worried that her hair might be messed up and the room looked untidy with their clothes scattered everywhere. Picking up her things she dived into the bathroom to dress and fix herself up. When she returned to the bedroom, Matt was still in bed waiting for her.

'Oh,' he said a little disappointed. 'Do you fancy that walk now?' He got up and began dressing. Kym nodded as she looked out of the window. The weather had changed, the rain which threatened to spoil their afternoon had stopped and the sun was glowing invitingly at her.

'Matt,' she said smiling, 'you couldn't have planned it better!'

After a romantic walk, they headed back to Kym's place.

'Shall we get something to eat about six or seven?' Matt asked. Kym's heart leapt relieved that Matt wanted to spend more time with her and hadn't been put off by her earlier modesty.

'Inside or out?' she asked, knowing she would be blissfully content with whatever he wanted to do.

'I need to pop home, to freshen up and get changed, let's go out for a nice meal somewhere?' Kym agreed instantly, it sounded perfect and they arranged to meet at seven o'clock at a bistro they both knew.

Matt arrived first, he waited for Kym at the entrance to the bistro, wanting to open the door for her and get everything right. Kym stepped out of the taxi, her long slim legs perfectly framed by a silver mini dress. Matt felt his heart pounding and his blood pressure rise as she bent over to pay the taxi. Twirling around swinging her long blonde hair, she moved gracefully towards him, smiling. He hugged her tightly, whilst closing his eyes and breathing in deeply. Never wanting to let her go again.

Matt sat up quickly when Kym's apartment computer greeted them with the date and time, early on Monday morning. He was completely naked and Kym loved that he was so comfortable in his own skin, whereas she still felt shy about her body. He was dressed within minutes and with a quick goodbye kiss, left her lying there.

'I need to go home before work,' he shouted on his way out, 'I will ring gorgeous you later.'

When he was gone, Kym lay there for a while. The side of the bed where he had slept was warm and smelt of his aftershave. Kym was going to be late for work but what the hell she thought, deliberately delaying getting up until the last possible moment. Showering slowly, thinking about his hands touching her and not wanting to remove the scent of his toned body, filled her with desire. She didn't have time to wash her hair and anyway liked the fact that it had a messy "been to bed" look about it. Nobody at work would suspect that she had made love not once but twice the day before. It had been hot, passionate and romantic all at the same time. She couldn't wait for Matt to come back and make her feel desired, sexy and beautiful again.

Kym seemed to be in a bit of a daze at work on Monday morning. Her only focus was on getting through the day quickly and returning home to wait for Matt to call her. Later, Kym stepped into a warm, soothing bath, the perfumed bubbles floating next to her skin felt beautiful. After making an omelette for tea, her phone rang. His voice was slow and sexy, they'd crossed the line in their relationship and now engaged in flirty banter about the night before and her needing a bath.

They arranged to get together on Wednesday

night and Kym reluctantly ended the call due to someone knocking loudly on the door. Mr. Right switched the screen to CCTV and she squinted across the room at the tall, slim man standing there, instantly recognising Anton. What did he want? She hadn't seen him in ages. Slowly opening the door she noticed he looked a bit nervy and burst into apologies for his intrusion. Just as she was about to invite him in he launched into concerns for Tom who hadn't been to work in the last week? That wasn't like him, she thought, but then what did she know. The last few years of her life had turned out to be a lie and she didn't know who Tom was anymore. Anton would have to deal with the problem himself, it wasn't anything to do with her and Kym certainly didn't want to know what Tom was up to. Anton wouldn't budge from her doorstep, he wasn't giving up and seemed really worried about Tom, but then he probably didn't know about the Knightsbridge episode. Kym couldn't believe Anton would have the nerve to question her about Jacqui. She should have just shut the door. Anton seemed to sense she was not prepared to talk any further and said his goodbyes. Would she ever be rid of Tom and the humiliation he had brought upon her? One thing she knew was that she didn't need him back in her life again, messing things up.

Kym tried to put Tom and Matt out of her head on Wednesday and concentrate on work. Shopping in her local area at lunch she selected a pasta salad and smiled happily as a warm feeling spread over her, remembering Matt's indoor picnic idea on Sunday. By 7pm that evening she was ready for Matt and looked confidently at herself in the mirror. Wearing seductive lingerie underneath a classic black dress, she turned from side to side, smoothing down the shimmering fabric, clinging to her slim frame. Upon hearing a brisk knock Kym rushed to answer the door, only to stop, startled, it was Anton again! What was going on, this man was turning into a bit of a nuisance. Matt was due any minute and she didn't want to go through another round of "where's Tom" with Anton who looked drained.

'Kym I need to come in, I have some bad news about Tom,' he said sadly and in that moment looking at Anton's face, Kym knew Tom was dead. Luckily Matt followed Anton in and held her while she listened to his sombre news.

Tom had died a few hours after their chance meeting, outside a bar in Knightsbridge where he'd been drinking alone. He was killed instantly after stepping out into the road right in front of a lorry. The lorry couldn't avoid him and the police wondered if it might have been suicide. He didn't have his wallet with him and had lain in the mortuary for twelve days until Jacqui had identified him late that afternoon.

Unknown to everyone, Tom's mobile phone still remained in the guttering above the pub, where it came to rest after flying through the air upon impact. It was smashed, but before it stopped working had recorded the exact time of Tom's death, as it stored Jacqui's unanswered call in its memory.

# Chapter Twelve

# Uncovered

Jacqui had spent another restless night tossing and turning, waking up feeling cold, only to wake an hour later feeling hot.  It had been two weeks since Tom's funeral, but it seemed much longer.  Every morning when she woke, Tom was the first thing she thought about and her last waking thought each night.  Anton had been wonderful, she could never have managed without him.  He'd organised the funeral and insisted on paying for everything, liaising between Jacqui and Kym to try and get everything exactly as Tom would have wanted on the day.  Their memories of him had been full of contrasts, when it came to the songs he enjoyed and his hopes and dreams.  Anton cleverly combined memories from them both to carefully construct the eulogy and arrange for Tom's favourite songs to be played. It hadn't been easy but he'd got there, avoiding anything that would upset either Jacqui or Kym on the day.

Luckily Kym had kept all of Tom's things together in her spare room. She had no desire to go through them again so Anton took on the role of sorting everything out and taking Tom's clothes to the charity shop. He boxed up the rest of Tom's personal possessions, taking them round to Jacqui's for her to look through, before he sold anything valuable. Finding an address book enabled Anton to use an internet service to trace Tom's parents and set the funeral date, giving them time to make travel arrangements to attend.

Anton took care of Tom's artwork moving his many pieces to his gallery where he catalogued fifty paintings. Kym only removed one piece before Anton took the rest. It was the portrait Tom had painted of her, which she couldn't bring herself to part with. Jacqui spent an afternoon at the gallery going through Tom's work, searching for a painting which would remind her of him. Flicking through the canvases of varying sizes, Anton looked on, thinking how well she was coping.

'Which one shall I take?' she asked after her third attempt at searching through Tom's work.

'The one that pulls you in and you don't want to

put down.'

'I just don't know, none of them are saying anything to me,' she replied looking perplexed.

'Why don't you leave it until another day, there's no rush,' Anton reminded her, stacking similar paintings together.

'No, I want to get it over with today, what about this one?' Anton looked at the small painting of a child on a swing hanging from the branches of a large tree. It was very different and looked older than Tom's other pieces. He inspected it closely and found the artists name at the bottom of the oil painting.

'It's beautiful, though not one of his works, possibly his grandfather's. I recall Tom saying his grandad was a talented artist.' Jacqui looked again at the painting. The child on the swing was Tom he must have been eight or nine years old. With his mop of dark hair and brown eyes it couldn't have been anyone else. A smiling, mischievous face stared back at her.

'I'm going to take this one,' Jacqui revealed, her hands shaking as she held the painting next to her heart. She didn't have any photographs of Tom growing up as a child, this painting was all that was left of him.

'That's great Jacqui, just great,' he replied looking tearful, his voice breaking as he said the words.

Jacqui had already stashed away Tom's many sketch books containing half naked drawings of her, some dating back to their university days. She had her own personal memories of Tom held within these many sketches and didn't need anything more. He had the sketches with him, in the small suitcase he brought to hers after leaving Kym, thankfully. Jacqui couldn't have imagined the embarrassment she would have felt if Kym or Anton had found them. How history repeats itself, she thought sadly. She would be a single mum just like her mother before her. Tom's birthday would have been the 4th of October and her child was due around that date.

Jacqui intended to take two more weeks off work, hoping her intense nausea would have stabilised by then. Most mornings were spent running to the toilet, especially if she smelt food cooking, which left her feeling tired and weak. She'd lost weight, having not really eaten properly since Tom's death. Every day she blamed and tormented herself for not letting Tom come home on that fatal day.

She'd finally taken a pregnancy test on the day of the funeral, wanting to tell Tom during her last goodbye to him. As she touched his cold, black lacquered coffin, she whispered the words, leaving him knowing that part of him was still with her.

Kym had brought her new boyfriend Matt to the

funeral.  Jacqui was appalled by how quickly Kym had moved on, thinking that she should have grieved for Tom before getting involved with someone else. Instantly recognising Matt from university, she curtailed her curiousity to find out how they had met up again, unhappy that he was at Tom's funeral.   Kym came over and hugged her after the short service at the Crematorium.

'He always loved you,' she whispered to Jacqui before walking away.  In view of everything that had happened, Jacqui was moved beyond words by Kym's kindness and as she walked to the car with Anton, something bothered her.

'Do you think Kym was acting a bit strangely?'

'What do you mean?' he asked.

'I felt that it was my long term partner who'd died and not Kym's.' Jacqui continued, Anton nodded.

'Yes, I thought that was a bit odd, perhaps it's just her way of dealing with things.'

After Tom's funeral Anton collected his ashes and brought them to Jacqui's apartment, deciding that Kym wouldn't want them after the way she had been treated. Jacqui wasn't the type to leave an urn on the mantelpiece, so they opted for a small farewell ceremony at the park where Jacqui and Tom had been reunited six months earlier.

Anton silently followed Jacqui through the park, noticing her tired and beaten demeanor as they made their way to a bench alongside the lake. Jacqui cried silently as her mind filled with thoughts of Tom. Picturing him walking along with his coat over his shoulder, looking ahead and quickening his pace when he saw her, five months earlier. She wept whilst shaking his ashes towards the lake as the afternoon breeze swept them up and dropped them into the gently rippling water.

'Anton, I have some news,' she said quietly as they watched the water glistening in the sunlight. Anton turned to look at Jacqui, his face filled with sadness.

'I'm pregnant with Tom's child,' she said slowly and carefully. Anton took both her hands in his, before hugging her.

'That's amazing, Tom is still with us after all,' he said, smiling through tears. They sat together for a while looking thoughtfully towards the water, not saying a word. Eventually his face lit up as he realised how he could help Jacqui.

'I can help you,' he said excitedly. 'I will be there for as long as you need me. I'll come to classes with you and be your birthing partner if you'd like me to. You don't need to go through this alone.'

Anton knew Jacqui had lost her mum and didn't

want to leave her struggling on her own. Jacqui was comforted by Anton's words, knowing he was a genuine friend, who could be relied on whenever she needed him.

'You're such a kind and thoughtful man,' she replied gently before hugging him closely.

'Come on you, let's go and get a cup of tea,' he suggested trying to lighten the mood.

Anton had come up with an idea before the funeral which he wanted to go through with Jacqui, as a personal tribute to Tom. It came to him when he was moving Tom's paintings into his gallery and he'd been waiting for the right moment to discuss it with her ever since. Now that she had told him about the baby, the time seemed right. As they sipped warm mugs of tea in the park cafe, he could wait no longer. Unknown to Jacqui he had spent the last two weeks, patiently framing all of Tom's paintings.

'Jacqui I've been thinking about holding an open day at the gallery to exhibit Tom's work putting all the paintings on display for purchase. What do you think?' She looked deep in thought before answering.

'Would anyone come though, he wasn't a well-known artist.'

'Maybe I could contact a local newspaper first to run a story about what happened to him, which might provoke some interest.'

'Hmmm,' she replied.

'I thought about giving any money made to charity, but now that you have told me about the baby, well it could go towards starting up a savings account, for the little one.' Jacqui smiled, cheered by Anton's enthusiasm, he'd obviously been thinking about this for some time.

'I love it, thank you. You've managed to cheer me up once again. I don't know what I'd do without you.' It was true after the cold, chillness that had remained with Jacqui throughout their time in the park, her heart felt lighter, warmed by Anton who never failed to lighten her mood. She hadn't thought about what to do with Tom's paintings. Kym didn't want any of them and Jacqui didn't want them around her place indefinitely.

The following week the local newspaper ran an article about how Tom had lain in the mortuary for days unidentified. The Gallery would be open to the public displaying Tom's work from 10 o'clock on Saturday the 30th March. Anton very much felt the pressure of the short timescale and spent hours hanging Tom's paintings in his gallery during the week leading up to the exhibition day. After much rearrangement of the canvases and changes to the lighting, he was finally ready, with only an hour to spare before the event started.

Anton told Kym about the open day, she wasn't sure about attending and he put it down to her not forgiving Tom's betrayal.  Jacqui was also undecided as to whether she would be coming.  Anton wasn't deterred by their lack of interest, it was what he wanted to do for Tom as a final gesture and had spared no expense to ensure proceedings went well.

Early on Saturday morning Jacqui woke feeling weak and tired, pulling the quilt back over herself, wanting to delay making a decision about what could be a horrendous day ahead.  She knew that it wasn't necessary for her to be at the gallery open day, Anton could handle it, he would understand.  Yet she was filled with an overwhelming desire to see Tom's work, hanging completed, ready to be viewed by the public.  This would have been his dream and silent tears slid down her face, knowing that he wouldn't be there to see his dream coming to fruition.  Tom would have been so excited, unable to sit still, constantly moving paintings around at the gallery, not satisfied with their positions.  She could picture him clearly standing there, glowing with happiness at finally getting his work exhibited and knew she had to be there.

Cereal seemed to stave off nausea for Jacqui, so it was her normal breakfast for weekends, replacing much loved bacon baps.  Getting dressed she turned and admired her tummy whilst looking in the mirror.  At three months she wasn't really showing.  Only a small bump protruded from her stomach which hadn't affected her wearing close fitting tops yet. Jacqui chose a bright coloured dress which Tom had always liked. A little baggy around the tummy area just in case. No black today she thought, it was to be a celebration of Tom's work.

When Jacqui found herself outside the gallery, a wave of nausea flooded over her and she delayed entering feeling light headed and unsteady. A stiff alcoholic drink on the way would have settled her nerves, but alcohol was on her banned list. Jacqui didn't want to take any chances with the life of her unborn child, wanting her baby to be perfect. Carefully climbing the three stone steps, she took a deep breath before walking quickly through the gallery door.

Hearing loud, excited voices talking, she stepped inside and gasped, startled. The small front room, was full of people all huddled together, sipping glasses of orange juice and sparkling wine. It was only eleven o'clock and the place was packed. Anton spotted Jacqui straight away and came over with a glass of orange juice for her, looking very excited.

'Isn't it wonderful, I had no idea Tom's work would be so popular, I've sent out for more drinks, it's fantastic,' he said, turning to attend to buyers around him. Jacqui stood alone, breathing in the atmosphere for several moments before making her way through the crowd, admiring Tom's paintings. They looked magnificent.  Anton had done an excellent job framing and presenting them to look better than she could have imagined.  Seeing Tom's paintings stacked in her lounge, she was unable to appreciate just how good some of them were.  Now Jacqui looked in awe at Tom's talent, finally uncovered and displayed for all to see.  Moving slowly, her eyes lingered on each painting, with Tom's voice filling her mind.

'*Wow, my work is amazing, I knew I would make it one day.  Look at this piece Jacqui, it's the one I did when...*' poor Tom she thought, quickly wiping her eyes.

Looking around Tom was everywhere, the room was filled with him and his colours.  Paintings of cascading waterfalls, valleys and hills.  Stunning red and gold sunsets next to lush, green woodlands filled with flowers.  Purple and grey misty hues clinging to mountains.  Snow and ice filled landscapes alongside warm sunlit, sandy beaches, surrounded by azure shaded waters.  Everything she saw oozed Tom.  She thought about how he had felt about his lack of achievements as an artist.  What a wonderful legacy he had left behind.  These paintings would last forever, unlike the work most people did.

The morning rolled into the afternoon and more people arrived to view and buy Tom's work.  Jacqui wanted to be part of everything going on, determined to see the day through.  It had turned out to be very uplifting and she felt proud of Tom.

It was Jacqui's turn to hide, when she saw Kym arriving with Matt. They looked like they were in love. He guided her around the gallery in a protective way with his hand next to her lower back. Jacqui felt a little jealous, Kym had come out on top again. Not wanting to spoil the afternoon, or to talk to Kym, she busied herself in the back room of the gallery until they had left. Whilst passing the time there Jacqui thought about Kym. Looking at her with Matt it seemed that she had forgotten about Tom very quickly. Kym hadn't put any effort into Tom's funeral, the scattering of his ashes or this open day.

Jacqui occasionally popped her head around the door, only to jump back quickly, if she saw them move, longing for them to go. Each time she returned to the leather chair in the back room the same words echoed in her mind.

*You couldn't have really loved him, not the way I did.*

By the end of the day they had sold all but one of Tom's paintings. It was a small painting of a stream, with a back drop of bluebells.

'I love this one,' Anton said gently, his eyes glazing over.

'You should have it, as a thank you gift, Tom

would have wanted you to have at least one of his paintings.'

Anton hesitated to reply. 'You've spent a small fortune on Tom's funeral and all the expensive frames around his paintings,' she continued, taking it down from the wall and placing it in his arms, insisting he take it.

'Yes,' he replied uncertainly. 'I'll add some money to the fund and we will say no more about it,' before disappearing into the back room with the painting clutched to his chest.

Jacqui yawned, overwhelmed with tiredness from being on her feet most of the day, she longed to be at home lying down in comfort. Anton stayed behind wanting to add up the sales figures and promised to ring her later. When Jacqui got home she ran into her bedroom, covered herself with her thick, warm quilt and cried until the room filled with darkness as daylight faded. That would be the last time she would cry for Tom. There was nothing more that she could do for him.

Jacqui was still in bed, half asleep when her mobile's tuneful ring caused her to stir.

'Hello there, how are you feeling?' Anton asked in his lively, enthused voice.

'Quite tired,' she answered, yawning.

'Have you had something to eat?' he continued, delaying disclosing the sales figures, wanting Jacqui to delve further to create a greater impact.

'Yes,' Jacqui replied anxiously, 'tell me how well we did?' Anton knew he could no longer prolong his announcement.

'Are you sitting down, I have some very good news, 250 thousand pounds worth of good news!'

'I can't believe it,' exclaimed Jacqui. 'Tom was always saying that the only way he would make money was when he was dead.' Realising what she'd said she started to choke back tears again,

'Don't upset yourself,' Anton managed to say, feeling a bit choked himself. 'Tom got the recognition he was looking for. Feel proud, like I do, he finally made it!'

As if on cue Jacqui could hear Tom speaking to her, just as she had earlier.

'*I knew I could do it, be somebody*' and in that moment she realised that he was successful, which was all that he'd ever wanted out of life.

## Chapter Thirteen

# Speechless

'Good Morning Kym and Matt, it is 6.30 am.' Mr. Right greeted them in his usual cheerful tone.

'What was that?' a surprised Matt asked, quickly sitting up in bed.

'What?' Kym replied playfully.

'Your computer just said my name!' he exclaimed, watching her face for a reaction. Kym smiled, pleased that Matt had noticed she'd added his name to her computer the day before. Matt kissed her gently, before teasing her.

'I suppose this means we are a couple then?' he asked, raising an eyebrow. Kym laughed.

'A couple of what, weirdo's possibly!' Matt was having none of this, he was on top of her threatening to make them late for work unless she said yes. Kym quickly gave in.

'Yes,' she yelled, leaping out of bed before Matt could stop her. Still naked and picking up a pillow to defend herself, Kym leapt from side to side trying to avoid his grasp. Unable to escape, they landed together, giggling on the bed, breathing heavily from their exertions.

'I love to hear you laugh,' Matt continued, moving her hair gently away from her face.

'Mmm and I love to eat,' she replied, before releasing from his arms and tying her kimono, around her slim frame. Matt sighed as she left the bedroom, her ability to display affection during intimate moments had taken a backward step recently.

The weeks had passed quickly since the gallery open day at the end of March, Matt wondered where the time had gone during the second week in May. Kym had tried to slip into her coping mechanism of spending more time alone, busying herself with work to hide her emotions from him since Tom's death. Matt had pulled out all the stops to avoid this happening. Whenever Kym insisted she was too tired after work to see him, Matt would arrive uninvited at her door with a takeaway and a movie. If Kym didn't fancy a day out at the weekend, he would turn up with a ready-made picnic, just as he had before. Matt loved being outdoors and was determined to rekindle Kym's passion for hill walking, beach strolls and pub lunches.

Kym seemed to have stopped doing the many things she had enjoyed as a teenager with her family in the Lakes. It was as if blanking out her childhood years had enabled her to cope with the death of her parents. Matt recognised this, as he'd done the same thing when Lucy died. It was far less painful than to remember. As time passed, he knew that memories had to be embraced as good times spent together. They had to be faced in order to completely heal.

Kym hadn't shared many of her childhood memories with Matt but he knew her family had kept dogs and spent lots of time outdoors. On one occasion after much prompting from Matt to talk about her past, she described walking on the fells with her dad, climbing rocky pathways for the best views. She'd forgotten how good it felt to sit and look into the hazy distance, after reaching the top of a steep hill. Finding what started out as a cold wind, turned into a heaven sent breeze, after feeling the heat from the ascent. How refreshing water tasted when you were thirsty and exhausted. How delightful that first drink in the pub at the end of miles of walking felt, when your feet were tired and aching. Matt shared her desire to get a dog in the future and move to the countryside, he was not a fan of the city.

Matt loved Kym, he would have done anything she wanted and aimed to spend the rest of his life with her, but was worried that it would be too soon for them to make plans. A hopeless romantic, he loved surprising her with flowers, chocolates or whatever gift he could find that might make her smile and fill her heart with joy. They were entering their thirteenth week together, long enough for Matt to know how he felt, but he wasn't always certain that Kym felt the same. He'd been patient but was finding it harder to handle her insecurities. When it came to discussing her feelings she'd mastered the art of changing the subject or joking, if she detected he was getting too serious.

With work commitments they didn't always spend time together during the week, but always kept weekends for each other. Matt loved waking up with Kym, her hair messy, her skin next to his, one of his shirts pulled on if she got cold in the night. Being with Kym felt like coming home. They made pancakes, bacon and eggs for breakfast, designed menus and took turns cooking and trying out new things. It seemed natural for them to move in together, though Matt was afraid to mention this to Kym in case she wasn't ready and it would ruin everything, but Matt wasn't very good at waiting.

One afternoon spent standing in the corridor at

work, Matt decided to take Kym away for the weekend. Somewhere neither of them had been to before, a small Cornish town next to the sea. Matt wiped sweat from his brow after booking a lavish apartment for the following weekend without asking Kym first. Telling her to pack a weekend bag and keeping the location a surprise. On Friday afternoon, Matt leapt out of the car, greeting Kym with a big hug, feeling his heart beat quicken.

'What are you up to?' she asked, smiling excitedly.

'Wait and see,' he answered. Kym intrigued, gazed into his eyes, her's filled with adoration for him, delighted that he'd kept everything secret, arousing her excitement. The romantic meal he planned to cook on Saturday night, flowers he'd lovingly picked, champagne and all her favourite foods, were hidden away in the car boot. Matt smiled, thinking she had no idea what he had in mind.

The apartment was fantastic, Kym's eyes shone with delight as she opened the large glass doors which led to a balcony overlooking the sea.

'I love the sound of the waves crashing,' she shouted, as her hair blew wildly in the wind. Matt was busy unloading the car while Kym explored each room with a satisfactory,

'Wow.' Matt's smile widened as she approached

him.  She looked happy, radiant and caressed the back of his neck with soft strokes of her fingers, before kissing him gently.  As she pulled away he saw a look of admiration in her eyes, wondering if it was love.

After a long walk, they arrived at an old smugglers pub at the end of a cobbled street, not far from where they were staying.  Finding a table near to one of the pub's open fires, they appreciated its warm, leaping flames, surrounded by a Cornish stone hearth.  Wonderful aromas of freshly cooked food wafted towards them, every time the door to the kitchen opened.  Kym noticed the many wooden beams supporting the low ceiling and Matt had to keep ducking to avoid hitting his head, to get to the bar.  She gazed through the small square windows containing tiny panes of thick, rippled glass whilst awaiting his return.  Matt had a pint of Old Habits ale and Kym sparkling wine as they took their time selecting local dishes from the lavishly detailed menu.

After devouring a platter of freshly caught seafood and two bottles of crisp, white wine, they looked longingly at each other.

'Shall we go?'  Matt asked, feeling the effects of alcohol coursing through his body, enhancing his desire to slowly kiss her intimately.

'Yeah,' a very tipsy Kym answered.

'Let's dance on the beach, feel the breeze on our

skin and run in the sand,' she whispered, 'I want to be reckless.' Her eyes twinkled as they stumbled unsteadily down a slope of large rocks which led to the beach. Arms around each other they laughed helplessly trying to stay upright after jerking momentarily back and forth in the refreshing breeze.

Kym twirled faster and faster with her arms outstretched, before tumbling onto the sand. Matt picked her up and brushed golden grains from her legs, before finding his hands move over her body as he stood up. They ran towards the sea, pausing to pick up pebbles before attempting to skim them unsuccessfully into the rolling, crashing waves, which they jumped backwards to avoid. Matt filled with exhilaration and anticipation for the evening ahead, chased her across the soft, golden sand. Picking her up and wrapping her legs around his waist, he kissed her passionately, unaware that other couples further up the beach were watching them jealously.

The heating was on when they got in, but it still felt cool. Leaving their sand filled shoes, just inside the door, Matt immediately set about lighting the fire. Whilst Kym struggled to remove fine grains from her toes, he opened a bottle of champagne, watching as foaming bubbles fell towards the slated floor.

'What's the celebration?' Kym asked playfully. Matt looked at his girlfriend, his heart pounding. Feeling crazily in love with her he knew that the moment was right to tell her there and then. Hoping it wouldn't turn out to be a mistake, he couldn't stop himself from pulling her towards him.

'Kym, the celebration is you. You are beautiful and I treasure every day that we are together. I love you and want to be with you always.' Matt waited for Kym's response, not quite sure what it would be. She looked serious and was hesitating and he was starting to feel hot under the collar again, how she liked to make him wait.

'I love you,' she answered, looking a bit misty eyed and that was it. Matt was expecting more from Kym, but in the absence of anything further, passed her a glass, attempting to hide his disappointment as they sipped the sparkling liquid.

'To us,' he said uncertainly, not sure what to do next.

'To us,' Kym replied, as she slowly and seductively began unbuttoning his shirt.

Matt wasn't going to give up, feeling like a man possessed, he knew he had to find out if Kym felt they had a future together. Kym had never taken the lead to instigate sex before. Now she wanted to control him, hurriedly removing his clothes. Heady with lust for her, he obeyed her commands, taking inspiration from Kym's wild, uninhibited moves. Her display of passion distracted him temporarily from what he needed to know. Afterwards as they lay naked next to the fire, Matt decided to take a chance and broach the subject once more. His fingers stroked her arm gently and he held his breath as he blurted out the words.

'Kym, why don't we move in together?' There it was Matt had finally said it, he just couldn't wait any longer, impatient to know and searched her eyes for an answer. Kym looked thoughtful and didn't respond straight away. How she makes me suffer, he thought.

'We could start looking for a new place, when we get back. Sell our apartments, maybe buy a house? What do you think?' he asked hesitantly, looking at the woman he loved with all his heart, wondering why she wasn't answering. Kym, taken aback by Matt's questions, knew she had to answer, but couldn't find the right words and wished she hadn't consumed so much alcohol.

'It would be great if we could move to the countryside' she finally said, smiling happily 'and get a dog.' Matt breathed a sigh of relief.

'Whatever you want, I will get for you, I would do anything for you,' he continued. Kym felt herself melt inside, he was going to get it for her, how wonderful that sounded. She wasn't going to be the one having to do all the work and pay for everything this time.

'We'll find our home together,' she answered

with tears of happiness in her eyes. Matt was her hero and nothing was going to spoil things for her this time.

Kym was quiet during the drive back to her apartment on Sunday evening. Matt worried that something was wrong. He was right. They had been so wrapped up in each other all weekend that Kym had forgotten something. As she packed away her toothbrush that morning, she noticed a pack of unused Tampons in her makeup bag. Her heart stopped as she stared at them, knowing that she was never late. The Pill kept her as regular as clockwork. It wasn't possible, it had to be a mistake with the dates.

During the next week Kym waited, but nothing happened. She didn't see Matt during the week so hadn't told him of her concern. An estate agent was visiting at the weekend and Kym busied herself making her apartment look its best. On Saturday night they went out for a celebratory meal as both of their apartments had been valued and they stood to make a substantial profit on each one. Clinking glasses they knew they could afford to buy the type of house they wanted. Everything was going well, Matt was bursting with happiness and Kym didn't want to say anything that might spoil their evening.

She knew that Matt loved her but how would he take the news if it did turn out that she was pregnant? They hadn't talked about starting a family, it was much too soon in their relationship and anyway Kym didn't want to be a mother, it would be a disaster for her.

After Matt left on Sunday evening, Kym took out the pregnancy test. Reading the instructions over and over, she knew that it could be put off no longer. Holding her breath, Kym looked away not wanting to see the words forming on the white plastic stick. Words from heaven or letters revealing her hell. The result was positive she was four weeks pregnant.

'Oh my God, oh my God,' she repeated, before dropping the stick in horror.

Kym sat on the cold tiles of the bathroom floor, numb with shock, staring at the words printed on a piece of plastic that was going to change her life forever. Stunned by her dilemma and trying to figure out how she could possibly be pregnant, tears of frustration stung her eyes. She hadn't missed any pills or been on medication that would affect her contraceptives. Kym put her hand over her mouth, gasping in disbelief at her misfortune in being one of the unlucky 1% not protected by the 99% effective pill. Suppressing sobs she envisaged the end of her career and more importantly her relationship with Matt.

Kym immediately decided the best outcome for herself would be to have an abortion. Attend a private clinic within the next couple of weeks without Matt ever knowing. Then her heart sank, realising that she had been one of the Generate group members who'd supported restricting abortions. There were exceptions but they wouldn't help her, she had no choice and would have to go through with the pregnancy, stuck in a situation of her own creation. Kym had listened to the news with interest when the new law was passed eight weeks ago, restricting abortions, with immediate effect. Happy that her idea had been accepted and action had been taken, never believing for a moment that she would be caught in her own trap.

'No!' she cried out loud, before wrapping her arms around herself and rocking back and forward with hysterical tears. Everything had been perfect between her and Matt and now their bubble of contentment was set to burst dramatically.

She took Monday off work and ignored her mobile phone. Spending the day crying, feeling sorry for herself and worried sick about her and Matt. Matt couldn't get in touch with Kym and sensing something was wrong, went straight round to her apartment after work. She reluctantly let him in, avoiding his eyes. Matt knew that something had affected her terribly and pleaded with her to tell him, but she remained silent. He took her hands in his, looking deeply into her eyes.

'Whatever it is, I'll still love you and we will sort it out together,' he tried to reassure her, but was unable to hide the panic in his voice. Kym burst into tears.

'I'm so sorry, I rushed you into selling your apartment, we don't have to move in together yet, we can put it all on hold, until you feel ready.' Matt continued frantically worried that he had caused her distress.

'It's not that Matt. I'm pregnant and I don't know how I can be,' Kym blurted out tearfully. She showed him the test - Matt stared at the words displayed there feeling the colour drain from his face.

'Four weeks pregnant' he said out loud. He looked at Kym, she was in quite a state. He knew that abortions were illegal and had no choice other than to disguise his shock from her. Somehow lifting his tone before speaking again and choosing his words carefully, he managed to say,

'Don't worry, we can do this. We'll be great parents, just think how good looking our children will be.' Kym wept with relief, knowing she'd had no other option than to see this pregnancy through, with or without Matt. She remained silent, looking up into his eyes, like a child totally dependent on him.

'We'll have our new home soon and Mum and Dad will be delighted.' It seemed to be working, Kym was looking more cheerful. Matt however, couldn't believe it. He needed time to get used to the idea that he was going to be a father but kept his disappointment hidden.

Matt continued to hug Kym close, whilst putting on a brave face, unable to tell her that he hadn't planned to have children, it was the worst news. Comforting her in bed, sleepless hours passed by as he looked at the woman he loved more than anything else. As she lay in his arms, quietly sleeping, he was filled with an overwhelming desire to protect her and their unborn child.

The next morning, leaving for work he felt like a shadow of the man who had walked through her door the night before. The thought of inevitable parenthood weighed heavily on his mind as he carefully closed the front door without waking her. The night before had been the first night they had spent together without making love. Kym was also aware of this, waking up, finding an empty space at her side, she shuddered, with past memories and doubts filling her mind.

Kym had worked out the dates and realised that their baby would be born during the second week in January of the following year. Almost twelve months since they had met at the Generate meeting, which had unintentionally caused their predicament. Matt and Kym sold their apartments quickly and found a detached house surrounded by countryside, within commuting distance of central London. They got over the shock and started to accept the situation and plan for their baby. Matt wanted to be involved in everything and Kym knew he would be a great dad.

She had been nausea free to date and seemed to be breezing through the first three months of pregnancy. Time had gone quickly and it was the last week in July, when they made their way to the Maternity clinic for the first scan of their baby. Holding Kym's hand, Matt breathed deeply in an attempt to stay calm, as they waited patiently to see images of their son or daughter. The friendly Midwife was taking her time, checking the screen carefully, before turning towards them smiling.

'I can see two hearts beating, four arms and legs, its twins! Congratulations,' she announced joyfully, before turning the screen towards the expectant parents, who looked at each other speechless.

## Chapter Fourteen

# Beating Hearts

Matt and Kym drove home from the clinic, convincing themselves that they would cope with twins no matter what.

'It might work out fine,' Kym said quietly, trying to recover from yet another unexpected thunderbolt that fate had dealt them.

'I've heard from other families that it's less work for parents who have twins,' she tried to reassure him. Poor Matt, she was thinking, he didn't look happy. He'd hardly said anything since they left the Maternity Unit.

'What a shock,' he replied. 'I certainly didn't see that one coming, there aren't any twins in my family, what about yours?' He looked inquisitively at Kym as if he was trying to apportion blame.

'None in mine either,' Kym answered sharply, he was arousing her irritation with his reaction, which seemed to be much more negative than when she'd told him about the pregnancy in the first place.

'Look it might turn out to be ok,' Matt replied, resigning himself to their situation and sensing Kym's impatience.

'They'll play together and keep each other entertained, leaving us to our own devices most of the time. I would have loved a brother or sister,' he added trying to lift the mood, sensing that Kym was about to burst into tears.

'Let's hope so.' she answered wearily, feeling the strain of more unplanned changes to her life, which was turning out to be far from the one she'd dreamt of.

Matt felt a little stressed thinking about his workload over the coming months. He wanted to get everything finished in their new home and started to plan the nursery. They were going to need two of everything. Cots, car seats, prams, high chairs. The list seemed endless, overwhelming. Kym would need much more care now that she was carrying twins, prompting Matt to change his work pattern so he could be available to help out during weekends and evenings. Beads of sweat appeared on his forehead every time he thought about the birth. Having heard first births could be difficult enough, Matt spent hours searching the internet for associated risks with the delivery of two babies. Not finding any reassurance he often sat quietly on his own, late into the night thinking about his fears. Matt hadn't been anywhere near a hospital since Lucy's death and didn't think he could survive another traumatic event.

With six months to go, he decided to spend the time getting their home ready. Hoping the extra work would leave him feeling exhausted at bed time and not lying awake, tossing and turning, fretting about what could happen. One morning, after waking covered in sweat from a nightmare about Kym, Matt decided that they should get married. She was sleeping peacefully, oblivious to his unending trepidation as he cuddled up to her.

'Marry me,' he whispered, knowing that she couldn't hear, though wishing she had, ending further turmoil for him. Matt recalled a conversation with colleagues at work, when one of them proposed and had been turned down. Poor bugger, he'd thought at the time.

'Lesson learnt,' his colleague confided in him, 'If you're going to ask someone to marry you, be sure they are going to say yes first!' Matt kissed the top of

Kym's shoulder gently, she still didn't wake and he inhaled deeply not sure what to do. What a disaster it would be if he went down on one knee in the restaurant where they had their first date as other diners watched and Kym said, no! Matt decided to start doing a bit of research first, taking his friends advice by dropping a few hints, which Kym either missed or was ignoring, forcing him to come right out with it one evening.

'Kym do you think we should get married before the twins are born?' he asked on the fifth attempt, having bottled out of the other four.

'Possibly,' Kym replied looking thoughtful. 'If you think we have time on top of sorting the house out, doing the nursery up and hospital appointments.' Matt didn't care, she hadn't ruled it out. All he could think about now was booking the restaurant for Saturday night and getting a ring. His sense of relief was enormous, knowing it would be one less thing for him to worry about on top of everything else. Matt was sure that Kym would only want their wedding to be a small local ceremony, being heavily pregnant. It wouldn't be exactly the wonderful romantic year he had planned for them both, proposing as they finished trekking up to Machu Picchu, or as they walked along a beach in Australia at sunset. Matt knew both of these things were on Kym's wish list, they had worked hard and could afford to go wherever they wanted. He shrugged, disappointed that fate had decided to halt their plans. A honeymoon locally was what they would have to settle for, their dreams to travel to the other side of the world would have to be postponed.

Kym's next appointment at the clinic was four weeks away, by which time she felt huge. Perplexed by her weight gain and scowling at the mirror, maternity dresses were pressed against her bump, only to be flung across the bed to join the pile of rejects already discarded there. Tears of frustration flowed freely down her face upon failing to find anything to wear that would conceal her swelling midriff.

'What if I can't lose it again?' Kym shouted to Matt. It was still early days in their relationship and she worried that the twins would ruin her figure forever. Matt was dismissive, he didn't see what the problem was.

'Some of my friend's wives have had more than one child and they quickly got their figures back afterwards, don't worry about it.' Matt could tell from Kym's face that she wasn't impressed by his answer and immediately regretted it.

'There's always my punch bag to work out on afterwards Kym.' He suggested, thinking he was being helpful. Kym thought she might need to start throwing punches before the twins arrived, if she got anymore answers like that one. It wasn't his fault Matt decided, putting Kym's short temper and stroppy attitude down to hormones.

'I hope they don't find any more in there!' Matt said hesitantly, trying to lift her spirits as they pulled in to the car park of the clinic. Kym actually laughed this time, which made a change, he thought, struggling to recall the last time he'd seen her looking happy. Witnessing her tantrum with the clothes earlier, Matt had tried his best to lighten the mood.

'It's a maternity appointment, not a cat walk,' he'd joked. Kym shot him a disapproving look, saying he was being unsupportive, which sent him scurrying to the safety of the car to await her arrival. Whilst sitting there Matt made a decision. He was going to contact a private clinic a colleague had recommended and arrange to have the "snip". The Pill had turned out to be unreliable and neither of them could take going through any of this again. Matt grimaced momentarily thinking about the procedure, knowing it wasn't something he wanted to rush in to.

They walked through the doors of the Maternity unit and Kym was amazed to see the amount of pregnant women in the clinic. Previously she couldn't recall seeing or knowing anyone who was pregnant. Looking around and searching for two seats, she realised that things had definitely picked up, the plans of the Generate group were truly alive and kicking!

'Maybe it's going to be a baby boom year,' Kym whispered to Matt, who felt a bit nervous being amongst so many pregnant women. Feeling slightly uncomfortable he hadn't looked around much as they sat down, but as he started to, he was pleased to see a good turnout of men in the clinic, he wasn't suffering alone.

He did a double-take as he spotted a familiar pair in the corner, waiting to be seen. It was Anton and Jacqui. Matt nudged Kym.

'Look in the far right hand corner, Anton and Jacqui are sitting there!' he whispered, smirking. Kym looked over, Jacqui instantly saw her and waved as Anton got up and walked towards them, with his usual big warm smile.

'This is unbelievable,' he remarked, shaking Matt's hand enthusiastically. 'Congratulations to you both, when is your baby due?'

'Its twins,' replied Matt still unfamiliar with the words. 'We're hoping they will have arrived by the middle of January.'

'That's just wonderful,' Anton replied hugging Kym gently.

'What about yourselves?' Matt enquired with an eyebrow raised mischievously. Anton explained that Jacqui's baby was due in October and that he was there to support her. When he had gone back to update Jacqui, Kym turned to Matt as they both worked through dates quietly trying to figure out whose baby it was.

Quickly realising that it must be Tom's baby, Kym's immediate reaction was to go over to see Jacqui.

'Jacqui how wonderful for you,' Kym said genuinely, feeling unexpectedly delighted that Jacqui was having Tom's baby. She sat down next to Jacqui to talk to her for a moment. Anton stayed with Matt, leaving the girls to catch up. After they'd both been checked over by their Midwives, Matt and Anton suggested lunch at a local bistro. The girls felt a bit awkward, but as the men seemed to be getting on well, had no choice but to go along with it.

'Does this mean you're getting married?' Jacqui asked, secretly thinking it was too soon after Tom.

'Next month, why don't you both come?' Matt replied.

'I don't see why not,' answered Anton. Jacqui shot him a questioning look, but it was too late. Anton told her later that his back had been against the wall.

'We can always decline, I was just being nice,' he added, feeling like a child that had just had their hand smacked.

Kym asked Jacqui about Anton. She hadn't meant to but her curiosity was getting the better of her.

'We're just good friends, he's been amazing supporting me by coming to all my appointments here,' she added. 'It would have been a completely different experience if I'd been going through it alone.' Her comments struck a chord with Kym who hated being alone and wouldn't have coped as well as Jacqui had, especially with the idea of having twins. By the end of lunch all four had relaxed and enjoyed each other's company, planning to get together again soon. No one had mentioned Tom. They were all moving on with their lives.

Kym and Matt got married in September. It was a beautiful autumn day and the short ceremony was held in the gardens of a luxury hotel near their home. Anton and Jacqui came after all. Matt's parents had been wonderful, organising everything for them, including a honeymoon in Cornwall. They would have liked to have done more for Kym, who they adored, but knew from Matt that Kym wouldn't want to travel far due to her condition.

Kym finished work when she was five months pregnant at the end of September. It was earlier than was normal, giving her the chance to relax and spend some time on her own. There was still lots to organise before the twins arrived in the New Year, but she was feeling relaxed for the first time in her life and loved it. Each day she would spend time in the nursery, feeling the softness of the tiny clothes they had chosen for their babies. Imagining them in the cots as their eyes watched pastel coloured lights slowly twirl above them. Matt had wanted to know the sex of the twins at their last scan, he was secretly hoping for a son, but said he didn't really mind.

Anton rang on the 4th October to let them know that Jacqui had given birth to a beautiful baby boy. He weighed 6lb 12oz and had a mop of black hair. Jacqui hadn't decided what to call him yet, but she was doing fine. Kym felt sure that Tom would figure somewhere in her son's name. She had a strange urge to visit Jacqui in hospital to see her new baby, secretly hoping to see some of Tom in his face. Anton suggested they could visit at the weekend when Jacqui was settled in with her baby back at home.

Kym and Matt went round to Jacqui's on Saturday morning. Jacqui looked great, most of her baby weight seemed to have gone, whilst Kym felt like a baby elephant in comparison. Tom's baby was beautiful and Kym held him for a while. She had never held a baby before and he seemed smaller than she'd imagined. Baby Daniel Thomas had his dad's eyes and Kym marveled at the small perfectly formed limbs of Jacqui's baby. It had been a good idea for them to visit. Not only to see Tom's baby but to help them appreciate how inexperienced they all were with babies. It was going to be a huge learning curve for Kym and Matt, but they looked forward to the day when they would hold their own daughters for the first time.

Matt and Kym attended the clinic shortly after Christmas for her final appointment. Matt was sat in the waiting room patiently, when he was called in to the examination room. Kym looked a little upset, when he sat down beside her.

'What is it,' he asked as his breathing stalled.

'One of the babies is in the breeched position and I have explained to your wife that she will need to have a caesarean section.' The Midwife continued to search for dates on the screen in front of her. 'Here we go, how does the 7th of January sound?'

'That's fine,' Kym answered, looking at Matt who seemed dumbstruck.

'You're all booked in then, see you in ten days.' Matt stood up, horrified and almost knocked the chair over.

'Ten days! Did you say ten days?'

'Don't worry too much,' the Midwife remarked, holding out an arm to steady him. 'The procedure will be safer for your wife and daughters than a normal delivery and quicker.' Matt somehow managed to smile but could feel his heart racing at the thought of facing a hospital much sooner than he envisaged. Kym hadn't noticed, she'd been more concerned with ensuring that the hospital would remove stem cells from each of her baby's umbilical cords and put them into storage. Now that she was not having a normal delivery, Kym didn't want this important process to be missed, knowing that stem cells could save their lives one day.

On the day of her caesarean Kym was shaking with nerves as she packed, Matt tried to reassure her, but was exhausted after spending another sleepless night scared out of his mind at the thought of something going wrong. Linking arms with Kym and carrying her bag down the stairs, he stopped for a moment and looked at the two little baby seats waiting in the hall. Removing a handkerchief from his pocket he dabbed at beads of sweat on his forehead, knowing that time couldn't stand still what was going to happen could not be prevented.

At the hospital, Matt held on to Kym's hand until the last possible moment, not wanting to let her go.

'I love you, see you very soon,' he said softly, kissing her forehead. She smiled back at him and then she was gone.

'Would you like a drink?' a pretty, young nurse asked, sensing his anxiety.

'No, nothing, I just want to be left alone,' he answered sternly, sending her scurrying away. When he was allowed to see Kym she was hooked up to monitors and the Midwife looked concerned as she moved one of the monitors over Kym's swollen stomach several times. Her cheerful tone disappeared as she rang for the Doctor. He quickly arrived and explained to Matt and Kym that they were having difficulty finding the heartbeat of one of the babies. They quickly prepared Kym for surgery who seemed calm, whereas a pale faced Matt was looking near to collapse.

'Don't worry,' she tried to reassure him. 'They have been kicking away at me all morning, I'm sure everything will be fine.'

The Doctor decided to take Kym straight to theatre, leaving Matt waiting alone outside in the corridor. He sat on a blue chair feeling worried sick, with his elbows on his knees. Looking down at the white floor tiles, cold shivers darted down his spine as he recalled Lucy lying there, dying. Matt took long, slow deep breaths, feeling sweat running down his face, he needed to get away, but couldn't move.

Then he heard a tiny, weak cry from inside the theatre and jumped to his feet, followed by silence which caused him to pace up and down outside the theatre doors like a caged animal. Minutes went by, but he hadn't been told anything. Just as he was starting to break with the strain of not knowing and moved towards the theatre doors, a Doctor emerged smiling broadly.

'You have two beautiful daughters, congratulations!' he announced, full of exuberance.

'We had to give your second daughter some oxygen, but it was just routine, she's breathing fine now.' Matt felt an emotional wave of relief sweep over him, longing to see Kym and hold her he lunged towards the theatre doors. Swiftly moving in front of them, the Doctor caught his arm.

'You need to wait outside for another few minutes. Your wife is just in recovery, you can see them all shortly,' leading Matt towards the seating area.

'I can't thank you enough,' Matt said in a very shaky voice.

'My absolute pleasure,' the Doctor replied before returning to the theatre and closing the doors behind him.

When Matt was finally allowed to see Kym, she was only half conscious and he looked with displeasure at the drip which sank into her hand. Squeezing her other hand carefully, she opened her eyes and smiled weakly.

'You did great,' he whispered, 'they're both fine.' Not wanting to let Kym see him cry, he turned and walked towards the plastic cribs the twins had been placed in.

'They're beautiful,' he whispered, his eyes clouding with tears. One of the babies looked a little smaller than her sister and as he reached to touch her, woke up and started to cry. Within seconds her sister joined in and the noise was deafening.

'Good pair of lungs they both have,' the smiling midwife remarked, then shaking her head she tutted. 'Three women in your house, you're going to have your hands full!'

Matt stared at his tiny daughters wriggling in their plastic cribs and instinctively put a finger in each of their tiny palms. They closed their fingers around his and stopped crying.

'Hello, I'm your Daddy,' Matt said softly, delighted with his daughters. The whole experience had moved him in a way he could never have imagined. Kym asked to see the babies and the Midwife wrapped each one in a white sheet and passed them to her. She tried to sit up.

'Careful, stay still, mind those stitches,' the Midwife insisted.

Matt was asked to leave again, while they made preparations to move Kym to a ward. Reluctantly he left, exasperated by being treated as if he was in the way. Sinking into the same blue chair, his chest felt tight, stressed by the day's events. After sitting still and taking slow deep breaths for a further few minutes, Matt got himself together and dialled his parent's phone number.

His mum was very excited, she wanted to know everything that had happened and how they all were.

'Recovering,' Matt advised thinking that was true for all four of them!

'What do they weigh?' asked his mum.

'I have no idea,' replied Matt, 'I couldn't even tell you what day it is.' His mum chuckled.

'We can't wait to see them, find out what time visiting starts and if we can visit tonight.'

'Ok will let you know, but right now I need to get some air!'

When Matt stood outside the hospital doors he felt the tightness in his chest ease as tension changed to euphoria. For as far as he could see everything had turned white. A damp flake drifted down and hit his cheek and looking up, millions of soft, silent snowflakes filled the sky and were fluttering down towards him. It was amazing, the ground had been brushed with glistening white crystals, which sparkled beneath his feet. Newly gathering and perfectly formed, they shone with a pure white glow in their untainted state. It looked wonderful, surreal, summing up the whole day perfectly. At last he could relax, he had two beautiful daughters and his lovely Kym was safe and well.

When evening visiting time arrived Matt and his parents walked hurriedly towards the maternity ward. The twins were fast asleep and wrapped up tightly in white blankets. Both had tiny plastic bands around their wrists stating their names. Clare Adams and Evie Adams. Matt's mum read out their names with tears of joy in her eyes, secretly knowing that she'd always longed for a daughter.

'How wonderful to have twin girls, they will never be without a playmate,' she whispered to Kym. Matt's dad seemed a bit choked as he gently stroked their delicate heads.

'Try not to wake them Grandad,' Kym urged, 'they've been screaming at each other for the last two hours.' They all quietly laughed and Matt's mum gazed at them lovingly before saying,

'That won't last, twins are always very close, friends for life.'

## Chapter Fifteen

# 24 Years Later

On the day that Evie and Clare celebrated their twenty fourth birthdays, Kym got up early and raced downstairs, in her dressing gown, upon hearing the letter box flap bang back into place. Gathering up the daily newspaper, she flicked through the pages whilst walking towards the sofa, colliding with the edge of its arm.

'Oww,' she cried out, wincing and rubbing her knee, 'that really hurt.' Matt looked up from where he was sitting near to the patio doors.

'Serves you right for pinching my paper, you

know I love to read it before you all get up. You're spoiling my bit of peace.'

'Not today,' she added, before sitting on his lap with her injured leg stretched out.

'What's so interesting then,' he asked smiling, before trying to take the newspaper off her.

'Just a minute, I want to look at something. Anyway isn't it time you put the coffees on?'

'Ok, but I'll be back in a minute, then it's all mine.' Kym found the headline on page two, "Restrictions on abortions lifted" and began to read, her eyes moving fast as she skimmed through the information provided. Matt returned with cups of hot, creamy coffee and sat beside her.

'Listen to this,' she continued excitement filling her voice. 'After years of campaigning women's rights groups have succeeded in getting the Government to lift restrictions on abortions. It says here that the UK population has grown by a million new births, every year since the twins were born.'

'Wow, that's incredible,' he answered pretending to be stifling a yawn. 'Bit late for us to be interested in that now though, isn't it?'

'Ha,' she scoffed, 'not easily impressed then, maybe this will get your attention.' Kym pointed to the second half of the article, 'Twenty Four years of stem cell storage benefits.' Matt snatched the paper off her, reading the words carefully.

'The UK is now the world leader for stem cell treatments and Dr. Kym Adams, has been nominated for a life time achievement award for her contributions to stem cell development and storage.' Matt read it twice.

'Kym that's fantastic,' he cried, jumping to his feet and twirling his wife around, her face shone with excitement. 'You must have known. Why didn't you say anything?'

'I wanted to wait until it was confirmed, before we celebrated.'

'Well, you've got that now, let's wake the girl's and tell them.' Kym caught his arm.

'No, wait, it's their birthday and I don't want to take any attention away from them today. It will be weeks before I get the award, probably at an evening event, let's just leave it for now.'

'Ok if that's what you want,' he replied, smiling broadly at his wife, 'I'm so proud of you,' before pulling her towards him. 'Clever, beautiful, sexy lady and all mine,' he whispered, then kissed her gently.

Later that afternoon, whilst Matt drove the girls

to the station, Kym turned to the internet to find out more about the population increases. It had been staggering to discover that half a million pregnancies had been terminated each year, prior to restrictions being introduced. The Generate group could be proud of their achievements as their efforts had led to an increase in the population of the UK within the time scale required. The amount of multiple births had been unexpected though. Kym read that in some areas many schools had classes filled with twins and one school had two lots of sextuplets. Studying multiple birth data she found similar occurrences in the United States during the nineteen sixties and seventies.

Kym sipped coffee, reflecting on how much she had personally benefitted from being selected as a member of the Generate Group. Never imagining when she first sat down in the meeting room, all those years ago, feeling miserable and dejected, that her life would alter beyond recognition. All the wonderful things that may never have happened. Matt and her beautiful daughters, who potentially would never have existed if the group hadn't chosen to restrict terminations. Although having two babies early in their relationship had been hard on her and Matt, looking back twenty four years on, she wouldn't have changed a thing.

The Generate group's second meeting had turned out to be an excellent forum for Kym to promote her ambitious stem cell storage proposal. Convincing the

Government to store stem cells from cord blood had saved thousands of lives. It was an expensive exercise, storing the cells indefinitely, but cancers and many life threatening diseases had been successfully treated and lives prolonged. Every baby born, including her own two daughters, had their stem cells stored, frozen indefinitely, hopefully never to be needed.

Matt was perplexed by the whole stem cell issue. It went right over his head. Kym remembered spending a whole afternoon trying to explain it to him.

'If you become ill and are given somebody else's cells to cure the illness, your body would reject them,' she patiently explained, looking at her husband to check he was listening.

'I've heard of this,' Matt said, nodding, 'don't you end up on drugs for the rest of your days?'

'Exactly, but if you had your own stem cells in storage, they could be recalled and implanted straight into your body. Then, because they are your own cells, your body wouldn't reject them. They could start their repair work immediately. Stem cells are amazing,' she continued. 'They can seek out damaged cells and grow healthy ones in their place, prolonging your life.'

'Does it mean that our girls will have the chance to live a very long life?' he asked.

'It means if they become ill, we have many more options available for treatment. They won't die before their time,' Kym replied.

Matt was beginning to understand how important Kym's fight had been.

'It's amazing. When you set out to ensure stem cells were stored, we didn't have any children, but what you have done could ultimately save them one day. You're a genius! You do realise you'll be famous from now on, not just here but internationally. A household name, imagine that!' Matt picked up his coat and wallet. 'People will be wanting your autograph,' he added, grinning, before heading out the door.

Hearing his car wheels crunch across the gravel, Kym dropped her waving hand and looked downwards as his words echoed in her mind. Her heart sank, not wanting anything to change in their lives, she was happy, content and certainly didn't want to be famous.

As Kym embraced retirement, Matt on the other hand hadn't felt any desire to finish work early. He was still enjoying working at Downing Street and playing golf with his friends. Golf had been his saviour providing both peace and relaxation, giving him the chance to adjust from being a bachelor to having a busy family. Bringing up two daughters had not been easy, sometimes he wondered how he had managed to survive it and remain sane.

Twenty Four years had passed very quickly. They had grown into stunning women. Clare was like her mum, tall and very slim with long blonde hair. Evie was smaller, with auburn hair, taking after his mum and had been the 'drama queen' of the family, much more difficult to manage than her calmer, easy going sister.

He loved that they were completely different, even though Evie had given them many sleepless nights. Clare had a maturity beyond her years, having the ability to see right through a person and know exactly what they wanted. Evie seemed foolish in comparison, wanting to learn from her own mistakes. You couldn't give her any sort of advice during her teens, at times it had been a very bumpy ride.

Matt loved sport and was secretly hoping that one of the girls would take after him, but they showed no interest. Kym had been kept busy throughout their school years, writing notes, excusing them from P.E. activities. Matt couldn't understand it, though it seemed to be the trend with the whole of their generation. Few cyclists, footballers or athletes had been found and trained from a whole generation either not interested or physically fit enough for sport. It was quite shocking how this had been allowed to occur.

Matt wondered, as he often did, what the future would hold for his daughters. Neither had a permanent boyfriend that he knew of. It seemed strange for their age but after some of the encounters he'd had with previous unsuitable boyfriends, it wasn't something he wanted them to rush into. He just wanted the best for them. Enough money had been ploughed into their education with Clare making the most of this as she excelled in academic subjects, whereas Evie wanted to "party" her way through College.

Clare had become an English and Spanish teacher, perhaps taking after Matt for her ability to learn languages quickly. Evie still hadn't settled on a career path, not wanting to stick to one job for long, always finding some excuse to move on. Matt sighed deeply, wondering if Evie would ever settle down. Her philosophy in life seemed to be to earn enough money to go travelling, come back home when broke and get a temporary job until she could afford to disappear again. Matt felt miserable when Evie wasn't at home. He would never get used to it and blamed her for his hair turning grey as he worried constantly about where she was.

It was the night of the awards ceremony and Matt got ready first, leaving much needed bathroom space for the girls. Pouring himself a small glass of whisky in the lounge, he glanced over towards the photo of the four of them and his lips curled into a self-satisfied smile. They were all together, a family once more and he swallowed, feeling a lump in his throat. Then his face darkened. An over protective Matt knew if anyone harmed them, he would leave no stone unturned to find them and couldn't be held responsible for his actions, heaven forbid.

Kym always looked much younger than her years and as she descended the stairs slowly, his face beamed with pride.

'You look fantastic,' he exclaimed, holding her hands and turning her around.

'Thank you, handsome,' she replied smiling brightly.

'Nice dress,' he remarked, whistling loudly, 'reminds me of our first date.'

'That was the plan,' she added, putting her arms around his neck and kissing him gently. Matt's heart leapt, he didn't think it would be possible to love anyone more than he did her and inhaled her perfume deeply as they locked eyes, with a knowing look. Even after all the years they had been together, she could still take his breath away at times.

'Oh no, not again,' a groaning Evie remarked as she walked down the stairs, looking stylish and pretty in a short crimson evening dress.

'Leave them alone, it's sweet,' Clare said, gliding past her in an elegant cocktail dress, similar to her mum's.

'All this beauty,' Matt added, looking in

admiration at the three women in his life. 'I'll have my hands full tonight keeping the men away.'

Walking hand in hand, Matt and Kym made a stunning couple, even though they were in their fifties. Looking happy and relaxed, they were seated at a large round table. Elegantly dressed with sparkling silver cutlery and red roses which created a stunning centrepiece. Shortly after their arrival, Anton, Jacqui and her son Dan arrived. Kym had invited them, they'd all remained friends after the birth of their children and she looked across at Dan noticing he'd grown into a very handsome young man. Dan quickly sat next to Evie before anyone else could sit there. Matt's parents were the last to arrive.

'Any objections to champagne?' Matt asked, knowing the girls loved it. Only Dan shook his head.

'Thanks Matt, but I'm not drinking alcohol tonight, I'm driving,' prompting Matt to think what a decent, sensible young man. Dinner was soon over and the awards ceremony began. When Kym's name was called she looked very nervous, hesitating to get up. Matt put his hand over hers, which was slightly shaking.

'You can do this, you look amazing and it's what you deserve,' he whispered encouraging her. Everyone was clapping as Kym got up very slowly, manoeuvering her long dress just above her high heeled shoes. Matt clapped loudly, watching her carefully as she made her way to the front, holding his breath, sensing her vulnerability. Kym made a brief thank you speech, her voice faltering occasionally, before walking tentatively back to their table and sitting down a bit too hard.

'That's it, no more, I can now relax and enjoy my retirement,' she looked relieved to be back at Matt's side.

'Let's hope you can still keep up with your toy boy when you're retired,' Matt joked, patting the back of her hand.

'Dad!' the girls said loudly, in unison, looking embarrassed whilst the others laughed.

Matt noticed that not for the first time, Evie and Dan had gone missing and wondered what they were up to? He gave his daughter a disapproving look when she returned, but Evie just shrugged and carried on talking with Dan. Matt glared at her, unhappy that she was monopolising Dan who had taken Clare out several times during the past month and now seemed to be completely ignoring her. Matt put his hand on Kym's knee and tried to forget it. Evie and Dan had known each other all their lives and were probably just having a good catch up. Relaxing, he realised that it was the first time they had seen each other since Evie had returned home. Dan was a solid young man, Matt liked him. He had a good job as a Financial Adviser in the City, turning out to be a genius with numbers.

When they got home Kym, was ready to let her hair down. Kicking off her shoes and sprawling across the settee, she let out a huge sigh of relief.

'Fancy a nightcap?' Matt asked, looking intently at his gorgeous wife and wondering what she was wearing underneath her dress.

'Why not,' Kym replied, feeling the effects of earlier champagne arousing her senses. Elated that the stress of the evening was over, she was eager to give Matt all of her undivided attention. It had been part of the plan, picking out her dress earlier she'd hoped it would stir up memories of first dates they'd had. Kym watched as he left the room, wanting him to return, half naked and look at her the way he had earlier when she walked down the stairs. Both the girls had gone straight up to their rooms, they wouldn't come down again. They managed another bottle of champagne before climbing the stairs, giggling and firing innuendoes at each other like a couple of dating teenagers.

'Sshh,' they whispered, putting fingers to each other's mouths and sniggering as they headed unsteadily towards the bedroom. Matt spent some time sprucing himself up in the en-suite bathroom, but when he returned Kym was fast asleep.

'Kym, Kym,' he whispered but there was no

response, so he kissed her lightly on the forehead, then turned off the light and fell into a deep sleep.

# Chapter Sixteen

# Secret

As soon as her parents had quietened down and she was sure they were asleep, Evie tiptoed out of the house, closing the front door carefully and quietly behind her. Dan had been waiting patiently in his car, with the lights turned off, at the end of the long driveway. Evie's breath quickened as she hurried towards his car, her heart racing at the thought of being with him at last. She'd been home for almost a month and this was the best thing that had happened so far. Life here was dull, boring. No more party nights or lazy afternoons spent lying in the sun whilst turning a deep shade of golden brown. No smoke tinged aromas wafting over from the beach barbeque at sunset, followed by dancing until dawn in skimpy clothes, lost under the influence of substances. None of those things would be happening anywhere near their country home.

Evie had only dragged herself home to be at her mum's award evening. All of Evie's friends knew about her mum's new found fame.

'You're the one with the genius mum aren't you?' she was often asked. To which Evie replied,

'Yeah and I take after her!' pretending to look hurt at their laughter. Evie loved her mum, she'd never let her down, always being the first to leap to her defence when Dad had yet another go about her unstable lifestyle. Clare had been his favourite and he'd spent hours helping her chose a top university. He'd also studied the "Latin's" and they had their own private conversations in foreign languages, which could be very annoying. Evie had never wanted to go to university, having managed to complete two years in college had been enough of an ordeal. She hated the endless hours of studying and memorising information, spending most of her college days peering out of the classroom windows, longing to be outside. Evie was a free spirit and hated the restrictions of routine. She'd had several boyfriends who her parents hadn't approved of and had therefore decided to stop telling them about her love life. Their constant nagging and the feeling that she wasn't good enough, left her longing to be away from them and the comfortable little bubble they had formed around themselves.

Evie kept out of the way by working until the early hours of the morning at bars in London, saving all her wages, until she had enough money to leave the UK for Europe or resorts in Florida. After experiencing the freedom and mind blowing fun that the rest of the world had to offer, she'd never wanted to return to the UK again, apart from just this one time. Evie couldn't understand her sister Clare's outlook on life, thinking she had no idea how to have fun and just let herself go.

They had fallen out plenty of times as teenagers and couldn't seem to get along. Looking back Evie felt a bit mean for getting Clare into trouble on several occasions, but found provoking her irresistible. Goody, goody Clare was "Miss Perfect" and it was unbelievably annoying, how dull her sister was. Evie loved clothes, the brighter the better and was forever changing her hair, introducing outrageous colours to her mid length locks to make her appear funky and the total opposite to Clare.

Dan was wild, fun and Evie adored him. His mum Jacqui had no idea what he was really like. They'd gone to the same college after finishing school and quickly became inseparable. When college ended on Fridays they would head for the lights of the city centre, with a crowd of friends, whilst their parents thought they were attending evening study classes. After drinking and dancing until the early hours, Evie and Dan would stumble out of a cab and into Dan's mum's apartment. It was great that Dan's mum had an apartment in central London, right in the heart of all the action. After creeping in through the front door, locked in a passionate kiss, they would occupy the kitchen away from his mum's bedroom and engage in some very physical activity. Dan's mum never mentioned hearing anything, though they weren't always that quiet. Evie's parents had no idea what was going on, they probably still thought she was a virgin. Deceiving them certainly added a new dimension to her sex life. Something she felt now, walking towards Dan's car.

Tonight had been the first time she'd seen him since returning home and his keeping her waiting, with no contact had worked. It had been unlike Dan to ignore her. Through social websites, he always knew when she was returning and they usually had a hot and steamy encounter not long after. What had changed? Maybe he had a girlfriend? Evie normally wouldn't have been bothered by this, but now was determined to control him once more, making him only hers. Sitting next to her at the table and out of earshot of their families, they planned their secret rendezvous, whilst enjoying the exhilaration of nobody suspecting.

...................

Dan started having sex at fifteen. Since then he'd had several girlfriends in between his encounters with Evie. He'd cut down on the alcohol and wild nights out lately and had taken her sister Clare out on a couple of dates. However, there just didn't seem to be any sparks with Clare, it wasn't like being with Evie. His mum had been delighted when he first went out with Evie's clever and sophisticated sister. To please her, he'd taken Clare out for a second time, but they were so unalike and he decided not to take her out again, no matter how much pressure he got from his mum.

When Evie returned this time he didn't contact either sister, not wanting things to get messy. Although he hadn't slept with Clare, he felt awkward about attending the awards dinner, anticipating more embarrassment as his mum tried to get them together again.

'I don't fancy going,' he admitted the night before, 'why can't you and Anton just go?' His mum was having none of it.

'Hark at you, Mr. Unsociable,' she remarked, 'Clare will be there,' she stated giving him a knowing look.

'That's exactly it, I knew you would have your matchmaking hat on, it's embarrassing.'

'Oh sorry,' she replied bowing her head. 'Ok, I

won't say anything and will keep my nose out of it,' Jacqui pushed her son's hair away from his face. 'I love showing the world what a handsome son I have and I need a lift, so will you do this one thing for me?' Dan sighed heavily, she wasn't letting him off the hook.

'Ok, but this is the last time and no interfering. You might have to make your own way home though.' 'Me interfering? I promise,' she answered as a self-satisfied grin spread over her face.

At twenty four years old Dan felt ready to have a steady girlfriend and make plans for the future. However it hadn't been easy trying to find another Evie. When he went out with his friends there were lots of attractive, scantily dressed, giggly young girls interested in him, though none of them matched up to Evie. She was his soulmate and the subject of all his sexual desires. Dan had felt the heat between them just sitting next to her at the table. Her hands had wandered during dinner and he'd felt his body responding, wanting more. What a good job he had only been on a couple of dates with Clare, it would have blown any chance with Evie if she'd found out.

Clare didn't seem to be offended that Evie and Dan were sat together, their plan to make it look like friendly, polite banter had worked. Evie's Dad threw him a few questioning looks though, maybe Dan was imagining it, but thought it better to meet Evie privately, just in case.

When Evie got into the car, his heartbeat quickened and his stomach tensed with desire as they kissed passionately.

'I've waited all night for this,' he whispered, breathless from their long kiss. 'You teasing me under the table, like that, I didn't know where to look.' Evie just laughed.

'You loved it,' she said confidently. 'Nobody could see anything, stop worrying.'

'I'm not so sure,' Dan replied. 'Your dad gave me a few stern looks, I'd hate to get on the wrong side of him.'

'You need to relax and have a drink, let's get moving,' Evie added, looking anxiously back down the drive.

'I definitely need a drink, look what you've done to me,' he added, gesturing towards his crotch. Evie's fingers found his bulge and stroked him gently, before turning up the radio and throwing her arms from side to side in the air to the beat of the music.

After leaving the car at his mum's place they walked the short distance towards the dimly lit streets of Soho. The place was heaving and Evie punched her fist into the air as they wandered past many bars and clubs, pounding with loud music, advertising topless and lap dancing. From time to time Dan stopped to press Evie up against the wall of a seedy club, kissing her passionately on their way to a bar that he had chosen, having been there previously to enjoy live sex shows, with his finance friends. They exchanged lingering looks as they took the stone steps down to the entrance of the bar.

'I need a drink, right now,' he said impatiently. 'It's been a long night, not having any alcohol to help me through the ordeal of waiting to be with you.' Evie smiled her sultry, sexy smile, looking at his lips as sexual tension pulled them closer. Dan could tell she was in one of her naughty, fun moods and took her hand as they searched for a seat. They found a small table near a raised platform at the front of the club and moved their chairs towards it. The small stage lit up and came alive with scantily clad bodies, writhing erotically around each other.

'Let's see if they can do it any better than we can,' Evie shouted over the noise of the music.

'You've no idea how much I've missed you Evie,' Dan replied, feeling growing excitement at Evie's closeness.

'Let's get a room here and you can show me,' she suggested feeling aroused by the stage acts and the electricity flowing between them. He went to the bar for more drinks and to book a room. The rooms were normally reserved for private lap dancing but you could also book them for an hour of sex. Usually for sex with one of the employees of the club, but as long as you paid for the room the club didn't care if you were using it for your own needs.

Dan handed over his credit card, wondering if his credit limit could stand it. Looking towards Evie, his temperature rose even further, worrying that they may be disappointed and was relieved when his PIN was accepted. An hour later they stumbled, giggling, back up the steps onto the street, which was much less crowded than before.

'What time is it,' Evie slurred, struggling to maintain her balance. Dan checked his watch

'It's just after four.'

'Four, you're kidding?' Evie's eyes widened and she stopped abruptly. 'I've still got to get home, or I'll be missed, what a pain.'

. . . . . . . . . . . . . . . . .

Back at home, Clare had heard someone leaving the house earlier and got up to go to the loo. Passing her sister's room she slowly opened the door, not surprised to find Evie's bed was empty. Returning to her bedroom, Clare lay there wide awake, wondering what Evie was up to. Frowning, she pulled the duvet cover over herself, but there was no way she was going to be able to sleep. As the hours crept by she continued to toss and turn, worried that her sister had gone missing and looked set to ruin what should be a weekend spent putting their mum first for a change.

. . . . . . . . . . . . . . . . .

Dan and Evie walked briskly back towards his car, Evie, leant on the door, looking exhausted. Dan looked up at his mum's apartment, there weren't any lights on.

'Evie, why don't you just stay at mine, it's too late to go back now.'

'I have to get back, if they find out, my life will be a misery. You don't know what it's like. I can't face a big row with them in the morning, it's horrible.' She looked near to tears and started to shiver. Dan couldn't bear to see her upset after the incredible night they'd had, it tugged at his heart. It was going to mean an expensive taxi ride and he'd already spent enough on the room, but it was his responsibility to get her home safely.

'I'll drive you back,' he reluctantly offered. 'We'll soon be out of the city and I haven't had that much to drink.' It was irresponsible and they both knew that, but an intoxicated Evie wasn't thinking sensibly.

'Great, problem solved, let's get going,' she replied, desperate to make a move, in case he changed his mind.

Dan hesitated, looking up and down the quiet street before he got into the driver's seat and started the engine. They drove carefully back to Evie's house, which seemed to take an eternity this time. Dan turned the lights off at the top of the drive so Evie could sneak back in unseen.

'Thank you, I owe you one.'

'You certainly do,' Dan answered, smiling. Evie looked happier as she kissed him lightly on the lips. With a quick wave he drove quietly around the corner. Massaging his tired eyelids had blurred his vision, causing him to brake. Dan was exhausted and knew he shouldn't push his luck any further by risking another hour's drive back home. Instead he bumped the car up onto a grass verge, intending to stay there for a few hours until the alcohol had worn off. Putting his seat back as far as it would go, he zipped up his jacket and quickly fell into a deep sleep.

Evie tiptoed up to the front door, quietly turning her key and slowly opening the door. Closing it again very carefully, she started to climb the stairs, stalling as she hit creaky boards to listen for any sign of movement before continuing. Gently closing her bedroom door she exhaled, long and hard, relieved that she'd made it. Down the corridor Clare stirred hearing Evie creeping back in and looked at the time it was 5.30am.

Clare frowned, she couldn't get back to sleep now that she was trying to figure out where her sister had been. Coming to the conclusion that it was Dan, Evie had been with caused her eyes to fill with tears. Dan hadn't asked her out on a further date and she'd accepted that but his cosying up to Evie in front of her and the family, had been galling. She'd noticed them disappearing a couple of times and that Dan hadn't been drinking any alcohol as he'd been driving. It all seemed to fit. Clare was convinced that Evie had been with Dan and was livid. Their sibling rivalry thing had gone too far this time. As for Dan, what was he playing at? She folded her arms, shaking with frustration, imagining them whispering about her, even laughing. Clare had told her parents about her dates with Dan, ensuring they always knew where she was going. She insisted on keeping them informed as to her whereabouts, after witnessing what they went through worrying about Evie. Now she shuddered. If her dad found out that Dan had been dating both his daughters, he would kill him.

At 5.30am Matt woke up as something had disturbed him. He'd heard a bedroom door closing, one of the girls probably. He couldn't get back to sleep and made drinks for himself and Kym at 6.30am. At 7am he got dressed, feeling wide awake, wanting to be up and about and let Kym have a well-deserved lie in.  It was a little too early to make her a surprise Sunday breakfast so he decided to go to the local shop and get the papers.  They both enjoyed reading the Sundays over breakfast, doing the crosswords, checking if there was anything of interest on the television later, even better as all his girls were at home for a change.

As Matt returned the empty coffee cups to the kitchen he thought about making pancakes for breakfast and checked the larder and fridge for ingredients.  The girls loved them and he wanted to do something special to impress them.  It was a cool morning and he quickly fastened his overcoat whilst walking onto the lane towards the village shop. Further up, a car was parked on the grass slope, which was unusual as the lane only led to their house. Passing the car, he looked inside, the driver was asleep and raising his arm to knock on the window, he instantly recognised Dan.  A wry smile spread over his face, of course it was Dan, he'd probably visited Clare last night, after they'd all gone to bed and didn't fancy the long drive back.  Matt crept by the car and walked on.  He liked Dan and was happy about his dates with Clare, though wondered why he hadn't stayed in the spare room.  Thinking that maybe the young lovers wanted to keep their after-hours meeting secret, he collected his papers and walked slowly back, taking a different route over the field, to avoid Dan's car.

It was a lovely morning and Matt's step was light

as he chuckled to himself, thinking about teasing his daughter. Perhaps make some remark at breakfast. Enough to make Clare aware that he knew Dan hadn't made it home, but not enough to embarrass her. The morning sunrise lit up his path as he walked down the drive to his house, with the prospect of a great day ahead, lifting his spirits.

# Chapter Seventeen

# Red Sky

Once back inside Matt took off his overcoat and felt a cold shiver run down his spine.

'Brrrr,' he uttered, realising it was a cool morning considering it was the first week in April. Throwing the paper onto the table he set about lighting the log burner. As the wood caught, he held his palms in front of the small fire, before sitting in his favourite armchair. The logs crackled as they heated up, wafting smoke from the burning wood embers into the air. Matt checked his watch, then frowned knowing he wouldn't have enough time to read through the papers. Shortly his peace would be shattered by the arrival of the females in his life. Matt had always been an early riser, only needing six hours sleep and wanted to

243

preserve the precious moments of the quiet, peaceful atmosphere as long as possible. He had a good feeling about today, which started when he'd opened the curtains earlier and was greeted by the most beautiful red and pink tones, giving the morning sky a striking appearance.

'Red sky in the morning, sailors warning, might be a storm brewing somewhere,' he muttered to himself. Then a smile spread across his face, thinking about Dan and wondering if he'd made it home yet. Matt toyed with the idea of going back to his car and inviting him in for breakfast, if he was still there. Then he decided not to bother, thinking how embarrassing it might be to have your girlfriend's father knocking on the car window. Instead he went into kitchen and set about beating milk, flour and eggs together to create a rich, smooth pancake batter. Depositing the mixing bowl in the fridge, Matt returned to the cosy warmth of the fire that he lovingly stoked.

At half nine, Kym emerged looking tired and dazed. This was Kym's usual morning look, she was never at her best first thing in the morning. Yawning widely she sat next to the fire and picked up one of the supplementary magazines from the Sunday paper. Matt knew there wouldn't be much conversation for the next hour, then she would burst into life and the day could begin in earnest.

Clare, who seemed to be in a very good mood, followed at 10am. Matt noticed she had a mischievous look about her as she placed her arms around his neck and hugged him.

'Morning Daddy what's for breakfast?' she asked, smiling. It was Matt's cue to jump into action.

'Pancakes, can you give your sister a shout?' Clare shot her dad a look which Matt recognised as one that meant she wouldn't be co-operating with his request.

'Evie,' he shouted up the stairs 'pancakes!' Kym put a hand to her head, not quite ready to cope with the noise of the morning. Noticing this Matt found headache tablets and took her two with some water. Just a normal Sunday morning, he thought.

He was busy tossing pancakes when Evie arrived in her dressing gown. Looking dishevelled she slumped into a chair at the table, massaging her eyebrows, without a word. Somehow Matt knew he wouldn't be getting any assistance with breakfast and dashed about, filling glasses with orange juice, banging the maple syrup down on the table inbetween making coffees for them all.

'Not much for me,' said a bleary eyed Kym joining them,

'I only want a coffee,' managed Evie through

245

half shut eyes.

'Why do I bother?' remarked Matt, wiping his brow with a flour stained hand. The kitchen smelt heavenly as he proudly placed the golden brown, freshly made pancakes in front of Clare.

'They look great,' she announced, her eyes widening at the large pool of maple syrup flowing across her plate. Matt looked at Clare, raising his eyebrows.

'Anyone seen Dan this morning?' Kym looked puzzled, Matt winked at her. He hadn't had the chance to tell her about finding Dan asleep in his car. Clare had been waiting for exactly this moment, not expecting it to happen so easily and responded enthusiastically with her well thought out answer.

'Not me, I haven't seen him since we left Mum's award evening. What about you Evie?' Matt looked concerned. Why was Clare asking Evie if she'd seen him? Evie shot Clare a disapproving look. Matt stared at them, confused, determined to get to the bottom of the mystery.

'You could have invited him in for breakfast Clare, it was a bit inhospitable of you to leave him sleeping in his car down the lane.'

Clare's face dropped, she looked angry with her Dad's response so Matt decided to stop mentioning

Dan and continued to read the paper. He looked up when he heard Clare inhaling deeply.

'I think you'll find, that it wasn't me who spent the night with Dan and got in after 5am,' she revealed. Everyone was quiet and Clare avoided eye contact as she looked down at the table, knowing that she'd landed Evie right in it. Clare bit her lip, to have her parents think that she'd spent the night with Dan was unbearable. She'd had to put them straight, whatever the consequences. It was the thought of her dad making witty remarks all day about Dan that had forced her to speak out. Clare and Evie exchanged frosty looks. Evie sat there motionless not saying anything. Matt noticed the tension between the girls, chilling the air, and began to realise the implications of what Clare had just said. Kym wondered what was going on, she was starting to wake up quickly, aware that there was trouble brewing.

'Evie?' Matt looked at his daughter angrily and she jumped slightly at the sound of his voice. Evie pulled her dressing gown tightly around her body, not believing what was happening. How had they worked it out? Typical that her sister couldn't be relied on to cover for her, what a sneaky thing to do. Evie looked defeated, knowing her secret had been exposed and she was in the family naughty corner once again. Normally, her sharp wit would have supplied her with a faultless, comical answer to give her some breathing space, but her brain didn't seem to be coming up with anything. Instead her defence mechanism kicked in causing her to throw a tantrum and storm off. She stood up sharply, her face full of rage.

'I'm so sick of this!' she snapped, running out of the room.

'Evie and Dan?' said Matt his forehead lined with anger as he turned towards Clare.

'Keep calm,' Kym said, touching his hand, 'it could all be a misunderstanding.'

'It's not,' responded Clare, but immediately after saying it wondered why she just couldn't keep her mouth shut. Clare couldn't resist getting revenge on her selfish sister even though she wasn't madly in love with Dan. However, dating two sisters was just something you never did. Not while her dad was still alive and breathing, what now looked like very hot air.

Matt got up, almost sending his chair flying, banging it down as he caught it and stormed after Evie. Kym would normally have stepped in, as she had in the past when both girls were arguing, but not this time. Too tired after the stress of the night before and fed up with Evie's tantrums, she groaned disapprovingly and held her head in her hands.

Evie slammed her bedroom door and flung herself across the bed, sighing, wondering what the big deal was anyway. Dan was a family friend, he had a good job, surely it wasn't the worst news. They hadn't had sex in her bed or indeed anywhere in the family home the night before. Her dad liked Dan, making it harder for her to understand why he was now giving her such a hard time? Pulling at her hair, Evie felt a tear run down her cheek. This was the reason she worked away from home so much, they were too controlling. She wasn't a child anymore and would show them that they couldn't treat her this way. Evie decided it was time to move on as soon as possible.

Her dad didn't knock, just opened the door and bounced angrily into her room.

'Are you having a relationship with Dan?' he asked his voice full of impatience, expecting answers. Evie, fed up with their suffocating style of parenting, glared at him.

'Well, yes and no,' she answered avoiding his gaze.

'What does that mean?' her dad asked raising his voice, unable to hide his agitation with her attitude. Evie looked at her dad, who was clearly seething and thought she'd better lie.

'Well we aren't having sex if that's what you're asking me, we went out to a few clubs last night and he drove me home afterwards.' Feeling safe that she'd rescued herself and the situation, Evie was surprised when her dad continued to look like he was about to explode.

'He's dating your sister, so why are you spending time with him?' Evie looked up, startled by this revelation. Matt could tell by the look of surprise on her face that it was news to her. What was wrong with his daughters didn't they speak to each other?

'What? You mean Dan has been going out with Clare? Are you sure? Why didn't anyone tell me?' Evie looked concerned, about to burst into tears. Her dad sat down slowly on the bed, astounded by Dan's behaviour.

'I don't believe this,' Matt said fuming 'he's been making a fool of us all. I am going round there to sort him out.'

Kym and Clare exchanged worried looks as they heard Matt stomp down the stairs and grab his coat. Before Kym could stop him, he'd slammed the front door. Clare watched, shocked by his actions.

'I wish I hadn't said anything Mum,' turning to her mum for comfort. None was forthcoming as Kym tried to control her breathing, she was livid.

'Evie's only been home four weeks and we're all at each other's throats again!' Kym spat out the words, frustrated by her daughters' turbulent relationship. 'Would it be too much for once to have some normal family time together?' Clare wanted to respond with, *it's not me you should be asking*, but decided not to say anything this time and ran upstairs to her room.

Matt revved up the car as he accelerated far too hard off their drive and out onto the open lane. Fortunately Dan's car was gone, Matt was still seething with anger and would have killed him if he'd still been there. Taking a few deep breaths to try to regain some control, he turned the volume up on the radio and drove faster than normal, towards Jacqui's home.

Matt hadn't thought about what he would do when he got there, he just hoped the hours' drive would help him to regain some level of rationalisation about the whole situation. Shaking his head, remembering his encounter with Evie, he didn't believe her for a moment when she said that they hadn't had sex. Her lying always followed the same pattern. Turning away from him, looking down at the floor, whilst twisting her hair anxiously. It always gave her away.

Hearing Matt roaring off in the car, Kym ran to the phone, to warn Jacqui that Matt was probably on his way round to confront Dan. Jacqui was shocked when Kym brought her up to date with events, hastily ending their call.

'Dan get in here!' she shouted furiously. Dan could tell by his mum's tone that something bad had happened and hesitated as he looked around his bedroom door.

'What the hell's up with you?  Dating Clare and now Evie?  What's going on?'  Dan could see she was mad and cowered near to his bedroom door afraid of facing her.

'Get over here.  Now!' she shouted.

'Ok, ok,' he cried holding his hands up, 'everything's not what it seems.'  Jacqui stood with her arms folded, waiting for answers.

'I love her, mum, always have done,' his voice started to falter.

'Which one Clare or Evie?' she snapped impatiently.

'Evie, I love Evie, but she kept going away and it was like she was stamping on my heart, over and over. I tried to get over her, but… well I just couldn't get her out of my head.'  Dan sat down on the settee, rubbing his face with the palms of his hands to stop the tears. Jacqui sat down beside him, her heart melting.

'When I saw Evie last night, I just had to spend time with her.  See how she felt. I didn't know it would cause any trouble.  We had a brilliant night together and now,' he looked at his mum, near to tears, 'now I might lose her forever.'

'What did she think about you dating Clare?'

Jacqui's voice softened as her anguish diminished.

'I never told her.'

'Oh,' Jacqui replied pulling a disapproving face.

'It's not entirely my fault, you just kept pushing me. I didn't want to go out with Clare, she's not my type. I only went along with it because you wanted me to. I tried but it didn't work out. I felt that once you saw that we weren't interested in each other that you would give up. Now everything is a complete mess.'

Jacqui was beginning to crumble, was she such an awful parent? Not having any idea how her son was feeling.

'Why didn't you tell me this? I would have stopped interfering if you had,' she replied shaken by his revelation. As they talked on, Jacqui suddenly became aware of the time. 'Matt's on his way round here,' she said her voice full of panic, 'he knows everything. You had better make yourself scarce before he arrives. I will explain what's been happening and sort it all out with him.' Jacqui felt confident she could handle Matt. He was a lovely guy and hopefully they could resolve everything over a cup of coffee.

Dan got up and went into the bathroom, catching sight of his face, he looked visibly white, scared. He wanted to stay and face Matt, but also wanted to run in case he revealed too much about him and Evie, making things worse. Dan splashed water on his face, picked up his coat and hugged his mum quickly, eager to get out of the way.

'Let me know how it goes. Mum, I'm so sorry about all of this,' he stressed, shutting the door behind him.

He rushed down the stairs of their apartment block which led to the basement car parking area. As he turned the corner towards his car, Dan's heart stopped, Matt was standing there his face full of rage, having already spotted him. Before Dan could say anything, Matt ran towards him punching him hard in the face. It happened quickly and Dan didn't have time to defend himself as he fell heavily to the floor. Matt stood over him, blood boiling in his veins at the thought of Dan trying it on with both his daughters. He kicked Dan hard, not holding back as his uncontrollable anger turned to violence.

'Don't you ever come anywhere near my daughters again,' Matt spat the words out at Dan, feeling his heart pumping fast against the wall of his chest. Dan remained lying on his side on the floor with his hands over his face, the pain from his nose was indescribable. He didn't dare to look at Matt or say anything to provoke him further. Feeling like he had done enough to teach Dan a lesson, Matt got back into his car, slammed the door and drove off at speed.

By the time he'd got back home Matt felt calmer, having found Dan and been able to unleash his rage. Dan had deserved it, although Matt now wished he hadn't kicked him so hard while he was down on the ground. That had been a total loss of control.

Kym met him at the door, her face stained with tears.

'What happened?' she asked nervously.

'I punched him, then I left.' Matt's eyes darkened as his body tensed, recalling his encounter with Dan. 'He's an ass and I don't want to see him anywhere near any of us again,' he snapped, impatiently. Kym had never seen Matt looking so angry before and knew she should leave him to cool off, but against her better judgement she continued to question him.

'Did you see Jacqui?'

'No,' Matt answered, walking towards the stairs, obviously not wanting to talk.

Matt was exhausted and lay down on the bed, needing some quiet time alone. He ignored Kym when he heard her approaching.

'Matt, Evie has left, she's packed a case with her things and she's… she's gone,' Kym whimpered, tearfully, 'and I don't think she's coming back.'

# Twenty Five

'Unbelievable,' Matt shouted, 'How I wish I hadn't got up this morning.' Kym started to cry, but Matt wasn't able to respond, he had enough problems of his own and needed some time alone to come to terms with what had happened.

'I can't believe it,' sobbed Kym, 'Evie and Dan, what a shock and poor Clare, how awful for her. Why did you punch him?' Kym asked. 'Was that really necessary? Was he ok when you left?' Matt put his hands over his eyes, as if trying to block her out.

'I don't know,' he screamed, 'I don't have the answers, can't you just leave me alone?'

# Chapter Eighteen

# Rounds

Dan lay still, clutching his side, quietly gasping in pain, out of the corner of his eye he could see Matt getting back into his car. Trembling and wide eyed, he feared Matt would drive over him as he exited the parking area. Matt revved his engine and drove towards Dan, just missing him to make a point. Dan rolled away from the car, screaming out as his weight moved onto his injured side. Another resident was driving into the car park at the time Matt pulled out and nearly collided with him. Spotting Dan curled up on the ground he stopped the car and ran towards him. Dan tried to sit up his nose was pouring with blood.

'What happened to you, who did this?' his neighbour asked. 'Was it the driver of the car that just sped out of here?'

'No,' Dan answered his voice full of fear not wanting to spark off another run in with Matt. 'I was attacked by a man trying to steal my car and the driver of the vehicle that just left was going after him.' Dan hoped he had said enough to deter his neighbour from involving Matt. The man wasn't leaving though.

'I'll call the police, we may have the assailant on CCTV,' he said, whilst reaching for his mobile phone.

'No it's fine, just help me upstairs, please!' Dan cried out, pleading with him. 'I'll get my mum to ring them.' Dan was panicking, why wouldn't this man just leave? He didn't need a hospital or anyone else interfering and causing more trouble for him. Feeling Dan's embarrassment at being attacked, his neighbour helped him up and took him to his door, knocking loudly.

'If I can help you further in any way let me know,' he said finally. Dan thanked him feeling relieved when he walked away down the corridor.

Jacqui expected Matt when she heard a loud bang on the door, causing her to jump up. It was obvious looking at Dan that she was too late to resolve things. Her son's nose was bleeding heavily and her hospital training took over. Dan didn't tell his mum that Matt had kicked him in the side, even though he was still in terrible pain there, it would be too humiliating. Round one to you Matt, Dan thought, you won't be doing that to me again.

This was the first time that Dan had brought trouble to Jacqui's door and she hung her head in despair. He'd had a few scrapes at school, but had studied hard and was a caring and loving son. Sometimes he came home drunk but what young man in their twenties didn't? For the first time Jacqui felt the loneliness of being a single parent and not having a strong man by her side to go and tackle Matt for her. Jacqui didn't know how to respond to this vicious attack on her son and had no-one to ask. She thought about ringing Anton, he would come straight over and they could decide what to do. Anton had always been there for her, however nothing romantic had ever occurred between them throughout their years of friendship. He'd been like an Uncle to Dan and wasn't in a relationship to Jacqui's knowledge. Thinking about it, they'd never really done anything for him. Anton never minded that, saying they were like the family he no longer had. Jacqui often wondered why his family had disowned him. Anton never discussed them and she hadn't asked. As if he was sensing his mum's indecision, Dan tried to stand up, wincing from the pain in his side, he carefully sat back down.

'Don't ring Anton, I'll be ok.' Jacqui tutted loudly as she cleaned up his nose and left him sitting still with his head tilted back, holding a white dressing to his nostrils. Jacqui rushed into the bathroom to hide her anger from Dan. Splashing cold water over her face, she stared in disbelief into the mirror. What was Matt's problem? They'd known each other for years and their children were all friends. Returning to the lounge she picked up the phone, wanting to ring Kym and tell her exactly what she thought about Matt's violent behaviour. Hesitating, Jacqui thought about ringing the Police instead and have him arrested for assault. Trying to decide what to do, she heard a light knock at the door. Jacqui looked at Dan, he was terrified, instinctively leaping up and dashing into his bedroom. What next she wondered, ignoring the knocks. They continued as she moved the curtains slightly to see who it was. A distressed looking Evie stood alone, with a suitcase by her side. Her heart went out to Evie, she was such a little thing, standing there with what looked like the weight of the world on her shoulders.

'It's Evie,' she shouted to Dan before letting her in, he returned and slumped back in the chair.

'Has my Dad been around?' asked Evie looking apprehensive. Spotting Dan's swollen, bloody nose, she knew the answer before Jacqui had a chance to respond.

'You look cold Evie, would you like a drink?' Jacqui asked trying to remain calm, in spite of the afternoon's events.

'Yes please,' she answered in a small, meek voice, before sitting next to Dan.

'Are you ok?' she asked, looking distraught as he removed the heavily blood stained dressing from his nose.

'He'll be fine,' Jacqui remarked as she placed a mug of hot chocolate in front of Evie. 'It's his pride that's hurting the most.' Dan would have reacted to his mum's comments but was in no position to, instead he picked up a clean dressing and pressed it against his nose.

'Where are you going?' Jacqui asked gesturing towards Evie's suitcase.

'I don't know. I haven't had time to think anything through,' she replied looking sadly towards Dan.

'You can stay here tonight, but only for one night, to give you time to think about your options.' Jacqui offered, biting her lip, not convinced it was a good idea. However, something in the way Evie looked struck a chord with her, she reminded Jacqui of herself at times.

'Thanks Jacqui but I will only stay if you promise not to tell my parents where I am.' Jacqui agreed, she certainly didn't want any more visitors at her door and it wouldn't benefit them, if Matt knew his daughter was staying with Dan.

'Ok, but only for tonight,' Jacqui answered thinking, what am I doing?

..................

Kym sat down on the bed, crying softly unable to understand why Matt was being so nasty, when they should be comforting each other. What was wrong with him? Why hadn't he put his arms around her, didn't he care? When he got up, without saying a word and walked towards the door, her impatience peaked. Fists clenched, Kym wanted to hit out at Matt for the unnecessary pain he had caused by not controlling his temper. Now Evie had disappeared and probably forever this time.

'If Evie doesn't come back I will never forgive you!' she said quietly and deliberately to Matt. He left the bedroom looking hurt and defeated.

'Are you ok Dad?' Clare asked as her dad came jogging down the stairs.

'Yes I'm fine, don't worry, I am going out for a while, I need to be alone.' Clare could see from her dad's face that something had happened between him and mum.

'Please drive slowly,' she added tearfully, not knowing if he'd heard her as he shut the front door. Clare sat on the bottom stair, looking at the door in disbelief. How she despised Evie and the chaos left behind every time she went missing. Although there had been many incidents provoked by Evie, Clare couldn't remember her parents reacting like this before. This time it could be serious.

The wheels of Matt's car screeched off the drive for the second time that day. After a couple of minutes, Clare went back to her room and put her headphones on as she lay on the bed to try and block everything that had happened out. She was feeling tired again but no one seemed interested in her problems. Clare felt exhausted most days, but today's events had been particularly traumatic and wearing. Closing her eyes, she removed her headphones and quickly fell asleep.

Matt didn't know where he was going so stopped at the first pub he passed and ordered a pint. Sitting at a small round table in the corner, he gulped down half of the thick, dark real ale, feeling numb inside. Disengaged from his warm, comforting surroundings he felt nausea rise in his throat, thinking about what he'd done. How easily he'd crossed the line, without thinking through the consequences. In his urgency to confront Dan he hadn't had the foresight to check the car park for CCTV, before attacking him and he inhaled deeply, appalled by his mistake. If Dan went to the police, he would be arrested and charged with GBH, he'd lose his job and end up with a criminal record. Caught in a situation that he couldn't control, Matt hadn't wanted to wait around for the police to arrive and bolted, unable to explain his concerns to Kym. Her having a go at him, hadn't been productive either. Snapping as she did, leaving him in no doubt that he was to blame for Evie leaving. Matt took another long drink of ale.

'Hmmm,' he muttered, thinking it wasn't a trait he'd noticed in her before. For the first time in their lives he needed consoling and she hadn't been there for him, instead she'd chosen to burden him further. Standing up, Matt returned his empty glass to the bar, banging it down, before leaving. The veins stood out on his forehead and his heart was still racing. Hitting Dan had pumped him full of adrenaline and he wanted to make something happen. Driving out of the pub's car park he looked to his right at the road to take him home, then turned left, driving above the speed limit towards the lights of the city.

Leaving his car in an overnight car park he walked briskly to the seedy side of London, Soho. Not knowing that his daughter had been walking the same streets hours earlier. Matt, disillusioned by conflicts at home, needed to be free of his problems and do what he wanted for a change. Crossing more lines than he could have imagined.

Whisky was the only friend he wanted to spend time with. Smiling he knocked back a double, whilst sitting in a sleazy looking bar, unsuitable for such a smartly dressed middle aged man. Matt hadn't noticed the decor of the bar when he entered, part of his brain had switched off, after the days traumatic events. All he'd needed to know was that it sold alcohol and that consuming large amounts of whisky would take his mind off his sickening, irresponsible behaviour.

It didn't take long for a female to take in the amount of liquor he was drinking. She caught his eye and smiled at him, before sucking long on a straw, protruding from a cocktail glass, not taking her eyes off him.

'Here I am girls come and get me!' he announced, dramatically to nobody in particular. Matt had never been unfaithful to Lucy or Kym, but tonight he wanted the company of an uncomplicated woman, who wouldn't give him any hassle or ask any questions. Matt had no idea why he felt this way, he just did.

Paradise he thought, allowing a small, curvy blonde to play with his bruised ego. Her lips were brightly painted with red and she seemed a bit drunk, slurring her words. Matt frowned, it was hardly turning him on. He glanced around at several other unsavoury characters occupying the bar, deciding it was time to move on. Several whiskys later at a more exclusive looking club in Soho, he sat alone at a table ogling a fit and very pretty, dark haired, pole dancer.

She turned to face him after every swirl around her pole. Slowly removing her glittery bra top and moving her pert bottom cheeks up and down the golden pole. Was it golden? Matt no longer knew, it could have been any colour. The whisky had damaged his senses which had ceased working properly and he tripped in a drunken stupor towards her. Taking her soft small hand, he was led into a backroom.

'Can you afford me?' she whispered seductively into his ear, caressing the lobe with her tongue. Matt opened his wallet, displaying a wad of notes. Enthusiastically helping herself to all of the money contained there, she let out a sexy moan, then whispered, 'yes, you can!' Matt in his drunken state, felt ecstatic, incredible. He hadn't drunk like this in years and was beginning to wonder why not. In a state of delirium, he watched as she moved and gyrated in front of him. Matt put his hands out to hold her tiny waist, she tossed her dark hair back and smiled at him.

'Naughty boy,' she tutted wagging her finger, 'No touching.' He smiled back, feeling dazed, it wasn't sex, just a bit of fun, what harm was he doing? Matt had never had a lap dance before and was enjoying the experience even though the girl was becoming a bit blurred.

Starting to feel very drunk, he touched his

forehead, everything was whirling around crazily and he knew the night was over. Once outside the club, cold air hit his face as he walked quickly on, occasionally stopping, disorientated, turning in circles. Finding himself on a main road he checked his wallet, to hail a cab, only to find all his money was missing.

'Damn, she's robbed me,' he muttered to himself. Steadying himself against a wall he breathed deeply, staving off nausea, wondering where he was going to find an ATM machine in what was now a hell hole, at midnight. Matt wandered the streets of Soho, unable to walk straight, putting his hand against brick walls to steady himself. It was only a matter of time before he came to the attention of two thugs waiting at the top of a dark street, for their next victim. They followed Matt as he swayed towards the service till, keeping a safe distance whilst checking that no-one else was around. They watched as he withdrew a stack of notes, waiting until he turned the corner before making their move. Matt felt the cold, sharpness of a steel blade against his back, causing him to stop and stand bolt upright. They'd got him. If he'd been sober he would have knocked them senseless, but in his drunken state knew he had no other choice than to hand over his wallet. As they ran off laughing, he sank to the floor wallowing in the depths of his self-made despair.

Somehow he managed to get back to his car at around 3am, after wandering aimlessly around for a further hour.  Matt felt tears of frustration fill his eyes after trying several times to open the passenger door. Eventually he got inside and sat in the passenger seat, fumbling about in the glove compartment, for anything to cure his unbearable thirst.  Relieved to find an unopened bottle of water, he kissed the label noisily.

'Best thing to happen today,' he cried huskily, before swallowing the cool, pure liquid.  Then everything went dark.  Matt stirred a couple of hours later, disturbed by the noise of refuse wagons emptying bins.  Rubbing his eyes with cold knuckles, before searching the floor of the car for his keys.

'Thank you,' he proclaimed, hands clasped in prayer, when he located them.  'For helping me survive the night.'

Slowly and carefully, Matt drove home and almost collapsed with relief upon opening the front door.  Everything he'd stored up for years was now out of his system.  Lucy's death, beating up Dan and losing Evie again.  In one night he'd dealt with it all. Nobody would ever know about Soho and Matt wouldn't be repeating the experience.  The only thing left to do was to contact his Bank and cancel all his cards, oh and hope Kym would forgive him for staying out all night.

.................

Matt had stormed out of the house at 3 o'clock,

leaving Kym speechless and distraught not knowing when he would be returning. She got that he needed space, expecting him to spend an hour walking his bad mood off and then return as his old joking self. By 8 o'clock she was pulling at her hair, pacing up and down in the lounge, staring through the window, checking her mobile every couple of minutes, anxious for news. Relenting, Kym sent another text asking how much longer he would be. By 11pm she still hadn't heard from him and with a heavy heart, rang his number, only to be diverted to voice mail.

Kym lay on the bed, staring into space, her head banging as she reached for more paracetamol, once again checking her phone. Still nothing, she placed it on his pillow and eventually fell asleep, waking at 2am surprised to find herself fully dressed. Praying as she reached for her mobile, her eyes filled with tears of concern. Matt still hadn't contacted her. Pulling back the curtains, Kym checked the drive for his car, only to return to bed, sobbing and flicking the television on to dispel the eerie silence of their bedroom. Nothing though could prevent her from sinking into despair, regretting saying that she wouldn't forgive him if Evie didn't return. His face was still etched in her mind as it crumbled, a look she hadn't seen before, of complete failure, she'd managed to destroy him with a few words. It was wrong and Kym needed to explain herself, but Matt wasn't letting her. This had never happened before. Matt always caved in first when they had an argument, unable to bear it when they had a fight. Not this time though and Kym feared that she'd pushed him too far this time.

At 4am she woke again covered in a cold sweat and trembling, wrapping the quilt tightly around herself the remote control landed on the pillow. Flicking channels on the television with the sound turned down and trying to watch a quiz show, sent her back to sleep, because the room was light when she next woke up. Her heart missed a beat upon hearing the familiar sound of a car engine, causing her to jump up and peer out of the window. Kym let out a sob when her much loved husband got out of his car, looking tired and disheveled. It didn't matter how he looked, Matt had returned safely and Kym exhaled long and hard, relieved.

Hearing him creeping up the stairs, she immediately turned over in bed, closed her eyes and pretended to be asleep. Kym wanted Matt to think that she hadn't realised he'd been out all night. Then they could cope with whatever had happened, no questions asked. No confessions laid bare and no more disastrous consequences that could change their lives forever. Kym knew this was a one off thing with Matt and decided never to ask him where he'd spent the night. Her man was sleeping soundly next to her and nothing else mattered.

# Chapter Nineteen

# Payback

Evie yawned, stretching out her arms.  She'd been awake for hours and still hadn't heard anyone stir in Jacqui's apartment.  Finding her phone she checked the time, 7am.  It was Monday morning and she knew Jacqui would be getting up for work soon.  The bed had been comfortable enough, but its surroundings needed some attention.  Evie stared at the crack running across the ceiling, thinking a lick of paint wouldn't go amiss there and on the marked walls.  The room was a dumping ground for empty boxes, an ironing board, suitcases of various sizes and a large box of Christmas decorations.  Lying wide awake, Evie decided as soon as she heard sounds of activity, she'd get up and start looking for work on the internet.

Without any savings, she knew it would be hard for her to get by initially, then her mood brightened, remembering the credit card Dad had given her for emergencies.

'Come on, one of you get up,' Evie mumbled, keen to get moving now that money wasn't an issue. Her dad had given her the card when she first went off travelling and a fiercely independent Evie hadn't wanted to take it at first. He'd persuaded her to keep it, for his own peace of mind, knowing she would always be able to get a ticket home if things went wrong. Evie had carried the card with her ever since, it remained unused in a pocket within her purse. Picking her purse up off the floor, she quickly opened it and exhaled sharply, relieved to see it was still there. Dad had been his normal generous self, arranging a £5,000 credit limit and as she stared at the white and gold plastic card a wide smile spread over her face. Kissing the card lightly, she knew it would do nicely, paying for her travelling and accommodation expenses until she found work. Then her mood rapidly changed as frowning she wondered if her dad had put a stop on the card. Her face was etched with worry as she threw herself back down on the bed, which creaked in objection. Evie, would have to ask Dan for help if the card wasn't working. However this would be a last resort, wanting her dad to pay for all the trouble he'd caused.

Finally, a bedroom door opened and Evie

giggled, hearing Jacqui's out of tune warbling.

'I'll protect you from the hooded claw, keep the vampires from your door, da da da da, la la la la.' Evie cringed hoping Jacqui wouldn't attempt any higher notes. 'Death defying love for you.' The kitchen door closed and Jacqui's singing became muffled.

Evie saw her chance and slowly opened the kitchen door.

'Oh, morning, did you sleep ok?' Jacqui smiled, looking slightly embarrassed.

'Yes, fine. Thanks for letting me stay.'

'Breakfast?' Jacqui offered, placing bowls and a metal rack of toast down on the small white table by the lounge window.

'Great, thanks,' Evie replied smiling as she tightened the belt around her silk robe and sat in one of the white chairs, with a padded cushion of bright red poppies.

'Dan….Dan,' Jacqui shouted, causing Evie to jump surprised by the loudness of her voice. Dan put his head around his bedroom door, looking bleary eyed.

'I'm not going in today,' he answered impatiently, rubbing his eyes and catching his nose in the process.

'Ouch,' he grumbled.

'At least have breakfast with us and I'll sort an ice pack out.' Dan went back inside his room, emerging several minutes later having smoothed down his thick dark hair and smelling of freshly applied deodorant.

After his mum had left for work and Evie had cleared up the dishes, they had an opportunity to discuss future plans.

'I guess you're leaving again then,' Dan asked, dreading her answer.

'Yeah, I'm going to spend the day on the net, it's the start of the season and I should easily get work on the Med.' Evie looked energised, her eyes shining with excitement.

'When are you going?'

'Friday at the latest,' Dan's face fell, that was only four days away.

'Are you ok,' she asked noticing, the sadness in his eyes.

'No, I don't want you to go, I mean I want you to go, with me.' He searched her eyes for a response, she didn't say anything, just looked away from him.

'I have savings to cover our costs until we get settled and find work,' Dan continued, putting his arm around her shoulders and pulling her to him.

'Evie, I have something to tell you. I .... erm, I love you, please don't go without me, I couldn't bear it.'

Evie turned towards him. Blinking away tears, she kissed him tenderly.

'I think I love you too, even with that big hooter,' she replied, though her smile looked to be tinged with sadness. 'You do realise that we could be slumming it for a while and it might not work out, what about your job and career?' Dan couldn't answer he'd stopped hearing anything she'd said after "I think I love you", his heart was performing somersaults and the pain in his nose and side had all but disappeared.

'I'm going with you no matter what. I've never been out of this country and I love listening to your adventures travelling around Europe, it sounds incredible. My job bores me out of my mind. I'll try and take a twelve month career break first, but if I don't get one, to hell with it all.' Their faces shone with happiness as they gently bumped heads together.

'We can make this work, I don't want to be without you again,' he replied, cuddling her with obvious enthusiasm.

'It's a pain that I need to leave here later and find somewhere to stay until Friday,' Evie reminded him.

'How about we book a local hotel until then, I can pay for it.' She looked thoughtful.

'I've got a credit card my dad gave me for emergencies, I can try to use that, see if it still works.'

Dan nodded, then his face darkened.

'It's not worth the hassle, he could find out where we would be staying and turn up there.' Evie pulled a face, panic showing in her eyes. Dan brushed the back of his neck with his hand, feeling the hairs tingling against his skin. He certainly didn't want to face Matt again.

'Don't worry, I'll talk mum round,' he reassured her, gently stroking her hair and moving it away from her eyes.

'Brilliant, let's get started then.' Evie kissed him on the lips, 'Where's your lap top?' she added, eyes wide with excitement, everything was falling into place and she banished her family from her thoughts.

. . . . . . . . . . . . . . . . .

Dan was sitting at his workstation bright and early the next day, eager to talk Ian, his manager, before he got involved in the day to day running of the business.

'Good Morning,' he greeted Dan, walking towards his office. Dan had no idea if Ian would allow him to take a year off work. Things had been quiet for a while, but he might have to complete a month's notice and that could give Evie the opportunity to change her mind about him accompanying her to Europe. Even worse, she may get out there and not tell him where she was, or meet someone else.

Approaching Ian's office, Dan felt his heart fluttering before he knocked lightly on the slightly open office door.

'Come in Dan. Is everything all right?'

'Not really,' Dan replied, his voice faltering, 'I erm, need to ask for some time off.'

'Oh, how long do you need?'

'Well, I've been offered an opportunity to work in Europe for twelve months and would like to apply for a career break.' Ian looked thoughtful.

'You'd better sit down,' he said. 'I had no idea, you wanted to work in Europe.'

'I wondered if it might be a good time to go there. We aren't very busy at the moment and I could return earlier if you need me.'

'Hmm,' Ian muttered. 'We are a bit quiet at the moment, when would you like to leave?'

277

'At the end of the week.' If possible,' Dan added.

'Right, I'll do the admin and let you know later, but I don't see any reason why you can't go.' They shook hands although Dan had wanted to hug his boss. He felt elated and couldn't believe how well things were working out for him. Dan would be free after Friday, with a chance to spread his wings and live with Evie, what could be better? Then he thought about his mum, she would be devastated.

Dan and Evie decided to tell Jacqui that evening. There was no easy way to break the news to her, so they just told her outright that they were leaving on Friday. Jacqui listened silently as Dan convinced her of his desire to travel and seeing the love in his eyes whenever he turned to Evie, knew to object would be futile. Scared of losing her son forever, she wisely put her feelings aside. Besides she had grown to like Evie, although her instability was a concern.

'Who am I to judge?' Jacqui whispered to herself, brushing away tears after they had gone out for a while.

On Friday she waved goodbye to Dan and Evie at St. Pancras station. They looked happy as they waved excitedly from the window of the train. The bustling station, turned silent after the train moved away and Jacqui walked back to the car park with her coat wrapped tightly around her, feeling slightly lost.

278

Dan had promised to let her know when they were settled, then she could come and visit them for a couple of week's holiday. This made her feel a little better, though her heart ached with the pain of having to let him go.

When she was safely back inside her apartment she started to cry. Looking around, the place was tidier but empty without Dan's liveliness and laughter. Jacqui shuddered remembering the last time she had been alone and the agony of absolute desperation, whilst she waited for news of Tom after he went missing, long before Dan was born.

'Please, please do this one thing for me and take care of him,' she prayed, 'and I will never ask you for anything again.' Then she got up and switched the television on, turning the volume up to dispel the quietness of her home.

. . . . . . . . . . . . . . . . .

By Monday afternoon, Matt's hangover had subsided and he groaned whilst thinking about the amount of effort that would be required to fix things. Frowning, his thoughts turned to Evie and the amount of heartache she'd already caused throughout her short life. Matt clearly remembered how the Midwife had struggled to find Evie's heartbeat, before she was born. The agony he'd endured whilst sitting in the chair outside the theatre, promising himself that if she made it, he would never let her out of his sight.

Evie refused to answer their calls and texts, which was typical of her, wanting you to worry for as long as possible. Matt knew from work colleagues that he could get a trace put on her phone and know by tomorrow afternoon where she was staying. He also knew, that it was time for him to let his daughter go. Evie was a like a beautiful, intricate bird, restricted by her surroundings, wanting nothing more than to embrace the careless path of freedom. Matt drew comfort from knowing she still had the credit card he'd given her and would come home eventually as she always did.

Clare was elated that Evie had left, as laughter and a peacefulness returned to their lives, she was visibly glowing. Clare considered her sister to be a disruptive, attention seeking drama queen and she'd exhausted her tolerance this time. Evie had demonstrated her unceasing jealousy by trying to ruin everything she did. It wasn't that Clare didn't love her sister, but her eyes stung with frustration when remembering Evie's relentless attempts to push her boundaries too far too often. Clare's counter attack would leave her filled with regret. Evie had spent a lifetime mastering this art and Clare secretly hoped that this time, she'd stay away for good.

On Friday night, Matt announced he was going out again. Kym switched the television to mute and stared at him.

'Where are you going?' she asked, confronting him with a puzzled look. Perturbed by his binge drinking session the previous Sunday and that he'd driven home over the limit, her heart stopped momentarily.

'I'm meeting a couple of acquaintances later,' he replied, before quickly leaving the room. Kym followed him into the bedroom. Her eyes found his, full of unanswered questions, but she hesitated, deciding to persuade him to take her out instead, steering him away from whatever he was up to.

'How about I come with you? It would make a nice change, I've been stuck in all day,' she suggested.

'Let's do something tomorrow night, go out for a meal somewhere.' He looked down, before moving towards his wardrobe, Kym swallowed hard unconvinced.

'Who are you meeting then, Sam from work?' she looked at him suspiciously, watching his every move.

'I've got to get ready,' he answered, looking flustered, 'I'll come down and talk to you in a bit,' he shut the bathroom door, leaving her standing there stunned. A subdued Kym walked slowly down the stairs. Surely he wasn't having an affair or some sort of midlife crisis, she wondered. Kym was now regretting that she hadn't challenged Matt about being out all night the previous week, thinking then it was just a one off thing. Now the affair idea was starting to grow fast in her mind, like a seed that had taken root there.

After avoiding her for the next hour, a secretive Matt was ready to leave. Kym studied her husband closely, noting he was very casually dressed as he picked up his baggy hooded coat, usually only used for cold, rainy days out walking. Not exactly the smart attire you would wear when going on a date or clubbing with friends, although Kym was sure Matt was lying to her about where he was going. She threw her arms around his neck.

'Don't go,' she urged in a choked whisper.

'I won't be late, stop worrying. I'm driving and won't be drinking,' he stressed, softening his voice whilst pulling on his coat. Fumbling in its pockets he checked for his gloves, then kissed her on the cheek and closed the door behind him. Kym walked slowly towards the lounge window to watch his car drive away. Standing there for a while after losing sight of him, her eyes watered, frustrated that she'd been unable to stop him.

Matt felt invigorated by a fresh surge of energy coursing through his body. He was on a mission, returning to Soho to find the two thugs who had robbed him the week before. Smiling and nodding his head up and down in time to the music, he drove steadily on.  Last week he'd been an easy target, this time it was going to be different.  Matt knew he was partially to blame by getting drunk and letting his guard down.  His body tensed and clutching the steering wheel with sweaty hands, his desire to find them increased with every mile.  A few years ago he would have knocked them out, drunk or sober, taught them a lesson.  Now it was time to settle the score, payback time!  Matt wanted the thugs to experience first-hand, what it was like to be unable to defend yourself and be robbed.  Something that they probably did to others regularly.  It had been on his mind all week as he pieced together the crime scene.  They'd planned in advance where to attack, away from the Bank's camera at the cash machine.  Matt was sure that when he found the same spot, around the corner from the ATM, there wouldn't be any CCTV cameras present.  He'd allowed plenty of time to stake it out before they arrived and now smiled, relishing the moment when he would pounce on them.  Despite being hammered the week before, Matt's training enabled him to memorise their faces, clothing and voices.  He wouldn't be making any mistakes tonight.

As part of his security job Matt had access to stun guns and had two fully charged and ready to be deployed in his pockets.  Recalling that the muggers carried knives, Matt didn't want to risk getting injured and planned to hit them with the stun guns first.  Then the fun would start as they rolled about on the floor, defenceless.

Turning onto the streets of Soho, looking around at the scene, he cursed himself, wondering why he'd chosen to spend the night in such a grimy, seedy, sex ridden place. However spotting the pole dancing club, caused him to frown, remembering the very expensive lap dancer who'd also mugged him.

'Bitch,' he muttered, shaking his head in annoyance. What a total idiot he'd been, letting the dancer help herself to his money. Two hundred pounds had been removed from his wallet, what a sucker, it must have made her day. Pulling up his hood he arrived at the cash machine, thinking what had possessed him to use it? Scanning the deserted street he understood why he had been targeted and kicked a loose stone high into the air in anger. Just as he'd thought earlier, there was a CCTV camera above the cash machine, he walked quickly past it, looking away from the camera with his head down. Rounding the corner, he surveyed the street, checking for further cameras. Unable to see any he put on his gloves and stepped into a dark, rotten wooden doorway. Matt's nostrils twitched and he winced at the rancid smell of stale urine. His heart beat quickened and his breathing increased as he waited, unseen.

The temperature must have dropped at midnight because he saw a cloud of moisture rise from his mouth during exhalation, although he wasn't cold. Poking his head out of the doorway and looking up and down the street, he fisted his gloved hands

impatiently.  Taking a few deep breaths Matt
reminding himself that it would be worth it in the end
and continued his silent vigil.  After ten minutes, the
hairs on the back of his neck stood on end, upon
recognising a voice shouting across the street at a man
walking alone.  Matt peered towards the voices, his
pulse raced, it was them.  His face twisted in anger,
realising it was their regular stake out place and he
watched, as they each grabbed the arms of another
drunken victim, escorting him right into Matt's path.

Matt was ready, his senses on full alert as
adrenaline pounded through his body.  Walking like a
man possessed right past them, without eye contact,
before instantly turning to deliver a blow from each of
the stun guns into the mugger's backs.  They dropped
like stones to the floor, writhing in agony, a sharp
knife rattled as it hit the concrete flags beside one of
them.  Their victim ran off, looking horrified, leaving
the three of them alone.

'Hello again boys, remember me?  You stole my
wallet last week and I thought I'd come back for it!'
He spat the words out at them, hatred and anger
unmistakable in his steely tone, before returning the
stun guns to his pockets.  Picking up the long blade the
first one had dropped, Matt tutted, looking at it in
disgust.  'Is this your weapon of choice?  How do you
like my weapon of choice?  Better isn't it?'  Matt's
face reddened with rage, tormented by a week of
waiting for this very moment.  Bending down he

roughly rolled the thugs over onto their backs, before searching their pockets. As he removed a large wad of notes from each of them, they began to moan as if starting to regain consciousness. Matt picked each one of them up by the front of their jackets, checking they were coherent and could clearly see the madness in his eyes. He smashed his right fist into their faces before dropping them hard, back on to the dirty, grimy gutters of the Soho streets.

'Lowlifes!' he mouthed at them with a self-satisfied look on his face. Matt didn't want to spend any longer at the scene now that he'd evened the score. Clashing with the thugs had only taken minutes, but now it time to move swiftly away, before anyone came by.

With the sights and sounds of Soho far behind him, Matt stopped to have a celebratory drink at a stylish bar, ordering a non-alcoholic lager, wanting to keep his promise to Kym. The pale gold lager chilled his throat as he drank steadily, feeling as refreshed as the label had promised. Sitting safely back in his car, Matt counted the money he'd taken from the muggers. He let out a high pitched whistle. There was almost fifteen hundred pounds. A chill ran down his spine, thinking that was some night the two had put in to enable them to amass that much. Hiding the money in the glove compartment, he decided to add another £500 to it tomorrow and pass it into the local childrens home. Matt would insist it was used to give the children a decent sized Easter egg each and a party.

Matt smiled, imagining their happy faces, a sense of well-being flooded through him as he selected his favourite tunes from the car's play list and started his journey back home. Driving onto the gravel and looking towards the front door, Matt sighed, feeling pangs of guilt, remembering the look on Kym's face when he left. Hesitating for a moment before leaving the car he knew she would never understand his compulsive desire for revenge. Matt decided it would be best to tell her he'd met his two acquaintances, but hadn't spent long with them as they'd both hit hard times. As in "the gutter", he laughed out loud, then composed himself, thinking he'd better leave that bit of satire out!

# Chapter Twenty

# Doorstep

Dan and Evie were having a wonderful time thanks to Dad's credit card. They travelled by train directly into Paris where they found a small hotel with a balcony overlooking the Seine. With arms around each other they cuddled up whilst sipping wine on their balcony and engaging in long, passionate kisses, whilst admiring the silver moonlight sparkling on the gentle rippling water beneath their hotel.

'So incredibly beautiful,' Dan announced looking towards the river.

'What is?' Evie asked, her eyes glazing,

overcome with relief that they were together in Paris.

'You are,' he answered, looking closely at her. Evie, inhaled quickly, her breath taken away by his words.

'That's lovely, thanks,' she whispered, before laying her head against his chest.

'It's beautiful, being with you, looking out at the stars… but,' his eyebrows arched up and down, causing Evie to shriek with laughter.

'But, let me guess, you'd rather be inside, in bed.'

'Well, the wines all gone,' Dan shrugged, picking up the bottle and holding it upside down, the last drop of Prosecco, splashed on his shoes. Evie continued to giggle uncontrollably.

'Right, that's it,' Dan cried, before picking her up off the chair and depositing her firmly on the bed.

'Ha, and I thought you were being romantic for a change,' she joked. Dan silenced her with a long hard kiss, stretching both of her arms upwards and securing them with one hand, whilst unbuttoning her blouse with the other.

The next morning Evie opened her eyes first and smiled in a dreamlike state at the man she adored snoring softly next to her. The pleasant aroma of warm home baked pastries was wafting up the stairs, inching under their door, floating towards them. Within minutes they were up and dressed, their stomachs groaning with emptiness. Sitting at a small round table with a pretty red and white checked tablecloth, they generously covered mouth-watering croissants with raspberry jam. They hardly spoke, but never moved their eyes from each other's whilst Evie swirled her tongue around the jam topped rolls and sucked the remnants from her fingers.

'Bloody hell,' muttered Dan, instinctively looking around to see if any of the other guests had noticed. They hadn't so he busied himself with pouring freshly ground coffee into their cups, before discussing plans for the day ahead.

Evie wanted to walk breakfast off and they sauntered along the river, holding hands, admiring artist's works displayed along the banks.

'Let's get one of them to draw us,' Evie suggested her eyes shining, dashing in and out amongst artists drawings. An older Frenchman watched Evie and a warm smile curled around his lips. He beckoned them over and before they could say 'non merci' had started to sketch their outlines onto a large sheet of white paper.

While they were waiting for him to finish, Dan breathed the fresh morning air in deeply and found himself thinking about his dad and how he probably would have loved to draw the many scenic elements of Paris. Dan wished he'd had the chance to get to know him and pursue some of the talent he'd passed on. His mum never really talked much about his father, she'd tried but usually ended up crying, leaving Dan with many unanswered questions. The trust fund he'd left behind would come in very useful for when they decided to settle down and buy a house. Carefully unrolling their drawing, they sat admiring the artist's work in a cosy bistro alongside Notre Dame.

'I love this sketch of us,' Dan whispered, 'We look happy.' Evie laughed.

'Oh yeah, it's really good,' she added, leaning forward to kiss him across the table.

'I'm having a great time and I never want it to end.' Dan continued, looking down at the sketch with happiness shining from their faces, contentment flooding his soul.

Strolling along the elegant streets to the Arc De Triomphe and squeezing up the tiny white staircase to the top of Sacre Coeur, Dan marveled at the sight of Paris laid out before them. As Evie paid for their entrance tickets to the Eiffel tower, he smirked thinking about how mad Matt would be if he realised he was paying for Dan's adventure with his daughter. What was it Matt said as he kicked him when he was down on the floor of the car park? That was it….

*'Don't ever come near either of my daughters again.'*

Round two to me Matt, Dan thought smiling widely. Revenge is definitely a plate served warm full of beef bourguignon and a bottle or two of red.

Their wonderful week in Paris soon came to an end as they made their way to the station, for the next stage of their journey to Southern Spain. With a heavy heart Dan boarded the train first, staring out of the window until Paris was out of sight. Evie though, couldn't sit still. Enthused by the thought of arriving in Spain, she'd turned into a giggly teenager, pulling faces at Dan, until he could no longer resist her playful mood.

'You can't wait to get there, can you?'

'Nope,' she answered grinning. 'Paris was great, amazing, but I need to get a tan now and party all night long.' Dan smiled, but when Evie dozed off, with her head on his shoulder, his face changed, saddened that the bubble of happiness they had enveloped themselves in might come to an end.

The holiday complex they'd chosen provided accommodation for its employees and Dan was relieved that they didn't have to worry about finding a place to live. Evie advised that the rooms would be basic, sparsely furnished, but he shrugged uncaring, living with her meant all of his dreams were coming true.  They withdrew enough Euros to get them by until they got paid, using Evie's dad's credit card for the last time.  Evie had decided she wanted to end the audit trail in France, not wanting anyone to be able to trace them from then on.  Dan went along with this, they were having too much fun and he didn't want to spoil things by reminding Evie that they'd promised to let his mum know where they were staying.

..................

With the hurt and rejection he'd seen plastered on Kym's face, after his run in with the thugs, Matt knew he needed to come up with something special to regain her trust.  Behaving like a model husband he was home on time each night and didn't go out alone at weekends.  However, he still detected sadness in her eyes when Evie was mentioned and decided to surprise her with a puppy, to make up for everything that had happened.  The following Friday after work he collected a twelve week old chocolate Labrador from a local breeder.

Arriving home, he crept in the door.  Kym hadn't heard him, but he could hear the sound of creaking floorboards upstairs.  Matt raced back to the car and picked up the puppy, placing it gently onto the doorstep.  It looked up at him with large sad eyes and let out a tiny yelp.

'Shush,' he whispered, 'Its ok,' and rang the doorbell, crouching out of sight behind the wall of the porch.   Kym opened the door wide, her face lighting up when she looked down at two big brown eyes, staring up at her.

'Oh look at you,' she cried, 'Whose left you here all alone,' scooping him up in her arms and hugging his warm, soft body.  The puppy tried to lick her face and Matt appeared smiling and looking very pleased with himself.

'Matt how wonderful, he's gorgeous, thank you, you're incredible.'

'I keep telling you that,' he joked, as she managed to reach up to his neck with one of her hands and kiss him full on the mouth whilst still supporting the wriggling pup.  Caught in the middle of their embrace, the puppy yelped and Kym placed him down on the floor.

'Ah look at him,' she remarked, watching as he sniffed around, exploring, then he turned quickly as Matt closed the door and rolled completely over.

'I'm going to call him Rollo.  Come on Rollo,' a delighted Kym announced.  The puppy sat up and followed her into the kitchen, it was the start of their inseparable relationship.

Over the coming weeks Kym spent most of the daytime hours playing and walking with her new found companion.  Which was a good thing, because

the summer passed without a single word from Evie.
Matt hadn't had a text from her on his birthday in June
and started to wonder if she was alright. She'd missed
his birthday before, it wasn't exactly unusual not to
hear from Evie and he soon realised why, when he
opened the post the next day. Evie within a very short
time had spent up the five thousand pound credit limit
on his card and he stared in disbelief at the pages of
transactions he'd received. Matt ran his fingers
through his hair, whilst letting out a deep sigh as he
carefully studied the multiple purchases occurring in
Paris. Restaurants, bars, hotels she certainly hadn't
just been using the card for emergencies as they'd
previously agreed.

'What the hell,' he muttered finding the amount
of euros she'd withdrawn in one transaction,
exhausting the card's limit. His heart sank, 'Shit,' he
cried out, tensing his muscles, reacting to her clear
message. She wasn't coming back. Although startled
by the amount spent, Matt knew she was still alive,
identification would have been checked at the Bank to
make such a large withdrawal, meaning it had to be
Evie using the card. Which was some positive news to
give Kym.

Matt put his head in his hands moaning at the
thought of having to trace his daughter with very little
to go on and the pressure Kym and his parents would
place on his shoulders to find her. Neither Matt nor
Kym had been in touch with Jacqui since Matt's attack

on her son, but if Evie didn't contact them soon, Matt would be forced to go and visit Anton at the gallery. It would be a last resort, hoping Evie had stayed in contact with Dan, saving him from following an unrewarding cold trail.

Clare came home from her teaching job a week after Matt's birthday in June looking pale and tired.

'What's happened,' Kym asked gently, before getting her to lie on the settee.

'I don't know, one minute I was walking towards the door, then I felt lightheaded, everything went black and I collapsed in the corridor.' Kym put a hand to her forehead.

'Your temperature feels ok, have you been drinking enough?'

'It was only a moment, mum, stop fussing, I'm fine now.' Kym didn't look convinced.

'Has this happened to you before?' she continued.

'Really, mum I'm just tired, please don't worry.'

'Ok, but if it happens again we will need to get you checked out, you will let me know?'

'Sure,' Clare replied, pulling the blanket her mum had provided over herself and falling asleep on the couch.

The summer passed quickly with the evening light fading earlier as the seasons changed into autumn. Clare hadn't had anymore fainting episodes and Kym's concerns turned back towards her missing daughter. By the end of September, Evie still hadn't been in touch and Kym decided to broach the subject again with Matt.

'Can't you get a trace put on her phone or something? It's been a long time since we heard from her, shouldn't we be doing more?' She challenged him, one afternoon.

'You know what she's like, preferring to make us suffer. It's the only tool she has right now, not answering our calls or texts,' he replied, trying to inject some reassurance into his voice.

'But there's been nothing since the transactions in Paris,' Kym stressed. 'It's going to be six months shortly and she's never left it that long without contact before.'

'Let's give her until the end of the holiday season, until I try to find her,' he suggested, wondering how he was possibly going to do that without any leads. Kym decided to send yet another text to Evie.

*'Don't worry everything is fine, we aren't bothered about the credit card bill, get in touch and*

*come home soon, we love and miss you.'*

Evie never replied. Kym continued to check her phone every hour over the following week. Matt could tell it was affecting her mood as she became snappy and short tempered. He tried to remain positive, with plenty of close hugs and helping around the house more often than usual. One afternoon he found her crying, with pieces of the phone in her hand, after throwing it across the room in frustration. Matt put his arm around her.

'It will be ok, she's probably changed her phone and not bothered to tell us, you know what she's like.' Matt wiped away his wife's tears with his fingers and kissed her softly, although his patience was also running out.

Clare experienced more blackouts during the autumn months, though wasn't concerned as they didn't last long. Noticing how much her mum was stressing over Evie, she chose not to mention their frequency, although Clare felt exhausted most days. Even a short walk with Rollo left her worn out. Clare spent the time lying on the grass as he bounded up and down, sniffing about and occasionally returning to plant a large warm lick on her face. Concerned by her lack of energy Clare decided to go and see the Doctor during the autumn half term week.

. . . . . . . . . . . . . . . . .

Evie and Dan worked long hours and partied hard throughout their summer spent in Spain. They were golden brown from warm, sunny days spent at the beach and as they lay in each other's arms, watching the deep orange sun sink into the sea, never thought about home. One morning Dan noticed Evie putting her hand out to steady herself against the wall when she got up.

'Whoa,' he cried out, reaching over and placing his arms around her waist.

'I'm fine,' she muttered. 'It happens occasionally but I quickly recover.'

'You might be dehydrated, try to drink more water…., please,' he'd add, knowing Evie never took advice and hoping his pleas would work. It did and Evie slowed down, took less evening hours work and reduced her alcohol intake. Evie shrugged the attacks off, more annoyed than worried, putting them down to the year's troubles and exhaustion.

Jacqui had kept in touch with Dan by phone and by the end of September was insisting they let her visit. It would be Dan's 25th birthday on the 4th October, he wanted to see his mum and there was nothing Evie could do to prevent her from coming over. Evie wanted to put home and the problems they had left in the UK behind them. She had already dumped her phone, not wanting to have parents finding them and interfering with their new lives.

Content with the intensity of their love, they decided to stay on at the hotel complex for the winter season. Evie hadn't done this before and had no idea what it would be like to entertain an older generation that occupied the resort during the winter months. What the hell, she thought, anything was better than going home to a confrontation and being separated from Dan.

By the end of October Kym had convinced Matt to do something to find Evie. Matt called at Anton's gallery for the first time since the showing of Tom's collection more than twenty four years earlier. It felt strange walking up the stone steps and he cursed himself for not ringing instead as he opened the gallery door. The bell above the door jangled and Matt glared at it, knowing there was no turning back. Anton stuck his head around the door of the back room where he had been busy framing prints.

'Matt,' he said, looking shocked. 'It's been years, I'll be with you in a moment.' Anton was a bit cagey and rightly so after what had happened with Dan. Before he got a chance to speak to Matt a customer came in to collect a framed print. He spent as much time with the lady as possible, wondering what Matt wanted. However, Matt wasn't going anywhere, he'd worked out from Anton's demeanour that he knew something and hoped he would co-operate. Anton took a deep breath before turning to face Matt, who had probably called round to find out if he knew anything about Evie's whereabouts. He shook his hand enthusiastically.

'It's great to see you, how's Kym?'

'Could be better,' Matt answered watching Anton's face carefully, spotting a nervous twitch underneath his eye. 'I wasn't just passing, I'm trying to locate Evie as we haven't heard from her in over six months.' Matt hesitated, but as nothing was forthcoming from Anton, he tried again. 'Do you know if Dan's still in touch with her?' Matt's face winced at saying the name, hoping it wouldn't be noticed.

Anton had always liked Matt and decided to put him out of his misery, choosing his words carefully, he cleared his throat.

'Last time I heard, they were both working in Spain, having a fine time by all accounts.' Matt squirmed thinking about the credit card bill and now realising why it had been so high. He swallowed hard.

'When did you hear from them?' Anton looked at him with unease, wondering how Matt would cope with the news that they were living together.

'Would you like a coffee?' he offered, taking quick steps towards the back room.

'No thanks,' Matt replied, 'If you know anything

please tell me.'

'They're together,' Anton revealed. 'Have been ever since they left home. Jacqui spoke to Dan recently and they've decided to stay in Spain for the winter season, but I don't know the name of the holiday resort they are working at.' Matt nodded slowly, hiding his emotions and resisting the temptation to punch the wall in anger.

'Thanks,' was all he could muster. Anton could see from his face that Matt was crushed by the news and tried to soften the blow.

'You can always get a message to her through Jacqui,' he offered, biting his lip in regret knowing Jacqui would probably lynch him.

'Thanks, I'll speak to Kym and see what she wants to do.' Shaking Matt's hand for a final time, Anton patted him on the back and watched as he closed the door, wondering if Jacqui would ever forgive him. Matt walked head down, back to his car, kicking the tyres before he got inside to try and relieve some of his anger. Kym loved Christmas and it would break her heart to hear that Evie wasn't coming home. Let alone tell her that she was shacked up with the bastard who had corrupted his daughter in the first place. He started his car then looked towards the inviting city lights, before driving in the opposite direction home.

Clare was not concerned that Evie wasn't going to be spending Christmas with them, in fact she was deliriously happy about it! Imagining putting up decorations with care and switching the lights on around the tree, she smiled, thinking about the wonderful, peaceful Christmas they would have for a change. No bickering over who had given the best presents or who was helping out the most with the dinner. It was a weight off her shoulders, the second good thing that had happened recently, enabling her to cope with sometimes feeling nauseous and light headed. She'd meant to make a Doctor's appointment during the October half term but never got round to it. Worrying her parents was not a priority, they'd only fuss and had been snappy enough lately with Evie on their mind.

What was more important was Clare's new boyfriend who occupied all her thoughts as she fell head over heels in love with him. The moment she'd set eyes on him, she'd known he was the one and clearly remembered the day he started working as a history teacher at her school, during the autumn term. Clare disliked going back in to work the day before the new term started. Her classroom seemed empty as she took down pupils work from the walls, indicating that the children she had got to know and love had moved on. Later sipping coffee in the staff room, she looked up just as he walked in. They locked eyes and her face lit up when he sat down next to her.

'Hello, I'm Clare,' she managed to say, extending her hand to meet his.

'Charlie,' he answered, smiling broadly and as their hands touched, Clare felt a warm tingling sensation spread up her arm and all through her body, flushing her cheeks. They hit it off straight away and quickly became good friends. Sharing the same taste in music, they started going to concerts together at weekends. Charlie was eleven years older than Clare and at thirty five had never married, saying he'd never found his soul mate before now. Exhilarated by his words, Clare fell deeply in love with her caring, romantic man. They arranged to go and see a band at the beginning of October and Clare couldn't wait as Charlie loved to jive and had been teaching her some steps. When the band played a rock and roll section they got up to dance, for the first time in public. Clare hadn't expected to feel nervous and the steps were faster than they'd practiced.

'I don't think I can keep up,' she gasped.

'You're amazing, don't worry, I'm feeling it to' he revealed, before slowing down and repeating the steps they had perfected. Looking flushed, Charlie wrapped his arms around her for the last dance which was a slow number and they ended up locked in a long passionate kiss.

The next evening Charlie took her hand and asked,

'When do I get to meet your parents?' Clare gulped, startled by his request, knowing that as they were now an item, she couldn't put if off much longer. Then her face darkened recalling the "Dan" incident. Her dad might cause a fuss upon finding out that Charlie was much older than her and she wasn't about to give him up.

'Soon,' she answered, 'It's my dad, he's erm, very protective, might be one way of putting it.' They laughed together, with Charlie not realising she was being serious. Clare continued to put him off until the night they had arranged to go to a dinner dance with his parents and her dad solved the problem.

Clare told them she was going out for the evening and had spent all afternoon getting her outfit right and doing her hair and makeup perfectly. This hadn't gone unnoticed with Matt and Kym who'd guessed their daughter had been spending time with someone special. She'd been out buying new clothes and shoes each weekend and hadn't been in for the last three Saturday nights. Did she think they were daft? Matt joked with her about it.

'When do we get to meet him?' he kept teasing his daughter.

'Who said there was a him?' Clare would reply, quickly exiting their home shouting 'Don't wait up.'

'I can always give you a lift somewhere, you

don't need to keep getting taxis,' Matt would say at breakfast the next day.  He was hoping his daughter would take him up on the offer so he could find out where she was going.

'I know Dad, but I'm trying not to be reliant on you all the time,' Clare would answer.  Her parents didn't care that they hadn't met him yet, he was making their daughter very happy and that was all that mattered.

Tonight though, Clare looked stunning, she definitely had a date.  Matt wasn't going to let her out of the door until he knew more.  Clare tried to avoid answering his questions but he wasn't giving up.

'What do you think Kym?  Do you think she has a young man in tow,' Matt asked his wife, with a raised eyebrow.  Clare decided to tell him something to shut him up if nothing else.

'Yes I have a boyfriend, we both love dancing and that's where we're going tonight, but he's not younger than me!'  Clare paused, waiting for her dad's reaction.

'Oh, is he about sixty then,' Matt enquired smiling, hoping his daughter was winding him up.

'Dad, he's ten years older than me, that's all.  I've been putting off telling you, knowing what you're like.'  Clare let out a huge sigh of relief, after unburdening herself. 'We work together, he's a history teacher,' she continued with new found bravery.

'Well anyone who can make you feel this happy has to be very special,' added a smiling Matt. He could sense his daughter's panic that he would disapprove and didn't want to say anything to spoil her night. 'We can't all have toy boys like your mum!' They all laughed, followed by close hugs.

'Bring him round to meet us soon, we're not ogres, you know,' Matt shouted after her as she stepped into the taxi. The taxi driver heard and laughed.

'Parents,' he remarked before driving away.

Clare hadn't told them that Charlie's mum and dad were going to the dance, not wanting to upset them. They had a great night, dancing and jiving with each other, It was the happiest Clare had ever remembered feeling. As they said their goodbyes, Clare felt a little unsteady. She never drank much alcohol so it was unlikely that was the cause. Charlie caught her as she started to fall to the floor. It didn't last long, but was embarrassing enough.

'Let's get you home,' Charlie said putting a supporting arm around her.

'You're very slim, are you eating enough?' asked his mum gently.

'I'm fine,' Clare moaned, wondering why it kept happening. She'd skipped meals all day to look slim in her dress and convinced herself that was the cause.

A week later Clare arranged for Charlie to collect her from home enabling him to meet her parents at the same time. They'd discussed it and decided to opt for a quick "hello" on the doorstep, when he arrived to pick her up, so both men could size each other up. It all seemed to go well, their first meeting was out of the way and hopefully that would satisfy everyone's curiosity for a while. Clare got into Charlie's car determined to put her parents out of her mind and just focus on Charlie for the rest of the evening. His parents were away for the weekend and they had the house to themselves. Clare had bought some new lingerie and stockings which she was wearing and couldn't wait to show them off.

Over the coming weeks Clare's parents had plenty of opportunity to get to know Charlie and they grew to like him. He was very popular with her dad, both were golfers and they arranged a golfing day out. Things were going much better than Clare could have hoped for. She needn't have worried about the age gap, it wasn't an issue, plus teaching at the same school was ideal, giving them many fun-filled days off together.

It quickly became clear to Matt and Kym that they were in love. Clare looked like she was bursting

with joy, her face glowed with happiness.  For the first
time in her life everything was working out perfectly.

## Chapter Twenty-one

# The Goldies

It was the beginning of November and as the temperature started to drop, after a long hot summer, the days felt refreshingly cooler in Spain.  Dan and Evie became engulfed by the whirlwind of changes at the hotel resort, known locally as the Golden Days. She would normally have returned home by now to boring England.  Lying on her bed, days would be spent reminiscing about another fantastic summer, longing to be back in Spain.  Craving the beach party atmosphere she'd left behind and the sound of waves gently lapping the beach, during evening hours, Evie quickly became fed up at home.

Not this year though, they'd stayed in Spain for

the winter and it was turning out to be great fun.  Evie had no idea what happened at holiday resorts during the winter months, quickly finding out that the party life she'd always sorely missed didn't happen anyway.  During winter the resort was transformed to accommodate pensioners arriving in droves.

Evie and Dan looked on with interest as the hotel complex was cleaned, freshened up and altered beyond recognition for the coming season.  The first thing they noticed was the change in attitude by the rest of the hotel resort's staff.  No longer kept up until dawn on late night trips or having to clean up sticky alcohol ridden floors and tables.  They became calmer, happier people.

The hotel was closed for a week to complete the transformation and staff members sang and whistled whilst going about their duties in an unhurried manner.  Dozens of Palm plants in large pots had arrived and were being arranged around the complex.  The indoor pool was completely drained and cleaned.  Fresh water filled its scrubbed sides and broken, plastic sun loungers had been removed and sent for repair.  Cushions were laid on newly cleaned chairs in the sun lounge and white lace tablecloths transformed the bar area into an afternoon tea emporium.  Floors were cleaned and polished ready for evening dances.  Golden themed menus replaced the summer ones and a salad bar was set up by the outdoor pool.  Freshly made fruit smoothies had been put on the breakfast menu, as a pick you up treat which were very popular with their expected guests affectionately known as the Goldies.

Evie wasn't impressed with her new work timetable. Normally activities didn't take place until the afternoon, due to late night outings. She cursed upon reading her new work plan, shocked that her day was going to start at 8 o'clock each morning.

'What a pain,' she moaned at Dan. 'I hate having to do anything before 11.'

'Tell me something I don't know,' he laughed, avoiding the pillow she launched at him. 'Ah come on, it can't be all bad, let's have a look.' They sat cross legged on the bed in their small room, comparing notes.

'You finish at 10 every night, that's got to be better than 3 in the morning.'

'Periods of adjustment,' she proclaimed, 'a girl like me, needs plenty of time to settle into a new sleep pattern.'

'Oh, do you now... and what have you been doing the last couple of weeks, nothing but sleeping.'

'Cheeky, sod,' she replied, returning to her agenda which caused more groans.

'It's all afternoon stuff, look. Market days,

cultural tours, golf and fishing trips, I can't do any of these.' A disgusted looking Evie, launched the papers into the air and turned on her side in a huff as they fell on the floor. Dan glared at her, then gathered them up and sat back down on the bed, playfully slapping her bottom turned towards him. He read through the daily events list.

'Well?' she demanded, without turning around.

'Well, I'm going to volunteer for fishing and cultural tours as a guide, it sounds great. Why don't you come with me?' She turned around and glared at him. 'Stroppy madam,' he muttered, before diving off the bed upon hearing her take a deep breath as if about to launch into an attack. 'I'm only joking, come here,' he gestured, opening his open arms, trying to defuse her aroused irritation. 'There must be something suitable, what about this… aerobics class?' Evie sat up and snatched the agenda off him, before looking up unimpressed.

'I tried aerobics once at a gym and hated it. All that twisting around and jumping with your arms in the air, it was a load of crap!'

'Hmmm,' Dan mumbled, what do you like then?'

'I don't know, I never liked sports or running,' she sighed, 'the only thing I was ever good at exercise wise, was dancing.'

'Dancing…' Dan repeated, his eyes scrolling down the list. 'Here it is…Ballroom dancing, most evenings and you'll be finished by ten. Spot prizes, no idea what they are and quizzes in the afternoon.'

'Great, I'm sorted then,' she snapped, lying back down and turning her back on him once more.

By the time the Goldies started to arrive during the middle of November, the hotel was ready and the staff had all been issued with Golden Days t-shirts and shorts which transformed them into a pristine looking workforce. Grinning they advised Evie that their new guests would be polite, charming and tipped generously.

Evie got up in plenty of time for the first morning's shift, her stomach tingling with nerves as she made her way to the outdoor sports complex. It was the level of noise that startled her first, before seeing the amount of people in their late 60's upwards, already engaged in lots of different activities. The lawned areas were full of groups chatting, laughing, waving and calling out to their friend's. The place was buzzing with a warm, friendly atmosphere. The hotels cycle area was busy as bikes were adjusted and Goldies, set off with bells ringing. Golf bags leant against the walls of the reception area, as golfers chatted, waiting for the bus to pick them up. The four tennis courts were all in use, with mixed doubles underway. Yoga stretches were being performed on one area of the lawn and what looked like a Tai Chi class had started in the shaded area near the foyer.

Evie looked around in disbelief, having never seen activity before noon within the holiday resort before. Normally the summer guests, aged under thirty, didn't appear until then. Lying motionless on sunbeds for the afternoon, with loud dance music pumping into their ears.

She paced the stairs two at a time back to her room.

'Dan you have got to see this! Dan,' Evie urged, shaking him.

'What's all the noise? What's going on?' Dan was still half asleep, not having to start his day until noon.

'It's the guests, they've all been up since dawn,' Evie answered. 'Come and have a look.' Dan turned over.

'Wake me up when they're all having afternoon naps and find out what vitamin tablets they take, you could use some!' Evie pounced on the bed, sitting astride his body, torturing him by tickling his sides. Dan, grabbed her arms and shoved her onto her back, kissing her hard before getting up and going into the bathroom.

'Oh and do something about that morning mouth,' she shouted after him, slamming the door behind her.

By 11 o'clock most activities ceased when the restaurant doors opened to commence serving tea and biscuits. Within minutes the place was heaving. Looking around, Evie felt sad, visualising her grandparents. She missed their warmth, kindness and love and thought about how cruelly she'd cut them off, knowing how worried they would be. They hadn't deserved it. All they'd ever done was to strive for her happiness. Spending lots of time and money with her and Clare as children, always wanting to give them a treat to make them feel good. Evie spotted a smiling lady, looking her way, she smiled sadly back realising that it had been too long since she'd felt her gran's warm hug.

After elevenses the Goldies seemed to be revitalised and made their way back outside into the mild sunshine. Just walking around the large complex, Evie felt tired and couldn't understand why the guests wanted to exercise when they were on holiday and should be relaxing. Chatting to several groups, she was impressed by their enthusiasm, leaving her wondering where they got all their energy from and hoping they would all be in bed by nine. Then she could finally rest.

The day carried on with lunch and afternoon teas,

followed by quizzes and competitions. The guests were charming, polite and the tips kept coming. Evie was surprised by how much she was enjoying the day, but had to return to her room to sleep soundly for an hour, before the evening shift began.

After evening meals had been completed the guests wanted to dance. Evie stifled yawns by ten o'clock though they showed no sign of going to bed. By eleven o'clock there had been a dramatic change and she punched the air in delight behind the stage curtain, when the music was finally turned off. The last few guests finished up their drinks and shuffled out of the hall. Within half an hour the hotel had fallen silent and Evie crept along corridors, closing fire doors quietly as she returned to her room. Closing her own door carefully, Dan got up off the bed to greet her.

'Bet we won't be kept awake tonight with slamming doors and drunken guests arguing in the corridors,' he whispered. Evie didn't answer.

'Are you ok?' he asked studying her face. Evie looked pale, unsteady. Dan put his arm around her as they walked slowly towards the bed.

'Not sure,' slurred Evie, nearly missing the bed as she sat down. Her head was spinning and Dan was fading back and forth in front of her.

'Dan,' she whispered, squinting, unable to make

out his features, reaching her hand out to touch him, unable to make contact, she closed her eyes.

'Evie?' Dan said quietly. There wasn't an answer. Dan covered her up and kissed her softly on the cheek, before getting into bed himself.

It wasn't until the end of the first week that Evie had managed to adapt to the early starts. However, she wasn't coping with the Goldies, who never seemed to stop. A lifetime of little or no exercise, left her feeling weak and opting out of games she was supposed to be supervising caused issues with her colleagues.

'Why don't you try one of those pick you up smoothies, the guests have for breakfast?' Dan asked one morning, noticing Evie's lack of energy.

'I'm too tired for breakfast, leave me alone,' she snapped back. Dan left her in bed, returning with a smoothie for her moments later.

'Thanks,' she said uncertainly, sipping the fruit drink slowly. 'It's delicious, have a taste.' Evie smiled, offering him the glass only to withdraw it and quickly finish the fruity, refreshing mix of exotic juices. Dan continued to bring her a smoothie every day from then on. Although they helped get her out of bed in the mornings they didn't seem to be helping with her energy levels. After more light headedness and nausea attacks, Evie started to convince herself that she may be pregnant and bought a test without telling Dan.  It lay hidden in her underwear drawer for a couple of days until she could put it off no longer, as her symptoms got worse.  After Dan left, Evie sat on the toilet waiting anxiously for the result.  It was negative and she suddenly felt a burst of energy, shouting out in relieved delight, only to sit down quickly afterwards as dizziness affected her balance.

With Christmas fast approaching, all the hotel staff were busy decorating the main hall with huge coloured baubles, which they hung from the ceiling, after wobbling on wooden steps.  Evie watched their antics and stood back with her eyes glistening in admiration at the cascade of colours streaming across the dance floor.  When they'd finished, Christmas cheer oozed from every corner of the hotel and for the first time since she'd left, Evie's heart felt heavy.  Dan found her crying, on the bed, later that afternoon.

'Evie, what is it?' he asked, wiping her tears away with his kisses.  'Shush, it's ok,' he continued stroking her hair, trying to soothe her distress.

'It's all the Christmas stuff,' she sniffed, inbetween tears.  'It reminds me of home.'

'Oh… what do you want to do,' he asked concerned.  'Go back?'

'No…. I don't know… maybe I'm just missing everyone and … well I always put the decorations up at home.'  Dan hugged her close.  'I wish none of this had happened and I could just go home for Christmas. Everybody probably hates me now.'

'That's not true, please stop crying,' Dan whispered, trying to remain calm.

'I need to know if I can go back. Would you ring your mum and find out if my family have been in touch?' Dan looked at Evie, she was pale and dark circles hung under her eyes. He picked up her arm, it felt light, thin, why hadn't he noticed this before?

'Are you sure? I mean, they might want to know where you are.'

'I don't know,' she answered sobbing loudly, 'they haven't even tried to find me and probably don't know I'm with you.' Dan held her tight.

'Let's not rush into anything yet,' he insisted.

'You're tired, try and get some sleep.' Within minutes she slept quietly, but Dan lay awake for hours tossing and turning, tormented by her distress.

For the first time since the girl's had been born, Christmas decorations remained in boxes untouched as the middle of December approached in England. It was Clare who mentioned the lack of colour around the house first.

'When are we putting the decorations and the tree up?' she asked on Sunday during breakfast.

'They're usually well up by now.' Matt placed his hand over Kym's, several cards had been strung over the mantle, but none from Evie which he though was heartless. Clare was right though the placed looked abnormally bare and he was surprised that Kym hadn't made an effort so far.

'How about we make a start this afternoon?'

'Yes,' Kym answered, 'absolutely.' They continued to eat in silence, each consumed by their own thoughts of Evie and the tears filling Kym's eyes hadn't gone unnoticed.

Matt's parents came over for Christmas dinner which kept them entertained. Everyone still missed Evie though, it wasn't the same without her. Evie was the one who always started the Christmas carols off, getting them to join in after a couple of glasses of wine. She was the one who insisted they play silly games after dinner, giggling away and providing lots of warm hugs if they lost, in her fun loving way. Try as they might, it was impossible to cover up the quietness of the afternoon without Evie and her vibrant spirit. Later, relaxing with a glass of warm brandy, Matt wondered why she always chose to punish them and especially her mum. It was unkind. He couldn't understand her motivation to stay away, surely she must be missing them to. Sipping away at his brandy, Kym dozing with her head on his lap, Matt held up his glass.

'Merry Christmas Evie,' he whispered, 'Wherever you are.'

.................

On the night of the New Year's Eve party at the hotel in Spain, Evie could hardly stand up for more than a few minutes. Dan took her back to their room and helped her into bed.

'Will you be ok?' he asked, she nodded unsure. 'I have to go, I'm sorry, but will come straight back after midnight.' Evie, closed her eyes after he left, wondering why the nausea and dizziness was becoming stronger, unpreventable. Could it be the manifestation of stress and heartache for not spending Christmas with her family? Her sickness increased at midnight when she heard distant voices singing Auld Lang Syne. Tears rolling down her cheeks turned into heartfelt sobs, realising for the first time in her life she was spending New Year's Eve alone. When Dan returned an hour later, Evie was in a deep sleep, but the shock of her earlier distress filled his mind as he lay awake wondering what to do.

The next morning on the way to get Evie some breakfast he rang his mum.

'Dan, it's fantastic to hear from you, Happy New Year?' Dan choked upon hearing her cheerful voice, he was near to tears.

'Oh mum, I'm worried about Evie.'

'What's happened?' she asked, her good mood fading.

'She's not been feeling very well since Christmas. I think she's homesick.'

'Get her to ring home. Matt called in to see Anton. He seemed fine about everything. I'm sure they would appreciate hearing from her.'

'She dumped her phone, ages ago and didn't keep their numbers. Do you think you could get a message to her mum? I think she wants to go home.'

'Of course, Matt gave Anton his number, he's coming round later for dinner and I will get him to ring Evie's mum and tell her the news.'

'Thanks mum, oh and Happy New Year.'

When Anton arrived later Jacqui told him about Evie and he immediately got his phone out and rang Matt. Although it was New Year's Day, Anton knew Matt would want to know his daughter had made contact and wanted to come home.

Matt asked him for Dan's phone number so he could ring Evie straight back. Anton hadn't anticipated this and hesitated not sure if it was the right thing to do. Dan would answer the phone and hearing Matt's voice would probably hang up. Instead he agreed to text Matt's phone number to Dan. Leaving it up to Evie to ring him back, not wanting to get involved any further, knowing how tricky their family could be.

By early evening, Matt had received a text from Evie.

'Kym,' he called up the stairs, 'We've had a message from Evie.'

'Oh thank God,' she shouted, clambering down the stairs. 'I knew this was going to be a good year.' After an exchange of texts between them, Evie advised she was coming home. The earliest that she could leave her job would be on the 5th of January, two days before her twenty fifth birthday. Evie's spirits lifted and Dan organised a small celebration with a bottle of cava and tapas. Her eyes lit up, as she constantly chattered about going home and her sparkle returned. Dan, however, was quiet and thoughtful in comparison, returning home was the last thing he would have chosen for them. Sitting alone on their balcony, he stared gloomily up at the stars, swigging from a bottle of sparkling wine. Something felt wrong, their dreams were coming to an end.

When Evie woke on the second day of January, streaks of sunlight touched her face and she smiled weakly, knowing her flight home was only three days away. Dan had gone to get breakfast, giving her time to wake up. Evie tried to sit up, her wrists buckled, causing her to cry out in pain. Lying back down she looked at her sore wrists and caught her breath, noticing her hands were grey and her nails had turned purple. Dan opened the door.

'Wake up sleepy head,' he announced, then stopped still, staring at Evie, she was white. Dan put the breakfast tray down on the floor. 'Hey, how are you feeling?'

'I'll be ok, just a little tired,' Evie answered breathless.

'You don't look it, shall I get the Doctor out?'

'No, there's no need, I'm getting up soon.' More shallow breathing followed.

'It sounds like you have a chest infection.'

'I'm ok, really, anyway it will cost a fortune and the last of our money went on the flights.'

'If you're sure,' he replied, holding a glass of fruit juice to her pale lips, as she struggled to raise her head slightly. Dan didn't want to, but Evie insisted he leave.

'You go, I will be up and about later. When you finish your shift, we can go for a walk.' Dan reluctantly left her, returning later only to find her still asleep in bed.

## Twenty Five

The next morning, Evie looked worse, she was very hot, sweating and complaining of a tight chest restricting her breathing.

'Evie, I'm getting the Doctor,' he told her.

'No, I'm ok,' she insisted, managing to sit up unaided, although it was taking the last of her strength.

'If you're still the same when I check on you at lunch, I'm getting the doctor no matter what it costs. Ok?' She attempted a smile and he hurried out of the door, forgetting to kiss her goodbye.

When he returned to check on her at two o'clock, Evie was lying on the bed in a very deep sleep.

'Evie, Evie,' he said gently, but she didn't stir. Dan poured some chilled water into a glass and sat down on the bed. He stroked her cheek, but she still didn't move. 'Evie wake up,' he shouted, picking up her hand, before dropping it and gasping in horror. Dan instinctively put his ear against her mouth. 'Evie,' he screamed, picking her up and shaking her, she was no longer breathing. 'No,' he repeated 'No,' holding her in his arms, sobbing her name.

It was too late, Dan couldn't do anything. His beautiful Evie was gone forever.

'No, no,' he moaned. 'Why wouldn't you let me get help?' Dan clung to her still body, whilst his tears soaked the strands of her auburn hair. 'Evie you're cold, let's get you warm,' he said, trembling, placing her lifeless body down on the bed and tucking the quilt around her. He lay down next to her, not knowing what to do with tears streaming down his face. Nobody heard him crying out. Nobody came to help him. Finally he kissed her cold, unmoving lips, before getting up and sinking to the floor, his body wracked with grief.

After another half hour of shaking and crying, he picked up the phone and rang Anton's number.

# Chapter Twenty-two

# Quarantine

Anton couldn't take in what Dan was saying.

'What, Evie's dead, are you sure?'

'Yes, she's gone,' he screamed, 'I found her lying on the bed.' Anton could hear Dan gasping for air, inbetween loud sobs.

'Have you called emergency services?' Anton sunk into a nearby chair, his voice faltering with shock.

'I don't know the number, I don't know what to do. Please help me,' he pleaded, sinking to his knees.

'Listen to me Dan, you need to get the Hotel

Manager.  Do it now, Ok?'  Dan seemed incoherent so
Anton repeated it to him several times until he heard
the phone drop and the door of the room opening.
After a few minutes, Anton put the phone down, he
was as white as a sheet.  Trembling he put his hands
over his mouth to stop him from shouting out in
absolute despair.  Numb to the core he picked up his
car keys and walked unsteadily to the car.

'My God, my God,' he muttered, his hands
shaking as he gripped the steering wheel and drove
unsteadily towards Jacqui's apartment.

Jacqui sank to the floor, when he told her.

'No, not Evie, it must be a mistake, what
happened?'  Anton guided her towards the settee,
where she sat trembling with both hands covering her
mouth, looking at Anton in disbelief.  He put his arm
around her and they both cried, heartfelt tears for Evie
and for Dan.

'How can this be?'  Jacqui, shook Anton's arms,
as if it was his fault.  'She's only twenty four years
old.  How has this happened?'

'I don't know, I can't believe it either.'  Anton
held on to her, 'Try and keep calm, you need to ring
him back.  Take a deep breath first.'  Passing her the
phone, Jacqui wiped away tears with her sleeve and
took several deep breaths, before giving Anton a look
of sheer terror as she listened to the ring tone.

'Poor Evie,' she whispered, biting her lip, 'And Matt and Kym, this will break their hearts.'

The hotel manager was already with Dan when she got through and had contacted a Doctor. Dan was crying, traumatised, Jacqui longed be able to hold and comfort him, pained by the distance between them.

'What happened, tell me everything that happened?' Jacqui asked, trying to steady her voice and glancing at Anton who pressed the speaker button, amplifying Dan's grief stricken voice.

'She couldn't get up, her chest was hurting. I wanted to get the Doctor out, but she wouldn't let me. Why, didn't I just do it mum?' he sobbed mournfully. Jacqui wiped away tears before continuing.

'Did you have a drink last night or anything?' Anton looked over to her shaking his head slowly from side to side, tears rolling down his face. Another string of garbled words filled the room.

'No, we didn't go out, she stayed in bed, it wasn't my fault, I had to go to work and left her and Mum, she was all alone, cold and alone.' Dan dropped the phone, unable to speak any further. The hotel manager picked it up and continued.

'Mrs. Lewis, Dan is in quite a state. I'll stay with him until the Doctor arrives and then I will let you know what's happening,' his voice was breaking with emotion as he ended the call. Jacqui sat crying for several minutes, then folded her arms and shivered as she said quietly,

'Anton what are we going to do? Shall we give the hotel manager Matt's mobile number?' Anton inhaled deeply, a troubled expression on his face.

'I can't let them hear about Evie over the phone. I'll have to go round there and tell them.' Anton picked up his coat with a heavy heart, mortified that pretty, full of life Evie was dead. Walking with his head down towards the car, each step seemed to take an eternity as he tried to figure out how to break the news to Matt and Kym, knowing their reaction would be too much to bear.

Anton drove for a long, slow, silent hour, wiping his eyes when he finally stopped his car on the drive of Matt and Kym's home. Anton knew only too well, what he would be facing. He knew what the devastation of losing a child looked like on the face of a heartbroken parent. The vision haunted him now as he walked towards the house.

Remembering the night he'd been out drinking heavily with friends when he was eighteen. How rough he'd felt the next morning getting up for the job he hated, working Sundays in a shopping centre. Turning the keys in the ignition, he backed out of the driveway without checking his path was clear and failed to notice his neighbour's little girl practicing riding her bike on the pavement, until it was too late. He hit her bike with the rear wing of his car and she fell hard to the ground, striking her head against the concrete flags, without the protection of a helmet. Then the chilling, blood curdling screams started as her mum rushed towards her unmoving five year old daughter and cradled her in her arms. There was nothing he could say, it was written all over her face that he personified the worst kind of evil possible. Anton remembered standing over them, cursing himself for not taking the train to work. A moment in time that he would give anything to change, that would remain with him forever. Breathalysed and arrested at the scene, Anton served a twenty four month sentence for her death. He'd never been able to return home and changed his name. Everyone, including his parents despised him. At nearly sixty years old, the look on the little girl's mum's face was still as clear as the day it happened. It remained with him now as he approached Matt and Kym's door.

Anton wondered whatever had possessed him to volunteer for such a horrendous task as he cleared his throat. Looking at the dark wood stained barrier that stood between him and breaking Evie's family's hearts, he hesitated, wanting to turn and run. It was several minutes before he found the courage to knock lightly, hoping they wouldn't hear him. Anton glanced at the three cars parked on the drive, knowing there was a good chance they were all in. He swallowed hard, hearing Clare first.

'I'll get it Mum,' she shouted in her sweet happy voice as her dainty footsteps approached the door. It opened and Anton knew there was no going back, he was going to have to tell them and watch them break down in pain right in front of him. He choked as nausea rose up into his throat.

It was a further six days before Evie's body was released and returned to the UK, her death certificate stated she had died of a heart attack. The same day that Matt turned on the television after another sleepless night and sat down, dumbstruck at the breaking news reported.

'Hundreds of young adults have died during the past week under a shroud of mystery. Early indications are that they have all suffered fatal heart attacks. Medical experts are baffled as to why so many have died suddenly.' Matt turned the volume up.

'Kym, Kym,' he shouted up the stairs. She sat up, Matt had hardly said anything for days and now he was screaming loudly, like a man possessed. Racing downstairs Kym could already hear the news reader's voice reporting.

'All the fatalities occurred in the UK. 'Tears flowed down her face as she listened to anguished relatives relating horror stories of how their children had died. The news report pointed out that they all had one thing in common, they were all approximately twenty five years old.

And so began their vigil. Sitting for days, glaring at the wall mounted screen in despair. Not eating or drinking, numbed by the constant reports of further deaths. A spokesman from the Medical Authorities investigating the deaths suggested that a mystery virus may be the cause. He added that they were working around the clock to determine how multiple heart failures had occurred amongst adults of the same age group. Every day the television showed more shocking images of fatalities arriving at mortuaries, displaying a blood churning count in bold black figures, sending shock waves around the country. A quarantine alert was issued by the World Health Organisation, borders were closed and movements restricted, but the death toll continued to rise.

The army was deployed and newspapers were filled with pictures of them placing body bags on to the back of army vehicles. Bodies were found all over the country. In streets, parks, shopping centre toilets and in cars parked at multi storey car parks. The Government declared a state of emergency and news channels gave hourly updates, interrupting programmes to show footage from Downing Street with ministers urging the public to stay calm and to stay indoors. Schools and large organisations were closed, hospital operations cancelled and public transport suspended. The Press gathered outside the gates of Downing Street and shouted questions at ministers coming and going.

'Is it still just 25 year olds in the UK? How many more have died today? What are you doing about it?' The Health Minister addressed them before leaving, walking towards them with his head bowed.

'We're doing all we can. I can confirm that it's not a virus and none of the bloods checked show anomalies.' Microphones were shoved in front of his face and his obvious distress showed as he tried to get through a sizeable crowd. 'I've got children too, as soon as we know anything more, we'll tell you. Please, this isn't helping,' he replied, batting away grabbing arms as he tried to escape the Press.

Hearing no answers, Matt and Kym focused on protecting their remaining daughter. They discussed travelling to Scotland and renting a cottage in a remote place away from everything and everyone, intending to stay there until it was safe again. Matt agreed and went to his local supermarket to get some supplies for their trip. He stared in horror at the empty shelves and smashed bottles and packets of food on the floor. There was nothing salvageable left. Tearing around the empty streets he ran in and out of every store he found, only to return home empty handed.

Matt's grief turned to anger which he directed at Dan, he was the reason Evie had left home in the first place, robbing them of the last year of her life.

'If that bastard hadn't taken her away she would be with us now,' he screamed at Kym that same evening, clenching his fists.

'It wasn't his fault that she died,' Kym whispered, shocked by her husband's outburst.

'Yes, but you could have taken care of her, saved her life. Clare is fine. Why is he still alive anyway?' Matt glared at her his face twisted with anger. 'The scumbag was twenty five months ago, why isn't he dead then? I'd better not bump into him or he soon will be!' Kym shot him a look, sweat was dripping down his tormented face.

'Matt, please stop, please' she repeated softly, trying to calm him. Kym's eyes flickered over his body, tensed with rage. 'At times like this you scare me,' she cried, running from the room. Weak with the stress of her family falling apart, Kym threw up several times in the bathroom before falling asleep on the bed that only she occupied these days.

Things got worse as people continued to die of heart failure in February and the Government still hadn't discovered the cause. Kym noticed that Clare was very quiet, getting up late and returning to bed exhausted most afternoons. She called their doctor and requested a home visit but was told that none were available. Panic had set in amongst parents of twenty five year olds and those soon to be twenty five and Doctors had suspended all home visits. As mayhem gripped the country, surgeries heaved with patients waiting to be examined and hospitals had to close their doors, overwhelmed by pushing and squabbling crowds arriving each day.

Kym, terrified that Clare was next, made her stay in bed, monitoring her heart and blood pressure. Matt continued to sit in the armchair watching news reports and only stirred when he heard Kym screaming his name.

'Matt, Matt help me.' He took the stairs two at a time. Kym was crying when he found her. 'It's her heartbeat it's fading, we need to leave now.' Gathering Clare up in his arms, they ran to the car and he drove like a maniac towards the hospital. Once again, Matt had to abandon the car at the roadside and raced with Clare in his arms, towards the doors of the emergency entrance. Rounding the corner he gasped in horror at the queues of people waiting to be seen, crowded around the hospital entrance.

Ambulances arriving with dead bodies stopped as near to the doors as they could, where members of the Armed Forces formed lines with stretchers, waiting to receive them. It reminded them both of the terrifying scenes during the flu pandemic years earlier. Not to be deterred, Matt forced his way inside, colliding with people standing in his way.

'I'm a Doctor, let me through!' Kym cried out and to her relief the crowd parted allowing them to squeeze past.  The corridors were packed and they struggled to make any further progress.  Kym looked around horrified at the amount of people, clutching their chests as they struggled in pain, dying in front of them.  The muscles in Matt's arms throbbed with pain, forcing him to stop and lie Clare gently down on the floor momentarily.  When her body touched the cold tiles, her head dropped backwards and she stopped breathing.

'Help us, please,' Kym shouted before attempting to resuscitate her daughter with rhythmic heart compressions, minutes went by and Kym's fingers stiffened but she continued, her movements becoming frantic as she compressed her intertwined fingers up and down, whilst shouting out for adrenaline.  Matt looked on silently, everything in front of him had gone into slow motion, Kym's voice was slurred, he couldn't hear what she was saying.  All colour had drained from his face and he shuddered locked in the spine chilling memory of Lucy's death.  He knew as soon as her head had dropped in front of his eyes that Clare was dead, there was nothing further they could do.

Kym collapsed on top of Clare, sobbing uncontrollably.  Matt just stood against the wall, unable to move in grim disbelief that history had repeated itself.  He looked at Kym, she was on the floor, next to their daughter.  He stared down at them both and then looked around at a mass of dead bodies lying in front of their parents. Matt jumped, it was as if someone had suddenly switched the sound back on and turned it up to full volume. All he could hear was loud wails of grief.

'Out of my way, get out of my way,' he shouted, shoving people aside roughly as he lurched towards the door, desperate to escape.

Matt threw up several times outside, something had been unlocked deep inside of him, hidden there since Lucy's death. It was going to take all of his strength to fight the desire to run and keep running from the pain which threatened to break him. Matt stood still, he couldn't move. He wanted to leave, but it wasn't simple this time, he loved Kym and had to go back and find his wife. Moving in a trance like state, back through hospital corridors, Matt stepped over grief stricken parents, cradling the bodies of their sons and daughters. Eventually finding Kym. He picked her up, placing his arms around her waist in support as her legs buckled underneath her.

'We have to leave now,' he said in a voice he didn't recognise, avoiding looking at Clare's lifeless body on the cold, hard floor.

'I can't leave her!' Kym screamed at him loudly, 'leave us alone.' They both sat down on the floor holding their dead daughter in their arms and waited. But nobody came to help them. Hospital staff were all too busy trying to save lives that couldn't be saved.

News articles began to report more victims of heart failures throughout the world. However the victims had all been born in the UK. By the end of March, one hundred thousand twenty five year olds had died of heart failure. It was unstoppable and tragically, a small number had taken their own lives fearing a painful and imminent death. Cremations happened en masse, with short, hurried services due to the volume of bodies arriving. Parents and relatives were given a date to attend and Matt and Kym joined a gathering of grief stricken relatives a week after Clare's death. They wept quietly when placing flowers on a body bag labelled with their daughter's name, lined up amongst dozens more. They said quick prayers, with other parents, as their loved ones were put onto a trolley and wheeled down towards the furnace doors. It was horrible and morbid beyond words. Ashes could not be collected, the whole system of dignity and civilised funerals had broken down.

By April, Medical Authorities and Government Investigators made up of coroners and pathologists, had reviewed ten thousand cases. They discovered the same defect in the heart muscle of them all which had led to fatal heart failure, but had no idea what had caused the defect. A report was completed on the findings and given to the Government, who chose not to release the information until they had a plan of treatment. One of the medical investigators was outraged by this decision. He had two daughters aged twenty one and twenty three himself and wasn't going to allow the Government to delay releasing the information for much longer.  Making his feelings known, he advised the Government to take immediate action or he would go to the Press.

During the middle of April, television news reports continued to blare out the grim daily death count, reporting that one hundred and forty thousand twenty five year olds had died of heart failure.  Every day it continued, it seemed that nobody could prevent the death toll from rising.

# Chapter Twenty-three

# Smokescreen

'What the hell is going on?' Kym shouted at the television, jumping to her feet. 'You must know something. Liar, liar,' she screamed at the Health Minister, pushing his way through a crowd of reporters. Pointing her finger at the close up of his squirming, red face plastered across her screen she launched her anger towards the Press. 'Ask him why it's taking so long to establish the links between the deaths. Why are they all the same age?' The news report switched to scenes of people dying in the streets and Kym stabbed at the remote button to turn them off.

Rollo, sitting in his basket, pricked up an ear,

then let out a loud bark, acknowledging her distress. Kym brushed away tears with the back of her hand.

'It's ok, I'm ok,' she said, lowering her tone in an attempt to calm both of them down. Rollo saw her interest in him as a cue to run towards the door and return with his brown, ragged lead locked between his jaws.

'Ha, I get the message, you win.' Kym fastened the lead to his collar, managing a wan smile as Rollo tugged and pulled her outside. Walking past the house, she crossed a field of tall grass intermingled with bunches of blue bells, before reaching a meandering stream that gently tumbled away from a sloping grass bank. Rollo's dry tongue scooped up some of the clear liquid, whilst Kym sat down, alongside and listened to the soothing sounds of the rippling water.

Watching Rollo's antics, her thoughts turned back to the frustrating television images shown earlier, whilst flinging a stick high in the air, for him to chase after. As a scientist she couldn't believe that the Medical Authorities were getting nowhere. Trying to wrestle the stick from Rollo's grip, caused her to smile as he snarled in playful defiance.

'They're missing something,' she calmly said. Lost in her thoughts Kym hadn't noticed that Rollo had disappeared out of sight. Instead she was busy constructing a plan. After several minutes he returned panting and licked her face fiercely with his warm, strong tongue. Falling off balance, Kym had no choice but to put her hand down into a pool of deep, black mud. With a loud squelch, she jerked backwards. 'Yuk, look what's happened now, Rollo,' she cried, before rinsing the mud away in the slow flowing stream. Crouching down, swirling her hand in the water, Kym stared at the deposits of mud clouding the stream and floating away. 'Come on, boy, let's go, it's time to get started.' Rollo's tail wagged excitedly as he darted around her revitalised steps on the way back, picking up on her newly found energy.

Once back inside, Rollo was dispatched into the garden, leaving Kym time to work on her computer. Calling up an empty page, Kym stared blankly at the screen, wondering where to start. After reading several articles on the causes of heart failures, Kym sighed knowing she'd already hit a dead end. Unable to gain access to tissue samples from victims heart's, threatened her task with failure, there was nothing else for it, biscuits and plenty of them. Whilst waiting for the kettle to boil, Kym wondered if researching the families of victims might be a way forward. Back at her desk and dunking chocolate rounds into her milky coffee, she began to compile a list of questions that might be significant, realising she would need to start at the very beginning.

Had the deceased been taking any form of medication or stimulants during their lives?

Did their mothers taken any form of vitamins or additives during pregnancy? The list went on and Kym crossed through several questions before deciding which ones to use for her information gathering exercise.

Within an hour Kym had put out an internet message on social network sites which contained a link to a questionnaire she'd compiled. By the end of the week she'd received eight thousand replies in her mail box. Scrolling through, Kym looked for plausible patterns within the answers, whilst Rollo sat at her feet waiting patiently for his morning walk. He tugged at her trousers in a playful way, while she continued to read responses and dropped his lead at her feet, wagging his tail expectantly. Kym reluctantly tore herself away from her laptop and turned to pat Rollo. He was no longer a puppy, now fully grown, her constant companion didn't take kindly to being ignored.

'Come on then Rollo,' she said in her soft voice, 'you first, then I have work to do.'

Although only wanting to spend a short time away from her research, as Rollo raced off into the fields, Kym realised they would be out for some time. It was a beautiful morning, with just a slight, mild breeze. She loved being out with Rollo on mornings like this, but today there was an urgency in her stride, driven by the desire to work through her inbox. Her eyes misted over and sadness clutched at her heart, thinking about how her days had once been filled with people and chores, without a minute to spare. Now with only herself and Rollo to look after, a filled inbox was the new stimulus she needed to keep her occupied.

It was taking weeks to get through them all and poor Rollo was neglected, running in and out of the back door, spending days digging holes in the garden. Kym knew he was unhappy but had to finish her crucial research.

'Not for much longer,' she shouted through the window, as he ran around in circles, chasing his tail. Staring out at the fading sun, lighting up the last section of the lawn, Kym exhaled sharply, hoping that she wouldn't discover her efforts had been nothing more than chasing around aimlessly for hours on end.

At first Kym had expected something obvious to stand out from the information she was collating, however, scrolling through the medication category of her questionnaires, she couldn't understand why there were no similarities. Kym groaned whilst shutting down her P.C. her heart felt heavy as she turned off the lights realising another day had been wasted. Switching on the television in her bedroom, it was more of the same. Shuddering, Kym, wrapped the quilt around herself, wondering how long it was going to go on for. One year, two years, twenty? Without answers people would go on dying indefinitely, potentially wiping out a whole generation.

By the end of April thousands more young adults had died, leaving Kym frustrated by her lack of progress. Then one warm sleepless night in May, she got up to get a drink of water and passed her computer. Something drew her to it and without a second thought, Kym sat down and switched it on. The date flickered, before blurring with her tears as she remembered it was the date she'd travelled to Cornwall with Matt, just before her pregnancy was confirmed.

It was like a light had been switched on in her brain, realising that the fault in victim's hearts could have occurred either at conception or during the first few weeks of development. Twenty six years ago she'd attended two Generate group meetings and their objective had been to increase the birth rate from the following year. Kym eyes flashed widely as she read through statistics from the year after the groups meetings had been held. A million more babies had been born.

'My God,' she muttered, stunned by the increase, the year before the meeting only ninety thousand births were registered. Scanning through the information on birth rates confirmed that each year that followed a further million babies were born. The colour drained from her face, how had this happened? What did the Government actually do with the Generate meetings ideas?  Shaking her head in horror, Kym knew there had to be a link, increased births started the year after the first meeting and now twenty five years later, they were all dying!

Kym tried to remember the details of the Generate group's meetings and its attendees, recalling how some members had not joined in discussions and instead handed in papers at the end.  What if one of the undisclosed ideas had been to change the makeup of the Contraceptive Pill?  Would that have been possible?  She started to scribble notes as ideas flowed quickly,

Changing the Pill's make up, multiple births, birth rate increases significantly - stimulants.  Placing her hand over her mouth, Kym looked at her notes, terrified by the word that screamed back at her. Stimulants.  They would certainly have caused a surge in the birth rate.  Kym switched off her computer, scolding herself.  She was going mad, probably due to sleep deprivation. The Government would have had to get a pharmaceutical giant on board to alter several well-known brands of the pill, it just wasn't possible. Her initial exhilaration at being onto something was now fading further.  Returning to bed the numbers kept going round and round in her head as she turned restlessly from side to side, unable to relax.

Lying exhausted, Kym looked at the clock it was 4am, but she couldn't stop thinking about the Generate group.

'Stop it,' she moaned, kicking off the quilt. Touching her stomach, revealed a layer of sweat, it was all over her body. 'What's happening?' Kym grumbled, sitting up and putting the light on. After a few minutes she turned the light off and tried to get back asleep, but her mind was wide awake. Trying to remain rational Kym thought back to when she'd collected her six month batch of pills, remembering that it had been during the first week in January and she'd started taking them straight away. Therefore the Generate group couldn't have been involved in changing the pill, because her pills had been produced before the first meeting took place in February and she'd got pregnant and her daughters had died aged twenty five. Now that she'd sorted this out, Kym was able to relax and quickly fell into a long, deep sleep.

Kym woke up disorientated with Rollo jumping on the bed and dropping his lead onto her stomach.

'What time is it?' realising nobody was going to reply, she grabbed the clock. It was almost nine. Rollo gave a loud gruff, needing to go outside desperately, he'd been waiting patiently at the door for the last hour. Kym opened the door and watched as he dashed into the garden, wrapping her silk gown around her frail body, for some protection against the morning's cool breeze. Leaving Rollo to play outside, she made a coffee then sat down at her computer.

Switching it on she twisted her hair around her fingers, whilst waiting for the screen to stop buffering. She just couldn't get the pill tampering idea out of her mind and wondered if it was really possible. If so how could it have been delivered to control an increase in pregnancies accurately for twenty years? Wouldn't everyone of child bearing years have got pregnant? What about the birth rate why had it now stopped increasing?

Hastily pressing keys, Kym scanned through news articles and figures until she found the answer. The birth rate dropped over a year ago when the Government changed. Restrictions on abortions were lifted that year also. Meaning the UK had almost twenty four years of unexplained increased pregnancies. Surely pills hadn't been tampered with for twenty four years? Her eyes flashed with panic.

'Please, no,' she cried out, realising that the UK could be facing the premature deaths of young adults for the next twenty four years. None of it made sense to Kym. How could her daughters have died of the same phenomenon if she hadn't been taking altered pills? Why had the Generate meetings been cloaked in secrecy, preventing future contact between attendees? What were the Government hiding?

It was then that Kym realised the enormity of her theories. The powers that be at the time of the meetings had already decided what they were going to do and had put their plans in operation before the beginning of that year. The Generate meetings had just been a smokescreen. With a pharmaceutical company in tow they had already started issuing altered pills, packaged under familiar brand names, so women wouldn't notice any difference. Kym's heart sank, she wanted to cry out loud, realising that her idea to restrict access to abortions may have helped the Government explain away the birth rate increases. Clouding over what they had really done.

Kym knew she would need compelling evidence to prove a pill tampering theory, which would be difficult now that affected pills were no longer issued. Scribbling away, before selecting a new set of questions, she chose the first ten email replies received and sent them a new questionnaire asking questions about the Contraceptive Pill.

Where you on the pill when you got pregnant?

What was the name of the pill you were taking?

When did you start taking it?

What was the dose?

Did you forget to take pills at any time?

Had you been ill and if so, did you use any additional protection?

Kym realised this was a long shot, as her

questions related to pills taken twenty six years ago there may be inaccuracies in the responses. However, Kym knew that one question would be answered correctly, was their pregnancy planned, that was something you would never forget.

A day later Kym had received all the replies and printed out the answers.

'Wow,' she exclaimed, leafing through them. Of the ten women contacted, all had been taking the same brand of pill as Kym. Their pregnancies were unplanned and hadn't been explained by missing pills or illness. Kym sat in silence, reading through the answers, searching for errors, there weren't any and a cold shiver slowly ran down the length of her spine.

Wasting no time the new questionnaire was dispatched to everyone who had responded to the original one. Within a few days, Kym had received seven thousand replies. Invigorated by her new challenge, she stayed up all night checking through as many of them as possible, immediately identifying a pattern. Several brands of the same pill kept cropping up. All the pregnancies had been unexpected and hadn't been put down to missing pills or illness. Kym had found the link she needed to prove the Pill had been tampered with. Yet she didn't celebrate, instead fell onto the bed exhausted at 6am.

By 10am Kym was sitting back at her computer, having sent Rollo outside for the morning. Checking through newspaper articles, several Doctors in small villages had raised concerns over increased pregnancies amongst pill takers with the relevant Medical Authorities at the time. The levels were significant enough to evoke action, although the authorities took years to investigate such issues. She now suspected that there may have been a cover up with Doctors completing reports that were never investigated.

Kym was convinced she had evidence that a stimulant had been added to the pill before Generate meetings were held. The questionnaire results also revealed which major Pharmaceutical company was involved. After a couple of pregnancies on the same pill, Doctors had probably switched patients to a different brand to give them better protection.

'Thank goodness you had the snip Matt,' Kym mumbled quietly.

The conspirators had got away with interfering with pills for more than twenty years, possibly putting control measures in place to keep births within the limits they had set. It was too much of a coincidence that twenty five years later, the adults whose births had been unexplained, were dying. Kym's theory was that stimulants added to the pill to promote pregnancy had caused a weakness within hearts that were destined to fail.

Now that she knew why hearts were failing, Kym

needed to start work on a solution to prevent further deaths. Would stem cells waiting in storage fix the problem? Kym sighed heavily, knowing she could not succeed in finding a solution without first having the might of the medical industry behind her, but how could she trust them after this? The guilty parties involved would collaborate together, even suggesting that they had acted in the national interest.

Armed with irrefutable evidence that the Contraceptive Pill had been tampered with, Kym had no other option than to go directly to the new Governing body, who had no involvement in the conspiracy and would instigate an investigation. Picking up the phone she called 10 Downing Street.

# Chapter Twenty-four

# Super pill

It was the 17th May and Kym was due to meet with the Prime Minister at 11o'clock to present her findings. Picking strands of blond hair from the back of her navy jacket had taken up several precious minutes and she sighed, knowing that her short retirement was over.

Walking towards the gates that protected Downing Street, she looked with unease at a large crowd of people gathered there. They waved banners angrily, shouting and screaming at the police standing behind the closed black gates. Kym hadn't expected this and stood staring through the intimidating mob for a short while before noticing an access area roped off at the side.  Getting as near to the front of the gates as possible, she shouted loudly to the nearest police officer.

'I'm Doctor Kym Adams and I have an appointment.'  Two officers opened one of the side gates, pushing back the crowd and guiding her through.  After being jostled and yelled at, Kym squeezed through and walked briskly up to No.10 as the officers continued to hold back the crowd whilst struggling to close the gate.

The door to No. 10 looked exactly the same as it had twenty six years ago and after spending hours checking through the data she'd collected, Kym had been eager to get there.  Now she hesitated at the door, tears in her eyes, unable to proceed.

'Matt,' she whispered sadly.  The lump in her throat was choking as she visualised meeting him just inside the entrance twenty six years earlier.  Kym searched for a tissue in her bag then dabbed away tears upon hearing his words echoing through her mind.

*It's Matt, we were at university together.*  Kym stood completely still, confused by her emotions, although she knew he wouldn't be there to greet her this time.  Just as she turned to walk away, a smartly dressed young man appeared from nowhere and touched her arm.

'Are you alright?' he asked gently, sensing

something was wrong. Unable to answer, she smiled at him sadly, lost in her thoughts. 'Can I take your name please?' he continued. Kym swallowed hard, she had to go on and try to hide the unbearable pain of being without the support of the man she needed most.

After Clare's death, Matt hadn't been able to face life with Kym and living at their family home. Although she tried to help him talk about what had happened, Matt locked himself away in a private world which nobody could penetrate. Spending the day, dozing off in his armchair whilst watching twenty four hour television, he refused to eat, talk, or move. Staring into space, hour after hour, lost in a trance. In despair Kym rang his parents. They came within the hour and led him by the hand, unspeaking to their car. He was still dressed in the same clothes they had left the hospital in days earlier. They had been caring for him ever since.

Time had passed quickly and it had been almost two months since Matt had left. Kym spent every Sunday afternoon visiting him. At first conversation had been awkward and mainly one sided with her doing all the talking, but during the last four weeks there had been a breakthrough and he'd accompanied her and Rollo for short walks outside. They never lasted long, Matt always seemed desperate to get back to the safety of his parent's house after half an hour. He'd given up working at No.10 and would probably never be employed there or in the security field again.

Kym longed for the day when he would return. She would never give up on him. They couldn't return to the family home, she knew that and dreamt of a new start for them one day soon.

Kym tried to focus, turning her thoughts to the enormity of the meeting ahead whilst following the young man down a long corridor. As he led her into a meeting room, she couldn't help but hope that he was over twenty five years old.

The Prime Minister greeted her with a brisk handshake and introduced her to the six other people present. A lady had already set up a screen and cabling needed to plug into Kym's laptop. Kym noticed her hands were shaking slightly and her mind went blank as she checked through her presentation. Looking up, her vulnerability was apparent as she let out a huge sigh and stood there staring at the Ministers present.

'Are you ready to start Dr. Adams?' The Prime Minister looked directly at her raising an eyebrow. His reaction unnerved her.

'Erm, I thought I would be speaking to you, alone, do we need all these people here?' Kym had emphasised the word alone and the P.M. looked troubled, before smiling.

'These are senior members of my cabinet and can be trusted, I need their advice,' he answered firmly.

'Then I'm sorry but I can't present my evidence.' Kym sat down, taking deep breaths to calm her nerves.

'Dr. Adams we need to hear what you have to say. I can assure you of the absolute discretion of all the persons here. If you prefer, only the Home Secretary and the Health Minister will stay, that's the best I can do.' He looked closely at Kym, having made it quite clear that the matter was not up for debate, leaving her no other choice than to agree.

It took half an hour for her to finish speaking, after which she sat down heavily in the nearest chair and looked down at the floor. Kym waited for questions as an eerie silence filled the room. After a couple of minutes of silence, the P.M. spoke first.

'Thank you Dr. Adams. Let's all take a short break, for fifteen minutes.' Standing up he exited the room, before anyone had the chance to speak.

Kym unplugged her laptop and waited patiently, looking around wondering what to do or say next. She felt sure the P.M. was locked in a private room, either on the phone or discussing her findings with cabinet members and continued to try and control her breathing whilst her heart pounded in her chest. The woman who'd helped set up her presentation returned with coffees, again smiling at Kym but not making any conversation as she left a tray of white china cups on the table. Kym's shaking hands caused some of the brown, thick liquid to spill, whilst stirring in a hard lump of white sugar.  Twenty minutes later the P.M. returned.

'Ah, good, coffee,' he remarked, his face remaining impassive.  After he'd placed sugar into his cup and they listened to the sound of metal clashing against china, he turned to Kym.

'Right, I have a few questions,' he continued with his lips curling into a slight smile.  Over the next hour they went through Kym's research in detail, subjecting her to a barrage of questions in an attempt to pull her super pill theory apart.  At the end of their discussion Kym's breathing was shallow, fear and anxiety had drained her senses and she wanted to leave.

'Interesting,' the P.M. stated.  'Can you wait outside, we need to discuss options, won't keep you much longer.'  Kym gathered up her things and left the room.  Tears of anger and frustration filled her eyes and she bit her tongue to prevent a sarcastic remark, threatening to expose her grief. *What other options do you have, do something,* she'd wanted to scream at the shabby excuse for a Health Minister who glared at her with beady eyes, patting his sweating forehead with a paper tissue, without saying a word.

When the door to the room opened the two ministers left and Kym was told to go back in.  Finally she was alone with the Prime Minister.

'Dr. Adams although you have convinced me that everything you have unearthed is feasible, I will have to take your research away and run it by experts who can advise me further. In the meantime, I would like you to start working on a cure, a treatment using your advanced knowledge of stem cells.' Kym felt her body tensing and looked at him bemused. Did he believe her or not, what was he saying? The Prime Minister continued asking Kym if stem cells could be used to repair defective hearts.

'If they can, how long would it be before a treatment could be available for use?'

'Oh,' he replied, pausing, after her answer of several months. In his mind he seemed to be calculating how many more people would die by then.

Kym folded her arms and stared at the man who she'd piled all her hopes on. Now filled with an ominous feeling, her breathing stalled, realising that she may have made a big mistake in coming to see him. The questions asked had not been the ones she'd expected and his reaction was suspicious, unsurprised. For the first time since uncovering the super pill theory, Kym suspected that the Government already knew about it.

'What I need to know is the name of the stimulant used in the creation of the super pill, then I can develop a cure within weeks, not months.' Her cheeks flushed, Kym had raised her voice unable to hide her frustration. Politeness was no longer an issue, people had to stop dying, nothing else mattered.

'I have to make sure that everything is done correctly,' he insisted. 'I have no idea what the implications of your super pill theory might be, if it became public knowledge. You're telling me that you believe Government officials, Medical Authorities and Pharmaceutical Companies have all conspired together and produced an untested version of the Contraceptive Pill. You actually believe that all of these bodies are responsible for potentially killing a whole generation?

'Yes,' she answered her voice shaking.

You must realise the seriousness of your allegations. I need time to verify your findings, before any investigation can commence.' Before she could answer the P.M. stood up and raised his palm at her, halting any further conversation.

'I'm sorry but I have to end our meeting as I have other engagements,' he said, curtly dismissing Kym by shaking her hand loosely. Opening the door of the meeting room for her, he looked perplexed, exasperated. 'Leave it with me, I will get to the bottom of this,' he insisted, before heading off in the opposite direction.

Unknown to Kym the P.M. had met with his medical investigators the previous afternoon. They too had worked out what had happened to the pill and had identified the defect which was causing hearts to fail. The investigators were also putting the Government under pressure to find out what stimulant had been put into contraceptive pills and who was responsible. Heads would roll. The P.M. had a meeting with the previous Government leader and his health ministers, later that evening. Now that he knew Dr. Kym Adams had also worked out what had happened and had substantial evidence, they would have to move fast, before she went to the Press.

Kym wasn't convinced and was slightly insulted by the way the P.M. had treated her. She'd wanted to remind him that her daughters were dead and a cure was too late for them. It was the reassurance that justice would prevail that she and other families needed. Fueled by anger at the idea of another Government cover up, Kym swore to herself that the truth would come out, no matter how long it took.

When Kym finally closed the door to her home, she sank to the floor, sobbing. Rollo came bouncing over, tail wagging to greet her.

'I miss Matt,' she whispered mournfully, 'I miss him so much.' Closing her eyes she could picture him standing in the corridor at No.10, smiling broadly, dressed in his smart suit with his blue eyes twinkling mischievously at her. With an aching heart she stroked Rollo's head in an attempt to try and find some comfort.

'Lucky Rollo, you have no idea what's going on,' Kym muttered as teardrops touched her lips. Rollo licked her face and whimpered as if he was experiencing her sadness, before running to get his lead, which caused her to laugh through tears.

Later, sitting with a blanket around her on the settee, the day's events kept running through her mind. The P.M's farcical, "Leave it with me," hadn't filled her with confidence. Then anger surged through her body tensing her muscles in the realisation they were all going to get away with it. Covering for each other, the finger of blame wouldn't point towards anyone this time. There wouldn't be a fall guy and probably not even an inquiry. Kym longed to confide in someone but there was only Matt. He was starting to improve but the horror of what she had uncovered would only set him back. Even Rollo wasn't listening and had taken to sulking in his basket with his chin on the floor, punishing her for not taking him out.

Looking at his sad eyes, Kym vowed that tomorrow was going to be different, it was time to re-focus her efforts on Matt and Rollo. A warm feeling spread over her as she thought about making a large picnic filled with treats and spending time with the man she loved more than anything else in the world.

Matt opened the door before she had time to knock, his smile was wide and he hugged her close. His warm, strong protective arms, melted her heart and she kissed his neck softly, smelling his familiar, comforting scent. Hearing Rollo bounding around, Matt's mum stuck her head around the kitchen door.

'Feeling a bit better then?' she said smiling at her son.

'I am now,' he revealed, looking Kym up and down and winking.

'How wonderful,' his mum added cheerfully looking at Kym. 'Perhaps you should start coming around more often.' They left the house strolling along with arms around each other, as Rollo bounded ahead. When they arrived at the gate to the meadow, Kym paused, captivated by the swaying golden heads of rapeseed, bowing in the breeze.

'Let's stop here,' she urged, breathing in the clean, sweet air.

'I know a spot, just over there.' Matt pointed towards a clearing, which gave unspoilt views across the countryside surrounding them. Kym spread out a picnic blanket and Matt rewarded her with a long, passionate kiss, which made her blush, although nobody could see them. Kym had brought all of Matt's favourite foods and lots of cake. They laughed and kissed as Rollo held out his paw patiently for sausage rolls to be thrown towards him. After they'd eaten far too much, Matt turned to Kym and picked up her hand, looking at her with intent.

'Kym,' he spoke slowly, 'I've been thinking. Would you and Rollo like to move in here with me for a while?' Kym moved by his unexpected suggestion, blinked back tears, but didn't hesitate to answer.

'Yes, I don't see why not,' she replied gently, smiling at her husband. 'It's about the same travelling distance to work, plus I wouldn't have to cook.' Kym continued happily, realising it was time for her and Matt to make a new start. Staying at his parents wouldn't be ideal, but it would be good to be spoilt for a change. Matt's parents were warm and caring and could certainly do that. Before she had the chance to say anything else, Kym noticed Matt's face had changed. 'What's the matter?' she asked concerned.

'Work? You said it's the same distance to work. When did you start working again?' He looked stunned by her disclosure.

'Don't worry,' Kym said her voice softening, 'I haven't started yet. I'm setting up a new lab and team to help prevent further deaths from heart failures.'

'You didn't mention this to me,' Matt replied looking disheartened, he felt Kym was hiding things from him.

'I only found out yesterday,' Kym explained. 'That's why I'm here today. I went to a meeting at No.10 and it brought back memories of us meeting there. I still love you more than anything Matt and want us to start again.'  Matt smiled, then his face darkened as he looked thoughtful.

'Why were you at No. 10?' he asked firmly.

'I know we never spoke about it Matt, but I had to tell them about the existence of a group I was a member of, remember I attended two meetings?  That's part of why I went back and it reminded me how much I loved and missed you.'  Kym smiled at Matt hoping she'd reassured him that everything was going to be fine.

'Please tell me you didn't tell them about the Generate group's meetings, what were you thinking?' His eyes flashed angrily at her.

'I wasn't thinking I just want all the dying to stop, nothing else matters.'  Kym could feel tears in her eyes, Matt was looking at her as if she was stupid.

'Anyway I didn't mention the Generate meetings. I couldn't.  I signed the Official Secrets Act, remember?  I just presented research I had completed on deaths from heart attacks, though they didn't seem convinced.'  Kym was beaten.  All she'd wanted was to spend a peaceful day with Matt and not to provoke a confrontation.

'My God Kym.  I hope you know what you're doing,' he answered, raising his voice.  Kym thought it was time for them to head back.  Matt looked tired and troubled, he was becoming anxious. Kym hadn't set out to talk about yesterday's events with Matt, the "work" thing had just slipped out. Matt was quiet and didn't mention moving in with his parents again on the way back to the house. Kym tried to lift his spirits but eventually gave in disappointed that she had wrecked any progress they had made. He looked deep in thought as they walked through the front door. Kym had a quick chat with his mum, who was disappointed that she wouldn't be staying for dinner.

'I think Matt's had enough of me for one day,' Kym explained, unable to hide her tears. Matt's mum put a comforting arm around her.

'It's still early days, give him time.' Kym smiled sadly.

'Would it be alright if I visit again on Sunday?' she asked, grabbing Rollo's collar before he could make a run for it. Matt had disappeared upstairs without so much as a goodbye.

'I'm sure it will be fine, don't give up hope,' she added hugging Kym goodbye.

Rollo licked Kym's hands sensing her sadness as she battled to get him inside the car. Kym struggled to make sense of what had happened during the drive home. Disappointed that Matt still wasn't ready for them to get back together, silent tears rolled down her face. Feeling his strong reassuring arms around her, reminded her of how much she relied on him. He always knew what to do, he was her hero and she was a lost soul without his presence by her side. It was confusing, at times he seemed fine, just like the old Matt, the man she knew and then his eyes would go dark and he'd look helpless, just as he had done today. Maybe it had been too much for him, bringing back memories of their first meeting. Kym knew she could never mention the girls during their conversations, Matt couldn't cope with that yet, but hadn't realised she had to tread carefully with everything else as well.

When Kym got home and closed her front door, for the second day running, she burst into tears. Shivering within the unshakeable cold cloud of loneliness that surrounded her, made worse by Matt offering her an escape, only for it to be cruelly snatched away. Wrapping her arms around herself, Kym thought about how Matt was definitely in a better place than she was. He had his parents to take care of him, but who did she have? Who did she have to help her through the long days and empty nights? Kym had horrific nightmares, waking up in a cold sweat most of the time, but nobody comforted her when she was scared witless.

Walking towards the kitchen, her footsteps echoed around the silent rooms that had once been their dream home. Flicking on the light switch, she stared in a trance like state at the gloomy emptiness, picturing the girls flipping pancakes high into the air.

It was no good.  She couldn't live there anymore,
today had been the final straw.  This house had lost its
heart, only ghosts remained within its walls.  Kym
walked slowly up to bed, leaving lights on everywhere,
even though they kept her awake.  Tomorrow she was
going to make a fresh start and look for an apartment
in the city.  Matt was going to need more time, but she
needed to get moving, vowing that this would be the
last week she'd spend alone.

# Chapter Twenty-five

# Foresight

By the next morning Kym had put everything into perspective. Realising it had been the trauma of the meeting at No. 10 that had led to her pessimism over Matt and their future, she tried to forget about what happened there. Matt's overreaction was probably down to his training. With her mind settled Kym made herself a coffee and returned to the lounge.

Recovering the remote from the floor, she flicked on the morning news channel just in time for the latest headlines. A female newsreader Kym liked was announcing some breaking news according to a bold lettered banner flashing across the screen. Kym sat up and listened as the newsreader began to speak.

'There has been a leak to the Press regarding a team of scientists who formed a group called Generate, twenty six years ago.'

'What,' Kym shouted out, horrified, turning the television sound up higher. The newsreader continued;

'The purpose of the group had been to come up with a means to boost the population of the UK by increasing the falling birth rate. Within a year of the group's meeting, the birth rate shot up by a million. Information received suggests that the Generate group were responsible for messing with creation, by tampering with the Contraceptive Pill. They created a so called super pill which caused mass pregnancies. The super pill, taken by UK women, caused babies to be born with defective hearts and is being held directly responsible for the deaths of 180 thousand twenty five year olds to date.'

Kym struggled to breathe as her throat constricted and her heart thumped rapidly, as she listened to the reports. Every channel she switched to was covering the same breaking story. Banners flashed across the screen,

*Super pill, kills thousands with birth defect…..* *Super pill, kills thousands with birth defect.*

Some reports showed masses of people arriving at No.10, battling with the Police to gain access to Downing Street. Their faces creased with rage and fists curled around the black rails of the gates that screened it off, trying to pull them down.

'Murderers,' they screamed. Some threw missiles of stones and bottles over the gates. A camera zoomed in on an officer's head oozing with blood.

'An update from the Prime Minister is expected within the hour,' the newsreader continued, with a face devoid of expression. Kym was stunned. Numb. She'd had the P.M.'s assurance that her presentation would be confidential and why was the news article blaming the Generate group? The super pill was already in circulation, a month before the group was formed. It was all a complete fabrication of the truth. How had they found out about the Generate group anyway? Kym certainly hadn't told them.

'What is going on?' she shouted at the screen, her heart missed a beat, terrified that it might now become public knowledge that she was part of the Generate group. Only days ago she'd been at No.10, what if that was also leaked to the Press, they could potentially name her.

Kym sat still, with her arms folded tightly in front of her, rocking slightly back and forward trying to figure out what to do. Should she ring the P.M. and find out what he was going to do about the Press reports?  Slowly she moved towards the window and carefully peered around the curtain.  Everything seemed normal outside, quiet.  Nobody on her drive, Rollo wasn't barking.  Kym sat back down, feeling her lungs rising and falling as she tried to concentrate.  Surely if her name had been leaked then the Press would be camped outside the front door.

Kym raced up the stairs taking them two at a time and quickly dressed.  Adrenaline energised her senses, awakening her brain as the sound of the television continued to blurt out more accusations.

'A full investigation into the Generate group, responsible for mass deaths, is to be launched immediately' the newsreader stated before ending her report.

Rollo bounced into the bedroom, ears pricked up, he looked at her before letting out an impatient bark.  Kym knew she'd have to open the door and let him into the back garden, but was terrified to do so.  Looking around before opening the back door slightly, a desperate Rollo saw his opportunity and squeezed through the gap.  As Kym was shutting the door behind him, her phone started to ring.

Kym expected it to be the Prime Minister, apologising for the leak and explaining that he was going to clear the Generate group of any responsibility for the super pill.  It wasn't a Government official, it was Matt who had heard the News reports.

'Kym listen to me, keep calm,' he spoke slowly and firmly. 'You know I love you,'

'Yes,' she gasped in tears.

'Well I need you to do exactly as I say. Trust me and don't listen to anybody else.' Kym could detect the panic in his voice as he urged her to pack essentials and leave the house within five minutes.

'Remember, you only have five minutes to get you and Rollo into the car. Then switch off your mobile phone.' Matt gave her details of a location where he'd meet her.

'Don't forget to switch the phone off before you leave, oh and get a move on.'

Kym ran back upstairs and retrieved a suitcase from the spare room. A thin layer of dust covered its leather exterior and she quickly blew it away, sneezing three times in succession. In her haste she grabbed at clothes, underwear and cosmetics, sliding the latter into the case from her dressing table with the side of her arm. After she'd finished packing, Kym sat on the bed and took deep breaths, wondering what she was doing. However, Matt's words remained clearly in her mind.

'Listen to me, leave now!' he'd shouted, panic stricken. Kym picked up her heavy case as if it was as light as a feather and grabbed her bag. Opening the back door she looked around.

'Rollo, Rollo,' her frantic shouts, caused him to respond by bounding over towards her holding one of his favourite balls between his jaws.

'Come inside, now.' Rollo cocked his ear at her and then returned to the lawn, where he dropped the ball and started to play with it. Kym didn't want to spend the next ten minutes running around chasing him, so grabbed a handful of dog biscuits and threw them on the floor in front of the door.

'Come on, biscuits,' she shouted, holding some in the palm of her hand. Rollo looked up and ran towards her. Kym caught him by the collar and pulled a whimpering Rollo away from the pile of treats towards the front door. Slowly she opened it and peered outside, breathing a sigh of relief. Everything seemed fine, still, normal. After locking the house and driving slowly away, she started to wonder if leaving had been really necessary. The P.M. would have made an announcement to the Press by now and the misunderstanding would be cleared up before she met Matt.

Her hands were shaking as she adjusted the rear view mirror, Matt had caused her anxiety with his demands for her to leave immediately and looking around with a pounding heart she drove steadily on. Eventually she found the spot where Matt wanted her to dump the car. Feeling like a tourist, strolling along, wheeling her suitcase was extraordinary when they should be out walking, enjoying the warm sunny morning, not hiding.

'Hmmm,' she muttered, deciding to do as he said, until things died down, though dumping the car and turning her phone off had seemed a bit over the top. Then she smiled, remembering how protective he was. It was instinctive for him to behave this way, after spending a lifetime working within the security services. That kind of thing never left you, Kym thought, dragging Rollo away from gaps in the trees he wanted to sniff out and investigate.

Matt looked tense when she met him. His face was ashen, and he immediately took her phone and stamped it into the ground, before flinging her sim card into the undergrowth.

'I've got new phones for us,' he stated, looking uncomfortable, constantly glancing around while he retrieved two new phones from his jacket.

'I was happy with the old one,' she remarked lightly, trying to break the tension between them. Matt stared at Kym in complete dismay.

'I've put my number into yours, don't add any others, these phones are just for us to use. Now let's get going,' he said firmly, taking her arm and carrying the suitcase in his other hand. Kym exhaled with relief, her eyes shone with love and respect for him.

Her husband was back. Being masterful, taking charge, just like he used to do. The old Matt had returned and she would happily follow him wherever he took her. That was until they arrived at an unkempt block of flats at the edge of a shabby looking street.

Kym followed him obediently up the concrete stairs to the first floor, taking in the grubby, neglected exterior of the block of four small flats. Speechless, she inhaled sharply when walking through the dank smelling, covered walkway that led to a dirty, white painted door. Once inside she hesitated, taking in the flat's squalid interior. It was partially furnished and needed a good clean. Rollo dashed around the four rooms, sniffing out the territory, before returning to Kym's side with his tail wagging excitedly.

After her initial exhilaration at realising Matt was his old self, her heart sank, appalled by his choice of accommodation. Sighing Kym realised that she was going to have to break it to him that she wouldn't be able to go along with his plans after all.

'Matt, I don't think we can stay here,' she began, hoping he wouldn't take offence. 'It's not me. Couldn't we stay at a hotel for a few days instead?' His eyes flashed with impatience.

'You've no idea what you've done. This is it. You need to stay here until its safe.' Matt could tell Kym was struggling with his course of action, but it was necessary now that he knew she was part of the

Generate group.

'Matt I swear to you that I had nothing to do with the super pill,' she insisted, looking hurt. 'I suggested restricting terminations and storing stem cells. That was all I did, it's all lies. The reports are all lies.'

'I know that Kym, but nobody else does and if they find out you were part of the Generate group you will be in danger.' Kym felt her heart stop for a minute, Matt was right, but how would anyone find out who attended the Generate group meetings. Only the previous Government had that information, surely they wouldn't release it to the Press.

'Sit down,' he continued in a softer voice. 'I'm going to cut your hair, then you'll need to colour it.' Matt produced a box of black hair dye from his rucksack and banged it down on the table, turning his eyes away from her.

'No Matt I don't think I can!' Kym protested, shocked at his proposal. She was beginning to understand why Matt was concerned for her safety, but cutting her hair off, she simply couldn't do it.

'Please,' he stressed, taking her arm, 'You don't have any choice.' Kym sank defeated into the crooked wooden chair he'd placed in front of her, her spirit crushed. Matt had thought everything through and produced a pair of scissors. Snipping away at her hair, caused Kym to flinch at the sight of her beautiful blonde locks falling towards the cracked tiled floor. Getting up with tears in her eyes she picked up some of the soft pile of light gold strands and then looked at Matt, heartbroken.

Leaning over a stained sink, Kym felt the cold, wet sensation of the dye being poured over what was left of her hair and being rubbed into the roots, causing her to shudder. After rinsing and towel drying, Kym glared at her reflection in the mirror, not recognising the older, paler face staring back.

'Oh, I do like this mysterious dark haired look,' Matt whispered. Placing his arms around her waist.

'I hate it,' Kym cried out, tears stinging her eyes, doubting Matt's sanity and wondering if their relationship could recover from his overreacting.

Matt undeterred by her tantrum, spent the next half hour taking Kym through what was going to be her new life for the time being.

'Your name is Jane Watson. I'm getting new identification for you tomorrow and need to take your photo.' Kym stood where he wanted, swallowing hard, feeling like she was under arrest. Matt gave her a thousand pounds in small notes, before reaching down into his rucksack, hesitating before pulling out a pair of dark sunglasses.

'Try these,' he urged, placing them over her

eyes.  Matt stood back, looking pleased. 'They look good Kym, nobody will recognise you now.'

'How long will I have stay like this?' Kym asked, trembling, her confidence diminishing with each embellishment of her new persona.

'I don't know Kym, sorry Jane,' he pulled an awkward face, 'honestly I don't know.'  Kym looked at Rollo who was lying down sulking after being ignored for the best part of an hour.

'What about Rollo, I haven't brought anything for him to eat.'

'Rollo, who is Rollo?' he answered.  Kym looked confused, was he going insane?

'This is Max,' Matt smiled, amused at his attempt to inject some humour into the serious situation they found themselves in.  Kym gave a wry smile.

'I'll take him back to my parent's house.  You could be recognised if you walk around with him.  Is there anything in your purse, credit cards?  Photos?' Kym reluctantly passed them to Matt, he'd done it, completed his mission, stripped away her existence.

'From now you can only use cash.  I'll bring cash when you need it, but I can't be seen outside with you.' Kym looked at Matt, searching his eyes for some reassurance that everything was going to be alright and he hadn't completely lost his mind. All she saw was concern and pain. Noticing her despair he pulled her close.

'It will be ok, don't worry. Write out a shopping list and I'll go and pick up anything you need.' He spoke in a softer, calmer tone, less troubled now that he had seen how different she looked. Kym, weary and forlorn, just shook her head, with no energy left to argue with him. Her earlier delight at him taking control, now flooded her mind with fear. Was this in her interest or was it a deliberate move by an insane man? Taking her hostage, stripping her of any dignity, torturing her by taking Rollo away.

Kym's mind went blank and she struggled to put together a list of essentials. She looked around the barely furnished room with just a tiny television in one corner.

'What do you expect me to do? Just sit here all day, waiting for you to return? I'm supposed to start working on a solution to save thousands of people from dying,' she snapped, angrily, 'surely all this isn't necessary?'

'You have to trust me, I know what I'm doing,' he insisted looking deeply into her eyes. Kym's anger melted seeing nothing but love there. Convincing as he seemed, she would only be prepared to stay hidden for a couple of days until everything had been cleared up.

Whilst he was away, getting groceries, Kym was reminded of a television programme she'd seen about the witness protection process. The people involved had left everything behind them, their families, their jobs, their lives. They were never seen again by their loved ones. Kym couldn't bear a life without Matt or Rollo. That wouldn't work for her, they were all she had.

When Matt returned Kym was ready to tell him how she felt.

'Matt I can't do this,' she whispered, broken and tearful. Matt immediately took her hands in his.

'Yes you can Kym, we've been through worse things than this and survived. Ring me if you need anything, but don't leave any messages, remember that, it's very important. Only talk to me and no one else.' With that Matt put Rollo's lead on and kissed her goodbye. 'I love you Kym, you mustn't go out, for your own safety.' With that, he was gone. Kym watched Matt and Rollo from the window of the first floor flat, until they disappeared from her view.

Switching the television on Kym let out a loud groan. The same breaking news statement was being aired on every channel, you couldn't get away from it. Why hadn't the Prime Minister spoken up? She'd remembered him saying that the implications of the super pill becoming public knowledge would be catastrophic. Then her face darkened realising what they'd done.

'Yes, very clever,' she muttered. Blaming the Generate group was taking the emphasis away from the people who were really responsible and she jumped up, clenching her fists.

'You bastards,' she yelled, venting her anger at the television screen. 'That's why you put the group together, to cover your own backs!' A stunned Kym, was also in awe of the person who, twenty six years ago had remarkable foresight to set up a group to blame if anything went wrong. Kym unplugged the television and slammed the cable against the wall. Closing her eyes, exhausted, she lay down and slept for several hours on a very uncomfortable settee that had seen better days.

When she opened her eyes sunlight streamed into the room, reflecting off speckles of dust floating around in the air. Kym reached out her hand to touch them and watched closely as they swirled away from her grasp. Bored out of her mind, she got up and splashed water on her face then shuddered, catching sight of herself in the mirror. Attempting to perk herself up she tousled her shoulder length hair, winding it around her fingers, scooping it up and holding it above her head. Picking up the dark glasses she'd discarded yesterday and placing them on, Kym frowned, but as she examined her image, realised that the disguise was effective. Matt had done a half decent job with her hair, in fact nobody would be able to recognise her. With her spirits now lifted slightly, Kym decided to venture outside for some fresh air, after making coffee and toast. She plugged the television back in and picked up the remote from the faded carpet. It took several flicks and swear words before the television came on and when it finally did, Kym put her hand over her mouth to stop herself from throwing up. A close up of her face was plastered across the screen.

'Dr. Kym Adams was a member of the Generate group that produced the super pill,' a newsreader announced. Kym sank to her knees, gasping for air.

'No, no,' she screamed, staring in horror at her face being broadcasted.

'I didn't do anything,' she protested, sobbing loudly. The sound of the phone ringing caused her to jolt. It was Matt. He'd just seen her face all over the News and knew she'd been set up, just as he'd feared.

'Kym, are you ok?'

'I don't know….Matt come round, please. Now,' she wailed, spluttering inbetween crying.

'I'll be there soon, you just have to hang on. Make sure the door is locked and stay inside with the curtains drawn.'

'Why can't you come now?  You sound distant, miles away.  Don't leave me here,' she pleaded, her voice shaking.

'I'll sort everything out and then I promise, I will never leave you again, I love you,' he said softly before hanging up.

Kym knew he would return and set about closing curtains, checking locks and bracing herself for more disturbing news reports.  Flicking through the television channels all showed images of hysterical crowds outside their house.  They hurled rocks at the windows and shouted her name as the glass crashed down and broke into hundreds of pieces at their feet.

'Kym Adams, Kym Adams, get out here!  Bitch, murderer,' they yelled.  The camera switched to the rear of the property, showing smoke billowing from the upstairs rooms.  Next, it zoomed in on the front door which had been kicked in.  People were falling over themselves, pushing, desperate to get inside, clearly on a witch hunt.  Kym watched in disbelief, weeping and shaking, crying out for Matt.  Her saviour.  If he hadn't got her out in time the crowd would clearly have torn her apart mercilessly in front of the cameras.

The News channel showed footage of her at the awards ceremony, before returning to scenes at the house, or what was left of it. The crowd had been pushed back to the bottom of the drive, whilst the fire service extinguished dying embers. Next to appear was her abandoned car. Matt must have moved it, as it wasn't where she'd left it. Kym covered her face and cried into already soaked hands. There was no escape, she'd been issued with a death sentence. It was hopeless.

The moment she'd walked into No.10 Kym had solved all their problems. Powerful people would be protected. She was their scapegoat, an unexpected, yet most welcome convenience, absolving them of all blame. Turning off the television, Kym knew what she had become. A fugitive, forever running. Faced with living the rest of her life with the consequences of one moment that she would never be able to change.

# Epilogue

By the end of the year, half a million twenty five year olds had died of heart failure and Dr. Kym Adams was the only person who had been linked to the development of the super pill. After publicising her involvement, the Government suddenly found out what stimulant had been used to create the pill, enabling them to produce medicines to counteract its effects. Once the medicines had been tested and proved to be effective, a programme of treatment commenced. No babies born in the last year had the stimulant present. All other children and young adults affected were treated with heart medicine which involved injections for years on end. After a two year treatment period patient's hearts began to show signs of strengthening. During the following year another 450 thousand twenty five year olds died. Those who were twenty four and had started treatment lived for a further two years. Those who were twenty three at the time of the treatment all survived.

A woman's badly burned body was found in the ruins of Kym's house. The body was removed for identification. DNA was recovered from hair strands found on the body, confirming a match to Dr. Kym Adams. The body was bagged up and sent for cremation along with other fatalities from heart failure, that same week.

Matt had spoken to Kym the day after the news story broke, before their house had been burnt down. She gave him a statement to be released to the Press, maintaining her innocence and declaring that the Government had set her up. Kym also disclosed that she herself was taking the pill and why would she have done that knowing it would not protect her from pregnancy? Accusing Kym, had meant that the scientist behind the super pill was able to give details of the stimulant used in its creation, without fearing prosecution. Kym ended her statement saying that her whole career had been spent developing stem cell technology to save lives and protect future generations. The Press aired her statement but it didn't change the public's opinion of her. The people responsible for almost 1.4 million deaths were never brought to justice.

Matt finally left his parent's house several months later, feeling fully recovered, with Kym's family inheritance and the insurance money from the arson attack on their home. A very affluent Matt would have been an eligible bachelor for any female but stayed true to his dark haired girlfriend Jane.

They fulfilled a lifetime dream and moved to Australia, renting an exclusive villa overlooking a secluded beach. They spent their days, strolling along the sands, hand in hand with Rollo bounding ahead. Keeping themselves to themselves, Matt never left the house without a fully charged stun device and his trusty switchblade knife. Jane never left the house without Matt.

# Fear's Burden

Fear's Burden is the sequel to Twenty Five and continues to follow the lives of Matt and Kym in Australia.  This haunting novel reveals Matt's darker side as they continue to battle for their sanity.  The first chapter follows and the complete novel is available to download now.

. . . . . . . . . . . . . . . . .

## Chapter One

# RUN

As she gradually returned to consciousness the first thing Kym felt was a crushing, heavy weight, pressing her into a thin, uneven mattress.  She tried to move away, straining and arching her body, but it was impossible.  Everything was pitch black, although her eyes were open, she couldn't see anything.  Trying to pull her aching arms downwards caused the rope to bite into the skin on her wrists. Blood oozed over its dirty strands as she cried out in pain. Muffled, choking sounds, suppressed by a vile, putrid tasting gag. The heat of his breath against her throat, sent her into spasmodic retching and he shifted his weight off her chest, allowing Kym's lungs to rise, inflating with short, sharp bursts of damp air.

The room was cold, musty smelling and in a skimpy summer dress she lay shivering, gasping for breath. The tight blindfold, produced a throbbing pain, piercing the side of her temple as she lay frozen to the spot. Kym tried to focus on the different smells that assaulted her nostrils, a mixture of sweat and urine, was it him or the mattress? A drop of his sweat fell on to her face and rolled downwards and she moved her head frantically from side to side, to avoid his foul breath.

The warm, wet flow of urine seeped down her thighs and Kym sobbed, knowing there was no escape from its path. He swiftly moved his hand to clasp her jaw and held it tightly in domination as his breathing increased. Then he moved towards the side of the bed, reaching for something. Terror swept through her body and instinctively she arched and thrashed her legs around in defence.

'Keep still,' he yelled, before stabbing her upper arm with a sharp pointed object. Everything went into slow motion and then black as she slipped back into unconsciousness.

One month earlier……

'Can you believe it's only two and a half weeks until Christmas?' an astounded Matt announced, looking over the daily newspaper.

'No, I hadn't really thought about it.' Kym answered, looking sadly across the beach at Rollo running around chasing gulls.

'It's easy to forget the time of year, sitting here in the baking sunshine,' he added, looking thoughtful. 'My mind tells me it's winter but I'm trying to pretend it's summer.'

'Me too. I don't think I can face Christmas this year,' she admitted, staring out at the horizon.

'Then we won't. Let's not mention it again,' Matt replied, quickly getting up, jumping the small gate that led to the beach and throwing Rollo's ball into the air, unaware that Kym was weeping silently.

Matt and Kym had been living in Southern Australia for the past six months, since fleeing the UK in fear of their lives. Before their departure, Matt had organised new names and passports, enabling them to leave England safely and remain anonymous. Kym, blamed for the deaths of over a million twenty five year olds, stayed hidden away, fearing attack. The death toll was still rising, although a successful treatment plan had commenced. Kym though, had sealed her own fate, by informing the Government about the development of the super pill and was a member of the Generate group held responsible for its creation.

They'd given up on trying to use their new names of Paul Collins and Jane Watson and now lived in a luxury villa looking out onto a beach of powdered white sand. Only their rented property occupied the small secluded bay, filled with a turquoise blue sea that stretched endlessly towards the horizon. Together they spent their days walking on the beach in front of their home, with only Matt venturing further for groceries. Still traumatised by the horrendous events that occurred in the UK before their departure, Kym, held in fear's grip, lost more of her ability to venture outside with each passing day. When Matt went out she'd sit watching through the window of their large single storey villa, feeling breathless and listening for any unexpected sounds. Her eyes glued to the steps leading to the beach, anxiously waiting for him to return.

Matt organised a rental property inland with the sole purpose of becoming a mail drop for bank statements and bills. He went there once a fortnight to pay the rent in cash and use the owner's WIFI to keep in touch with his parents. Matt was never late back, he couldn't afford to be, after witnessing Kym having a panic attack a couple of months earlier. At first everything had been fine and she would accompany him on short walks along the coast. Then one afternoon everything changed for no apparent reason.

'Matt, I can hear voices, people, nearby,' she claimed, halting abruptly. Matt listened and waited.

'It's nothing, just the wind or the gulls,' he tried to reassure her.

'But, I saw something, a flash of light, over there.' Kym stood completely still pointing towards the wooded area at the end of the bay. Matt put his hand above his eyes, shielding them from the bright sunlight as he scanned the beach.

'I can't see anything,' he remarked, looking at her frightened eyes.

'Can we go back?' she urged, trembling.

'Ok,' he replied, 'come here first,' reaching for her hand. She snatched it away and looked at him terrified.

'No, we have to go now… run.' Kym tore across the sand, leaving a dumbfounded Matt staring after her. When he reached the villa, she was banging her fists hard against the door.

'Let me in,' she screamed, 'let me in.' Matt pulled her away from the door.

'Kym, what is it?' he asked smoothing strands of dark brown hair away from her tear stained face. Kym was covered in sweat, her breathing laboured.

'I can't go out anymore, it's not safe,' she protested. 'I keep telling you, but you never listen. Stop forcing me, leave me alone!'

It was hours before she calmed down. Matt stayed by her side, holding her in his arms, until she fell asleep.

The following day Matt wanted to go outside but couldn't cope with distressing Kym again, still shocked by her reaction the previous day. Throughout the morning, he busied himself around the garden, putting up a large umbrella on the decking and encouraging her to sit with him in the shade. Kym seemed happier and hadn't mentioned the previous afternoon, which led Matt to believe she'd got over the incident. He looked out towards the beach, longing to go for a walk.

'Kym, how would you feel if I went out for a while?' he asked scrutinising her face. Turning towards him Kym stared down at the decking, her mood changing dramatically.

'Can't we just order what we need online?' she suggested, her voice shaking.

'Not really, if we use the phone here we could be traced, I can't chance that. Look, I won't be long, stop worrying.' Kym still didn't make eye contact and Matt feeling guilty, knelt in front of her.

'Is there anything I can do? Please tell me,' he asked, putting his finger under her chin to raise her eyes to the level of his.

'It's just that… it's just that I hate being alone. I can't stand it when you're away,' she said, looking past him, towards the incoming waves.

'Then come with me. I'm not going far, only to the grocery store. How about if you stay in the car, if you're worried about being seen?' Kym looked at him horrified, before staring back at the floor.

'I'm staying here,' she insisted, 'I can't go out today, it's too soon.'

'Okay, but I need to go out, there's things I need to do.' Kym nodded.

'Can you at least leave me some sort of weapon,' she blurted out. Matt couldn't believe what he'd just heard and startled, looked closely at her.

'A weapon, what like. A knife or something?'

'Yes, anything,' she snapped. 'It's alright for you, I'm the one that's trapped here. I'm the one whose supposed to be dead, you can go and do whatever you want.' Tears of protest filling her eyes

'Oh, okay, okay,' he kissed her forehead softly, though wondering how she could possibly defend herself against an intruder. Sighing in resignation, Matt went into the bedroom and returned with a small Swiss army knife. Reluctantly placing it next to his wife, even though it seemed absurd, he dutifully obeyed.

'Why don't I leave Rollo with you?' he offered, hoping she might feel safer with their faithful, chocolate brown Labrador by her side.

'No. Rollo needs a walk, but don't be too long.' Kym got up and went inside, checking windows were locked and pulling down blinds, before returning to the lounge. When he locked the front door behind him, Matt heard her putting the alarm on and shook his head slowly from side to side. She wasn't going to be fine and it took all of his strength not to turn around and rush back inside, but he didn't. Exhaling deeply, Matt knew that one day the storm would eventually pass and they could start to rebuild, it would only be a matter of time. Until then she would have to manage as he desperately needed some crucial alone time.

When he returned, earlier than agreed, Kym was still sitting in the chair looking out through the window, as if she hadn't moved the whole time he'd been away. Retrieving his knife, he wondered if their lives would remain like this forever. Looking over your shoulder every time you went out. Peering through windows to check if anyone was on the beach, although there was never another soul in sight. Reacting to every slight noise heard during the night, which had turned them into insomniacs.

'Did you hear that?' Kym would whisper, sitting up in bed suddenly, listening carefully for any unusual sounds, scared, terrified.

'It's nothing,' Matt replied after listening for a few minutes. The property was alarmed and Rollo's basket was stationed outside their bedroom.

'Stop worrying. If anyone was inside, Rollo would be barking and he hasn't stirred.' Within seconds, he would be snoring again, whilst Kym spent another sleepless night listening to every creak and thud inside her self-made prison. Afternoon naps had become a frequent arrangement in their household, with them dozing off for half an hour at a time, exhausted due to sleep deprivation.

After another week with Matt disappearing for an hour each day, they agreed to try an hour and fifteen minutes. Kym seemed to be coping, but still wanted him to leave her a knife and sat staring at the small winding graveled path which led to their door, eagerly awaiting his return. Matt brought plants back, hoping to inspire her into spending time in the garden creating a new flower bed.

'Can you put them outside, in the shade,' she asked, without thanking him.

'Yes, and then maybe we could plant them tomorrow, decide where you want them to go.' Kym shot him a disinterested look and the next day made excuses as to why she couldn't go outside.

Matt's impatience intensified as the flowers lay unattended in their pots. Frustrated he threw water over them, noticing that the leaves were wilting as they started to fade. Opening a bottle of red wine he sat on the decking with Rollo by his side, slowly sipping the comforting red liquid. Admiring the burnt orange and dark crimson hues forming across the sky by the sun, fading into the ocean, felt just like his beautiful wife. Fading into nothingness, prevented from living. Not exactly what he'd intended, when choosing Australia for their escape. Startled, he looked up, hearing a strange sound of female voices, fading in and out,

'Stay...,' Matt couldn't make out the last two words. There was the same sound again,

'Stay....'

Matt leapt to his feet, scanning around trying to decide if he'd just imagined it, or if it was the wine or the crashing waves. There wasn't anyone about so he sat back down and poured himself another glass, downing it in one go. The words of the mysterious voices continued to run through his mind as the sun finally sank into the sea, plunging the bay into darkness.

Printed in Poland
by Amazon Fulfillment
Poland Sp. z o.o., Wrocław